Dungeon Core 101

R.J. Triveri

Published by Level Up in the United Kingdom in 2020

Cover illustration by Sippakorn Upama
Cover by Claire Wood

ISBN: 978-1-83919-328-6

www.levelup.pub

For my wife, my son, my friends, and my readers:
You only have yourselves to blame for this.
Thank you.

Rebirth

Through my research, I have learned many things about the world both seen and unseen. I have fought kings, dragons, and Dungeons. I have slain every beast to walk this world save one, gathered every rune and enchantment available to the living world, and learned to manipulate magic on a world-wide scale. And yet this is nothing.

Everything I have done, everything that I am, everything that I have accomplished, it all pales in the light of the knowledge I have won. Knowledge that I now freely share to those curious enough to wish to join me.

Death can be only the beginning of a greater journey if one has the willpower to overcome one's limits.

Final words of Grandmaster Ansith, Wizened Artificer and Runesmith of Copperforge

Chapter One

Rem

The sun was high above the treetops and streaming down into the lower forest in a rare spectacle after the rains of the night before. The entire forest was alight with rainbows, and someone with an eye for natural beauty would be taken aback. I had an eye for natural beauty, but it wasn't the kind the forest provided.

"Rem!"

Saria always had such a lovely voice. It was even more so when she was trying to pelt me with rocks. She was beautiful when she was angry. Dangerous as a viper after you've stepped on it, but cute all the same. The fire in her eyes made it completely worth it.

Of course, I had set those pests in her satchel, but it wasn't like medusa frogs were dangerous. All they did was eat flies, they couldn't hurt a Foxkin. Well, most of the time they couldn't. Unless you count when they're scared, turned to something equivalent to granite, and thrown like magic missiles at the back of my fleeing head, otherwise they're completely harmless.

I had two legs back then, a full head and chest of snow-white fur, and my tail. I loved my tail! It was long and graceful, and with it I could perform great acts of balance any human would kill for.

I just grinned to myself, dodging the fearfully-solidified frogs as they flew with preternatural speed at my back as I dashed though the forest undergrowth. I didn't have to look very hard since it was still the middle of the day in the summer season and the leaf-litter wasn't very thick; so, while I was still jogging away, I turned and yelled back "I thought you liked frogs!"

I shouldn't have turned to gloat.

Before the final word could leave my lips, the next amphibian projectile slammed straight into my nose and shattered it like cheap dwarven pottery. I could feel each piece of cartilage split and force themselves against my skull. My ears folded forward as blood began streaming down my face, dying my white fur red wherever it landed. Saria had just ruined my plans for the night. With the way my blood streamed down and was matting into fur and fabric alike, I'd have to spend far too much time making myself look presentable.

Thankfully, the frog-storm stopped when the orange-furred Foxkin felt that she had done enough damage. Well, that or she had run out of frogs and come to finish the job herself. I lost count of the projectiles after eight or ten of the magical amphibian buggers since she was using both of her hands by that point and laughing like a possessed maniac as they whizzed by my head. Honestly, it was hard to believe I'd gotten sixteen of those things in her bag before she had noticed.

To her great and wonderful credit, Saria didn't feel inclined to continue the fight as I was prone on the ground, holding my pained nose. In her eyes, she'd gotten what she wanted, and, as she loomed over me, I'd wholeheartedly call her victory total.

Saria took one look at me and winced in a pitying way as I felt the warm liquid trickle down my face. "Guess I overdid it again."

I tried to say something witty, but all that came out was a whimper and more blood as a river of gore flowed from my face.

Seeming to pick up on the fact I couldn't speak quite yet, Saria stooped close and inspected the damage a bit closer, gently moving my head to one side to the other, no doubt to check for more serious damage than my shattered, bleeding nose. "Don't you have any of the Cure spells yet?"

I shook my head meekly under my own power this time. Sure, I was an Oracle. In theory, I could heal small wounds like this... in theory. There were two ways for someone of my class to learn magic: hard work with magic healers, learning the ins and outs of anatomy; or through divine intervention. In either case, I hadn't gotten around to learning or being gifted with those ability Nodes yet. I had chosen to branch out a bit, to learn a slew of cantrips to make myself more versatile before I had to specialize in healing magics. I may not have had strong Rank One Oracle spells like Heal Wounds, but I had a lot of the easy, flexible spells in my arsenal. Out of these cantrips I had a few that I had mastered and crystallized into Nodes around my mana reservoir. Useful spells like Invisibility, which I used to sneak into Saria's post; Will-of-the-Wisp, to distract others; Mend, to fix things I'd broken…

In retrospect, everything so far in my life was probably just my punishment for not living up to whatever divine force turned my fur white in the first place. I really wasn't the best Oracle to my people yet, but what did they expect? I was only eighteen winters old.

As I came back from my mental wanderings, I noticed that Saria had moved from her place next to me and was just looking me over dumbfounded. Heat rushed across my face as my tail and ears fell in time.

I was going to get around to learning to Heal Wounds! I really was, but the work was always so bloody. You needed to know everything about how bodies and muscles worked, or you'd royally screw up someone's muscle structure. How was I supposed to know the difference between tendons and ligaments? They all looked the same when someone was squirming in an operation tent! I didn't even like my own blood, let alone that of others. I did have the basic ability to magically stabilize the wounded and could forbid an action against me though. Not that I particularly wanted to be close enough to stabilize a bloodied body, but it came with the class I was born into. Forbid was a different story entirely, but I could only use that once a day, and it didn't work against creatures more than a rank above me. The more skills someone mastered and the more mana someone had access to did something to buffer the effects of mental magic, go figure.

Saria pulled a rag from her pocket and handed the cloth to me with a long, drawn-out sigh. "Why don't you just do your lessons like the rest of us? I'm already a D-Two Ranger, and my instructor says I'll be at the C Ranks soon from how fast I'm building my new Nodes. Have you even progressed a little this month?"

I knew the answer already, but I focused inward anyways and checked my Nexus.

4

Oracle
Class Skills Mastered: 2
Secondary Skills: 3
Oracle Rank D2
7/9 requirements met to reach Rank C
Mana Types - Celestial
Mana Reserves:
Celestial - 80/80
Class Passive for Mastery:
None Earned

Word of Power: Forbid
Unique Primary Class Node - Active - Oracle
Evolution Potential - None
Cost: Base - 20 Celestial (Scaling)
Effect: Spend mana to bend those to the power of your Patron. Word of Power: Forbid prevents a target from taking a specific action. The power and cost of this spell depends on the will of the target and the complexity of the command given. This spell cannot stop biological functions such as breathing.

Stabilize
Primary Class Node - Active - Oracle
Evolution Potential - Minor
Cost: Base - 20 Celestial (Scaling)
Effect: Spend mana to stabilize a fallen creature. Stabilize will quickly mend critical injuries and restore lost blood by responding to specific magical and biological cues. The power and cost of this spell depends on the severity of the injury and the power required to mend critical injuries. This spell has no effect on a non-critically injured party.

Invisibility
Secondary Node - Spell - Cantrip
Evolution Potential - Flexible
Cost: Base- 10 mana per minute per creature per five feet radius (Scaling)

Effect: Spend ambient mana to bend light around you and appear to vanish. Cost of the spell increases based on movement, environment, and size of the spell's target.

Mend
Secondary Node - Spell - Cantrip
Evolution Potential - High, Flexible
Cost: Scaling
Effect: Spend ambient mana to attempt to repair a mundane or magical item. Repair cost is based on knowledge and complexity and the severity of the damage of the item.

Will-of-the-Wisp
Secondary Node - Spell - Cantrip
Evolution Potential - Flexible
Cost: 5 (Scaling)
Effect: Spend ambient mana to create a sphere of light in the color of your choice. Cost of this spell changes based on size, intended duration, distance from user, and color of the sphere.

It took less than a breath for me to take stock and sigh. Nope, no changes there. I still had a long, mysterious way to go.

I still couldn't speak to Saria, so I shook my head as the rag continued to steadily turn red. I couldn't see any changes to my mana reservoir or in the skills I'd mastered around it since the last time I checked, but maybe I just wasn't able to focus as a result of the rapidly adding up blood-loss. It wasn't too serious and I'd probably get better faster with some help, but my advancement was the real problem. Healers and clan sorcerers could only teach me so much thanks to my stupid fate. Divine mandate and skill manifestation came from prayer, they said.

Saria knew none of that though, sighed again, and offered me her hand. I took it without a second thought and pulled myself up. With my nose covered, I was finally able to speak.

"I'll get better." I managed while the rag plugged up my nose, but my words were off sounding, garbled just enough to be funny to the girl as a smile crossed her face: even if the blood still continued to stain the gray square of cloth.

"Sure you will," Saria laughed. "Just like you'll heal your nose and meet your patron before the end of the season."

That stung, and I don't just mean the more-than-likely broken cartilage in my aching nose.

"You'll see," I said simply, taking her words as a challenge. "I'll bet you I'll be Rank C by the end of the week."

"Oh really?" she grinned taking a step closer as her tail swished evenly from side to side with each and every step. "If you do that, Rem, I'll reward you myself."

What? That got my tail wagging more than I cared to admit. My ears stood to attention listening for any trick, and the new focus helped the pain lessened ever-so slightly. "Oh really?"

She leaned in, pecking my cheek, letting her tail caress mine ever so slightly as she circled me, looking me over as she let the answer drag from between her teeth. "Yep."

And with that, I had a whole new drive to be the best I could be.

Before I could give her any sort of a real answer, a horn's bellowing call burst through the air, and Saria's ears twitched as the intonation changed. As a Ranger, it was her job to patrol the outskirts of the village for danger, and apparently one of her kin had found something. The modulating tones of the Rangers' watch could mean anything from feral monsters to an envoy from one of our neighboring clans, with the difference of just a few moments of sound. From the look of her face and the sway of her tail, it didn't seem to be too threatening.

"I've got to go, Rem," she said with just the slightest hint of disappointment. "Duty calls."

"What is it?" I asked while the rag continued to collect blood. The words weren't as clear as I'd have liked them to be, but Saria picked up the meaning easily enough.

"Nothing dangerous," she said simply, listening for any final echos. When none came, Saria took one last look at me and grinned. "Before you ask, keep it. I don't need your bloody scent attracting predators."

I raised a brow but kept the rag in place as she bound off, giving me quite the splendid view. It was a real problem. I loved when she was around, but I also loved the sway of her body as I got to watch her leave. There was a comfort in the back of my mind this time as she bound away though the greens of the season. If I played my cards right, I'd be seeing her again real soon.

***

After a quick visit to the Clerics, who once again scolded me for my antics and told me how my patron would be disappointed in me, I was on the move. I didn't even bother to change or clean myself before I took my scrolls out into the woods, sat against my favorite tree, and began to read. The only thing on my mind now was building more Nodes, forcing my mana reservoir to expand, and getting a serious chance with the fox of my dreams. Bloody or not, if something came along, I'd have a great target for my Forbid spell.

Determination was my name now. The task at hand was a great one, but it wasn't impossible. I would learn at least Cure Poison. It wasn't that hard compared to Heal Wounds. Then, with my third Oracle spell, my Node network would be populated enough to be classified as Rank C, and my mana would be forced to expand. Then, if the Clerics were right, I would somehow learn how to commune with my as-of-yet-to-be-known patron. Then, I would impress Saria!

It was a good plan if I did say so myself, and I did say so.

Not ten minutes into my studies, I was a bit distracted from my work as I was treated to the worst splitting headache of my life.

It was also my last.

Feeling your spirit leave your body is an odd thing though I didn't quite realize what it was until it was over. The best way I could describe it in the moment would be vomiting—without the terrible taste of bile and the unpleasant smell—out of every single follicle and hole that had a home on my body; it was wholly unpleasant, disorienting, and would have made me sick if I hadn't suddenly lost that ability.

So, my soul was vomited forth and looking down on what was left of my body. It wasn't pretty. My head was bashed in like an over-ripened melon, rind and all. The weapon, a large, silvery mace, still rested within the remains of where the rest of my face should have been. The pain of my death was as sudden as it was intense, but it didn't last. After seeing the dripping chunky remains that were me, I was very thankful for that. Then I had bigger concerns, questions like: what in the Pantheon had killed me? And why in the Mists did they do it? My mind raced as it tried to process everything at once, but it wasn't the fact I was dead that worried me most of all.

I was bleeding all over the scrolls of the elders.

I'd ruined the scrolls. I'd ruined the elders' scrolls! My blood seeped into the fabric, blotting out all knowledge, all vision, all learning for the future generations of the clan. I was all nerves at that revelation. The elders would kill…

Oh… right…

Then, I began to panic. I tried to scream, but no words came out. I couldn't talk, I couldn't yell, I couldn't even move as something tethered me to that location. My body was still somehow fixed to my soul, leaving me trapped. With my limited motion, the best I could do was move a little from side to side and turn in place. I was less than thankful for that little bit as a pair of someone's boots finally came into view.

There were two of them, human adventurers. A shimmer of illusion passed over them, removing itself and making them visible again. One of them was short and stout, another was a giant of a man who may or may not have made me question what it was to be strong.

The larger of the adventurers unceremoniously nudged at my leg with his stupidly over-sized boot as his large mace continued to rest in the tree in the space where my head had been only moments before.

"Aw, sket," the giant man said as he pulled back his mace from the remaining section of gore with a sickening crack of wood and bone and a quick sucking sound as my skull tried to hold onto it. My body fell a moment later into a growing pool of its own gore. I barely heard him as I watched myself slump forward and bleed like a decapitated chicken. "It's one of them Foxkin. Not worth a lick of coin to the guild."

His friend wasn't nearly as placid about the whole situation as the larger man cleaned my blood and other choice bits of my skull off of the smooth surface of his weapon. "Zoa, you idiot! Look at its fur!"

The man did. He looked at it for a long time, staring at something he thought he should see. He used his foot to flip me over when he didn't find what the other wanted, and I was nearly sick again. The wound was so much more real when I was staring down at my face. Well, where my face should have been. Finally, he turned back to the man and shrugged. "It's white? So what? I thought he was a werewolf, Cecil. They're white too, ya know."

I looked at them stupidly, not even registering what they really looked like besides human. I'd have growled if I could. They thought I was a werewolf? How stupid were they? It was the middle of the afternoon!

The second man, Cecil, looked from side to side as if checking his surroundings for some unseen threat. Then, he turned back to Zoa and slapped him across the face with a resounding crack. I was surprised the man could even each that high. "You killed their Oracle, you idiot! Do you know what kind of shitstorm you just started, Zoa!"

Zoa rubbed his face, taken aback by Cecil's unprovoked attack. "Aren't they those healers?"

"God. Touched. People." The man reminded him annunciating each word of the phrase slowly and clearly. "God touched people are Oracles, not Clerics! A God favored him of all his race, and you just killed him because you thought he was a werewolf!" Cecil was getting twitchy now and talked to himself instead of the large oaf. "We have to fix this. If his clan finds out that guild envoys did this to their Oracle, there'll be trouble. Lots of trouble…"

If I could have, I would have ripped their throats out myself. As it was, I was just an angry spirit, watching in disbelief as his body was more or less desecrated.

"Oh," Zoa said as he looked down at the blood-soaked scrolls. The man was more oblivious than a pet rock and not nearly as adorable as he picked them up, wiping the bloody objects against the clean fur of my arm in what I could only imagine was an attempt to salvage them. "Can we get money for these at least?"

Looting my corpse was not okay!

From the anger in Cecil's eyes, at least he felt the same way as he smacked the scrolls out of the larger man's hands.

"Are you simple!" The man's eyes began to glow and began looking around. "We have to do damage control before anyone finds out!"

I didn't like being referred to as damage control. That usually meant bad things. My damage control was cleaning up my messes, but I doubted reconstructing my head, putting my spirit back into my body, and parting ways with an apology was part of theirs.

After a few soft words, the man's eyes began to leak a hazy gray mana. It was a familiar spell that the Clerics had tried, and failed, to teach me: Astral Vision. It was a low-rank Cleric skill that let anyone see lingering spirits or things obscured by spirit magic. As I realized what he was doing, I raised my middle finger at him. It was a simple gesture but one universally understood since my words seemed to be failing me.

Cecil nearly fell back as he turned and faced me, and I grinned darkly.

"He's still here," Cecil said fumbling for his pouch. "Cover me, Zoa."

Cover him? What was I going to do?

The large man nodded and set his pack down next to my body as he pulled out an even larger hammer from the bag. It was easily the size of my body and had to weigh at least twice that. That wasn't the most reassuring thing I'd seen this day, but it was far from the worst.

I raised another finger on my other hand to stress my annoyance, but Cecil ignored me and pulled out a stone from his bag. Was it to appease me? If it was, I wouldn't be so easily bought, but it was a rather nice-looking chunk of mana stone, Celestial mana if I wasn't mistaken, although one marred by a large vein of purple.

What was I thinking? I'd just lost my life! I'd just lost any chance with Saria! What did I care about a rock? It kept teasing my attention towards it though. Something about it kept drawing my gaze to it as if I were a crow and it was a shiny object. It was pretty, to be sure, but not as beautiful as the chance they'd stolen from me. Rage gave me back my focus, shaking the strange allure of the item off. With what little I could do, I kept my fingers raised as high as I could while Cecil began chanting something in Dwarven, or was it Elvish? I had such a hard time with those languages.

11

Either way, I knew a language they could understood and kept my fingers raised high as the gem began to glow brighter, and the draw of the stone became stronger. Even then, I resisted. More words came, and the allure of the stone wasn't just in my mind. It, too, became a physical pull, dragging me towards it with no regard for my want.

I tried to resist, but the only resistance I could muster was to keep my fingers raised all the way up until my soul touched the surface of the Celestial stone, and everything went black.

Chapter Two

Divine Interventions

I don't know how long I was out for, but when I came to, I am not proud to say that I began to freak out just a bit. I mean, I couldn't feel my legs or my arms. Then, it all came back to me.

Well, the important part of it did anyway.

Oh yeah... I was dead...

When the moment of anxiety and existential dread at being in such a state passed as much as it would, I tried to get some kind of bearing to look around. Really, I thought that it'd be hard to look around without a head, but I quickly came to realize that I didn't have to. I could see everything around me at all angles. It was a little distorted around the top and bottom of my sight, but I had a vague sense of everything that surrounded me. The strange way of seeing took some time to process even if all I could really see were the walls of my crystalline prison. The walls looked thick and opaque even from the inside, and they pulsed softly with an opal, almost silvery light tinged with an unnatural violet tinting it across the center. Even if the light wasn't blocking me, I couldn't see though any part of it.

Okay, it was time for a new plan. I would push my way out of the stone! Ghosts could move through objects, right? What was stopping me from doing the same?

Without hands or feet, I had to use my consciousness to force my ethereal body to change position. As easy as that sounds, I took up everything within the stone, and it was an exhausting feat trying to move myself as a whole. I could move small parts of me easily enough by pulling myself closer to where I felt my center was, but my entire body, if I could even call it that, wasn't as easy. When I pulled myself closer, it felt like I was getting... thicker? Denser? I resisted my own thoughts. My body wanted to stay mostly circular, filling the stone's every facet. Whenever I finally managed to figure out how to 'move,' the dark purple vein of light shocked me. It shocked me, and it hurt! I was a ghost, why did it have to sketing hurt! My entire body recoiled like I'd been struck by lightning, and I could feel that I was back where I had started weaker for the effort.

Great. Just great.

Cecil, the bastard that he was, had trapped my soul. Now, I knew that much at least, and that meant just one thing. Cecil was a Necromancer, or he was working with someone that was. Necromancers were usually bad news, and that was especially bad news for me. Not because of who I am - or was, I should say - but because of who they were. Necromancers were demon-touched mages by blood or by pact. They were resistant to holy magic too and usually very annoying. Not that they were all bad, but they had a habit of monologuing or being, dare I say it, cryptic? They were able to heal by manipulating bones and dead flesh, but more often than not they used the bodies and souls they found to create weapons and minions. More than likely, a worse fate than that waited for me. Talented Necromancers used the souls they captured to imbue items with a tremendous power, to fulfill their demonic contracts, or they just blew them up for fun and profit. Considering that I was god-touched, I had a bad feeling that I might fall into one of those two categories.

Whether it was the effort of thought or my attempts to escape, I began to feel light headed again. I struggled to hang on, but Oblivia's embrace was just too tempting. I just couldn't stay awake anymore...

That was when things kind of went off the trail.

That's when I started to dream.

***

Yes, I'd dreamed before. Dreams were pretty standard for an Oracle. I had been taught that Oracles first had to control dreams before they could speak to the Divine. I'd learned that about as well as I'd learned

14

everything else. It wasn't perfect, but I could have a sense of self, lucidly dream, and just generally enjoy my time napping. I say that because as an experienced dream, this… well, this was something different entirely.

I didn't have to work at it to form my body, I didn't need the tell of the blue rose in my hand to know I was dreaming, and I certainly never could have imagined the woman standing before me. She was beautiful, which I can't fault myself for, but she wasn't Foxkin like my normal dream cohorts were. She was beautiful, but she was nearly nine feet tall and dressed in a long, flowing white robe that was seemingly made from a single piece of fabric. Besides the abnormal height and odd dress of my literal dream woman, she was very much human or elven in her build. There wasn't a touch of fur or claw to her white skin except for her nine, beautifully fluffy tails. Another dead giveaway was that we didn't need masks to give us ears or elongated faces, and one completely covered her face. The mask itself was interesting, made of some polished white stone with gold accents. It was seamless except for a pair of openings for her eyes, one purple, one gold, and a spot cut for her golden lips.

Yes, she was beautiful, but she still wasn't a Foxkin. Not that any of these things were deal breakers for me, but something about it struck me as odd even by my standards. I'd never dreamed of other races before, and my thoughts kept coming back to the tails and the mask. They tugged at me like a memory, like something should be coming to mind, like…

"Hello, my Oracle."

Sket.

Like, I should have been smart enough to realize when Vul, Goddess of Tricksters and Illusions and the soul Patron Goddess of the Foxkin race was standing in front of me.

The only other part of her face under the vulpine mask that I could see, a pair of golden lips on pearly white skin, smiled at me and chuckled.

Oh, sket. Oh, sket! This wasn't a dream. This was not a dream!

In my panic, I noticed that the smile on her face grew a bit wider as every part of me from my ears to my tail began to show every single

15

sign of panic and excitement they could muster outside of me actually wetting myself. Thankfully, that wasn't a worry in the real world anymore, though whether or not I'd embarrass myself in front of a goddess in a dream was still up in the air.

Please, please don't piss yourself in front of the goddess of your people, Rem. If anyone found out, you'd never hear the end of it.

"No, you wouldn't," she said, almost teasingly, with that nearly vulpine smile." Though having my Oracle lose so much credibility in so small a time would hurt your image as much as my own."

I took a deep breath, which was completely unnecessary, and sighed. At least she did have a sense of humor. "Thanks?"

"You're quite welcome, Rem."

In the beautiful field of dreams, we stood facing each other. Like an idiot, I simply stared. I was talking with our goddess. The one who created us, the one who nurtured us, the one who gifted us with so many things to make us unique. What did you say when you meet your creator?

"Am I dead? Really dead, I mean."

It seemed like a valid question at the time.

Her smile fell just a bit, and I wondered if I'd said something wrong. There was another pause, as if she were picking her words carefully before speaking again. "No, Rem. You are not 'really' dead. You've been put into a sleep by the one who captured you."

Cecil, that bastard. If I ever saw him again—

"He is quite dead, Rem."

"Oh." Well, that made revenge either really easy or really hard.

"Never the less, you are alive, but only so that you can continue to serve me and your people."

And she had my attention again. "That sounds a little hard, being trapped inside a rock and all."

Her tails swished, leaving a cascade of colorful light in their wake. "It's not a rock. Where you're trapped is a soulstone. A very special soulstone that will open up an entirely new world for you, a world for the entire Foxkin race."

I'd worked out the soulstone part, but I didn't see how it was special, let alone how in the Mists it would help our entire race. "I don't mean to be dense, but I am a rock, and it sort of comes with the territory, but how can I help anyone?"

Her laugh was as beautiful as the songbirds on a summer morning. More importantly, I made a goddess laugh! She liked puns! I was set as an Oracle now that I knew that. I could see why she picked me to represent her.

"Rem," she chuckled. "What do you know about Dungeons?"

I shrugged. "That you don't want to find yourself inside one unless you're into that sort of thing?"

"Other than that?"

I thought again. "They're buildings that people keep their prisoners in rather than killing or reforming them?"

This time she nodded. "While that is true, that's a dungeon. The word is the same, but the meaning is quite different. A Dungeon is what you will become."

I didn't think I was going to be a building, but I was a stone now. Maybe she was going to use me in some Celestial prison or something...

"No, I'm not going to use you as a brick." With that, Vul simply sighed. "You've never heard of Dungeons, Rem? Never in all your time?" When I shook my head no, she was not the happiest of deities. "What did the clan teach you, Rem? How can you not know what a Dungeon is?"

I thought of more than one way to say I don't know, but I doubted any of them were appropriate in the presence of a goddess. With that in mind, I opted for the honest response. "They didn't let me interact with the other races much, never let me explore or ask questions, and said I had to discover everything on my own. I'm sorry, but I've never heard of the other kind of Dungeon before."

Something akin to pure noise came through her lips, and my ears bled. She made my dreamy, fake ears bleed, and all the joyous noise of nothingness became actual nothingness. I don't even know how that works.

After a time, she calmed down and sat cross legged in front of me. My ears were still bleeding as she spoke, so I waved my hands to get her attention and pointed to my ears.

Her lips made the shape of a woman's laugh before one of her tails stood on end, glowed a soft gold, and just like that, my hearing returned. Ah, the sounds of sweet, sweet nothingness.

"Words of the divine language aren't meant for mortal ears, Rem. I apologize."

I shrugged, joining her as I sat on the cool grassy plane of the dream. "We all say things we don't mean when we're angry."

She gave a curt nod and sighed. "We have a lot of work to do, and so little time to do it."

That was curious, and slightly ominous. "Why?"

"Because you're going to have to be presentable when you go to meet the other races."

Like I hadn't heard that one before.

Chapter Three
At the Core of Things

Time passed weirdly in dreams. Normally when I had control, dream time lined up pretty well with real time. I'd spend eight hours or so exploring strange places in my mind to find hints of new divine spells, learning about myself, or more often than not, spending the time goofing off in a way that wouldn't lead to be getting in trouble with the clan elders.

That was another strange thing.

I had no control here, no inkling of how Vul controlled the dream if that was even what this was. How she spoke next though, made me think that we were moving at a much, much slower pace than the outside world though.

"Rem, tell me, what did they teach you?"

No one wasted time like that unless they had plenty of it.

Her question was vague though, so I took it at the base level. "I was an adorable kit which, I guess, thank you for that, Goddess Vul. I had a wonderfully boring childhood full of lessons and training, and I didn't even bite too many people."

We both knew that last part was a lie. I bit everyone I saw as soon as I could crawl. Mists, that's even how Saria and I met. Vul knew that, but I wanted to see just how much I might be able to get away with.

"Hm," she tapped a finger on her exposed chin as she thought. It seemed I could get away with very little. "As much as I enjoy a good story, how about we start with your Nexus, and depending on your answers, I'll move this in a better direction."

She really did want to go basic. At least I wouldn't be totally embarrassed to start with.

"Our Nexus defines our ability to cast spells, manipulate mana, and reinforce the skills and body that we already have," I began almost reciting what I'd been taught by the primary teacher of the clan Faw. "As we practice skills, they crystallize in our Nexus as Nodes that we can call upon at a moment's notice and use to reinforce our mana reservoir to stop it from damaging our soul. These Nodes exist in the form of Primary Nodes that determine our primary skill set, our class, secondary Nodes that complement the nature of our class, and cantrips, Nodes that anyone can use." I was particularly good at that last set, the rest… not so much. "The reservoir only expands when we master enough Primary or Secondary Nodes to support our primary mana type and perform tasks our bodies deem necessary to show progress in our Class."

She seemed to mull the idea over in her head, her tails moving in time with her thoughts like a hand drumming against the earth before she nodded. "Adequate, but you're missing some details. For now, I can let that slide, as I want to see your face when you figure it out for yourself." She grinned, and I got the distinct feeling that a mouse must have before a cat ends their game with a brutal swipe. "Now, how does this affect your Rank?"

At least they were simple questions so far. "Nodes are a requirement for increasing your Rank along with other tasks that the class needs to perform like—"

"You misunderstand me," Vul said holding up a hand to stop me mid-sentence. "What are your requirements to Rank up, Rem?"

I hesitated. I figured my Rank F requirements were the same as everyone else's, so I thought about the E and D Ranks. "I know I need at least three Oracle Nodes to advance right now."

"And?" she pressed.

"And… that was it for the move to Rank C."

She seemed to consider that, nodded, then shook her head just as quickly. "That's just to Rank C-Seven, Rem. What about C-Six, Five, Four, Three, Two, and One?"

That… I did not know, and this ignorance was probably written on every fur on my face.

Typically, progressions were normal, natural feelings that slowly unlocked your strength and increased your access to mana. I mean, to break out of the F-ranks, you only had to be alive, walking, and breathing for the most part. Without much thought, most people progressed past D without any problems either. Those on unique paths, like say when someone was born as an Oracle, didn't have it so easy. There were just so few of us to know what pushed us through the ranks. My clan had only seen one in all our recorded history.

Thankfully, she read it on my face and saved me the embarrassment of my having to tell her so. "Well, I can't tell you directly…" she leaned in, giving me a conspiratorial look as she whispered, "but completing D-One and ascending into the C Ranks has something to do with me."

If she was worried about telling me anything directly, she had nothing to worry about. That hint was about as direct as a pebble in a tornado thrown by a baby. That did, however, bring my mind back to the topic at hand.

"What does this have to do with being a dungeon?" I finally asked when no more questions came.

"A Dungeon," she corrected, putting extra emphasis on the initial syllable. "As for what it has to do with being one, it has everything and nothing to do with it."

I was beginning to see why she'd chosen my people as hers. She loved puzzling things out, but I wasn't picking up on whatever she was hinting at. "So… it has everything and nothing to do with it," I began, speaking aloud to help my mind work with the pieces. That only meant one thing logically. "So, they have some things in common and other things they don't?"

She grinned. "I don't want to ruin the surprise," she began, "or maybe I do. Being a Dungeon isn't the same as being an Oracle. Dungeons only have a few skills from birth and learn no others. It's also a lot easier to Rank up as a Dungeon and gain more power. There are no requirements to rank up other than gathering mana and gathering

21

knowledge to grow your Nexus. Both of which are easier to come by than a blade of grass in a field."

Unlimited growth, power, and I'd already know all the skills I'd need to master? Any one of those on their own would have been tempting, but together? That was a bit more than interesting. I could feel my tail showing as much, but I didn't want to reign it in. Vul knew she had me so far, so what was the point?

"Go on…" I urged eagerly.

She grinned under that mask so much that I could see her cheeks rise. "Imagine being able to do whatever you want, however you want. Imagine having the power to make life from the ground up, to build a new life for yourself where you control your entire world, to control everything the world has to offer and more. Some would even say I'm offering you the power of the Pantheon itself…"

My tail twitched from side to side like I was a kit again as I leaned forward, eagerly drawing in what she had to say.

"… where your power will influence your people; where the Foxkin will come for help, where they will test themselves and advance all because of you,"

While I did like being important and I did want to help, that was starting to sound more like work that needed a body, and I was still mostly dead…

Then, as if she knew I was starting to waver, her words began to build momentum. "Where you can prank countless people to your heart's content…"

Less like work…

The crescendo of her voice picked up, and her tails stood a little taller as she finished her pitch with the sweetest words of all. "And show adventurers all around the world that you and the Foxkin clan are not to be crossed, Rem Snowfur of the Wildwood!"

There we go! Pranks and revenge were two things I could very much get behind! I was as attentive as a warbear smelling honey. Power was good, pranks were great, but being able to get back at the bastard adventurers that killed me? That was all the influence I needed. It almost sounded too good to be true…

Which meant it probably was.

"There's got to be a catch," I said, trying to control the swishing excitement that was my tail. "If that's what it is to be a Dungeon, why haven't I ever heard of them before? Why wouldn't the clan know about them? Why would you need me?"

She must have been expecting that. The smile never left her face as her tails began to dust rainbows across the backdrop of the scene once more. "I'll answer the only one I can, Rem. I need you because you're the only one I can turn to."

Well, that wasn't reassuring in any way. Being the default never felt like a good thing. It made me feel like a puppet, not that that seemed any different than usual. That was what had gotten me killed in the first place! Vul frowned at me as soon as the thought passed through my head and my tail quit its circuit.

"That isn't the only reason I chose you for this, Rem. If you'd been an idiot or weak minded, I'd have waited another hundred years if I had to. No, your spirit is strong enough, your will is great enough, and your creativity and cunning are a credit to your people. I need a think-ing, creative, bright soul that can forge a path for our people and keep their lives alight with wonder and challenge."

I still liked the sound of that, but it just didn't sit as well as it had. For power over creation like she described though? I could probably get over it. Still…

With a flick of her tails, the world changed around us. The sea of luscious green grass and the cool air of the new season were gone. In its place was a crisp cold, white snow, and a ceiling of the sky itself. All around us, the stars twinkled and gleamed with their deep, unknowa-ble-ness. As we stood there on the snow-covered ground, I was able to identify a few of the markers I'd come to know and love: a collection of stars called The Kit's Treasure; a stream of reddish-green-gold clouds that never moved called the Pantheon's Stoke; and of course, our moons, Luna and Sola, the Twin Defenders. The memories turned bittersweet a moment later. I can't even begin to count the number of times I'd bugged Saria to join me on a clear, summer night, or how many times she'd found me when I didn't.

I caught Vul smiling again as I came back from my thoughts. "I'm sorry, Rem, but you can't have this again, but you can make sure that the others can always be sure to have the peace they've come to know and love."

Mists, she knew how to drive an offer home.

With another flick of her tails, the scene changed again. We were above the clan's village. Small buildings made of stone and wood pressed against one of the cliffs of the Wildwood. Some buildings hugged the wall of stone, digging into it to make more rooms, storage, and any number of other things. I saw the Clan's Kit hut, and the sulk of kids running rampant against the few caretakers. I saw the clan Watchers in their robes around the village in their towers; the Rangers patrolling around the outermost areas, the normal Foxkin laborers and citizens gathering around the village square. Then, my heart ached. I saw Saria in the center of it all still wearing her leathers and pointing out something to a smaller group, then another, then another as they moved off in all directions. She never gave orders though…

What I wouldn't give to hear her voice again.

"You can make sure that everyone gets stronger, Rem. If you accept my offer, you can make everyone else's dreams come true." Another smile, and her tails swished, sending us back to the cool winter night. Her tone changed as she addressed me this time. "I could release your soul, Rem. I could shatter the stone at your word and send you back into the cycle of rebirth. I can't say what would await you there though, or what might await your people. I am not Dante nor the Traveler. I do not control or read Fate, I can simply advise my people."

Translated, that meant "Rem, if you know what's good for everyone you know and love, you'll heed my call, but hey, if you don't they might survive."

Power over creation, the power to protect people, the ability to make my clan stronger, and the power to get revenge against adventurers? It was too good to pass up.

"You win," I said with only a bit of resignation in my tone. "I'll become your Dungeon."

"Good!" The goddess's voice was a melodious symphony of joy that I'd yet to hear. I guess getting her way did that for her. Who knew? "Now, I cannot help you directly on your journey…"

"Of course."

She ignored me, naturally. "But soon you'll have all the help you need. Sleep well, Rem, for when you awaken, your entire life will be the stuff of legends."

Before I could ask her to elaborate, the world around me went dark again.

Then, it wasn't.

Waking up as a spirit was weird. Though, weird seemed to be my normal state of being lately.

There was no grogginess, no lagging between being alertness and oblivion. I was asleep then I was awake. It was sort of like blinking. I did a body check… which was pointless I quickly realized. I was still very much stuck inside the soulstone Cecil had put me in, but there was something different.

I don't know how far they made it or how long I was out for, but I could sense myself sitting in something. Something I quickly identified as bloody, muddy water. There was blood and magic everywhere around me. I can't explain how I knew it, but I could feel it through the walls of the crystal that I was submerged in the stuff. Blood and mud were churning around me like a maelstrom.

Saying that something had changed was a tiny bit of an understatement.

I could feel nearly everything about the world around me maybe a foot in every direction now: the blood suspended in the mud around me, the air that popped in and out of the churning, the earth below the churning mud, and… something causing the storm of bloodied soil. The force felt warm, but what it was doing was horrible for me. I couldn't exactly see or feel it, but my senses told me enough as I was knocked back and forth. Flying around with completely blurry vision was the least amount of fun I'd had since I died, and I wanted it to stop.

On command, the essence of my body responded, lashing out like a whip from my center to attack the force. Even away from me, I could feel my 'body' working to meet my command. I could move it, control it with a thought as it exploded against the… thing?

No…

25

I knew this feeling. It was a familiar feeling, warm and inviting down to my very soul. I couldn't forget the feeling, no more than I could forget Saria's touch on the tips of my ears or the length of my tail swaying as I ran. The thing whirling around me was a spell, and my power was trying to exert its will against it, countering it… with myself in bursts of raw power.

The result went about as well as I could have expected.

I hadn't been a great Oracle, but even I knew the theories of spell-work and magic. Unless you had the proper counter-spell Node mastered, a strong spell needed a stronger or smarter counter-spell to work against it, usually of an opposing or neutral element so things didn't explode everywhere. The problem was that my instinctual command to attack, to counter, was neither of those, and I regretted the choice instantly as I felt my power wane against the storm outside of me. It absorbed my power like a sponge and grew more wild around me. With my soul added to the storm, the empowered fury of the wind was able to pick me up and carry me through the air like a pebble in a stream. All the while, I kept fighting against it.

Needless to say, it wasn't pleasant, and I was feeling sicker by the moment.

It wasn't a physical sickness or vertigo from trashing around in the air. It felt like when I cast too many cantrips without resting. It felt like my personal mana reserve was gushing out of me like a spring, and, as it did, the soulstone prison became more and more spacious as I lost density and volume. If I had a spine, a chill would have run through it as the result of what was going on hit home, and I screamed at myself to stop.

It was spell fatigue.

Just as it had started, my brute force counter-spell ended with a snap and my consciousness swam, both from the knowledge of what had happened and of what my trapped form truly was now.

My body was gone, and my soul trapped within the white soulstone had become mana. I was pure, conscious magic. I was now pure mana, the most powerful force in the known world! Upon further introspection, I even still had my Nodes intact!

The thought was exciting, and if I still had it, I'm sure my tail would be twitching with the potential I now had. As it was, no, my tail could not twitch. This would have been so much more exciting if I wasn't dead.

Being dead sucked the fun out of everything.

Well, at least that explained how Necromancers worked with soul-stones. If I had studied a bit better, I probably would have already made that connection. I always thought there might have been more to it. Even that brought about more frightening ideas. Were all soul-stones alive like me? Were we always spending our souls when we used magic? Is that why we felt empty when we used too much, why we got sick, why some mages died doing grand spells?

I shook the thoughts away. Right now, my mana was me and that's really all that mattered. I might have had all the power in the world, but it was pointless if I couldn't do anything without risking my consciousness.

Around me, the world began to calm. Either the spell was natural and ended when it overloaded with my power, or whoever was casting it had lost control from the unexpected resistance. Either way, I was settled in a nest of leaves in some crater nearby. The blood was gone too, so that was good. I tried to 'see' further, but outside of the crater, there was nothing. The world was a haze of faceted white, and nothing else existed. I knew it did, I had just been there, but it didn't seem to matter to my limited senses.

A noise interrupted my thoughts. I didn't have time to catch its meaning, but not a second later something new entered my territory. The large, fleshy thing wrapped around me while sharp stones clicked against my surface. My sight and senses were drastically limited now, and it was too late to do anything before I realized the danger. It was a mouth.

Something was trying to eat me?

The thought made me furious. I'd been killed, stuffed in a crystal, finally met my goddess, and fought a magical storm for what? Some stupid thing to eat me?

I couldn't even begin to describe how wrong that was.

No! I thrashed as the thought radiated through my being. I need to make the goddess proud! I needed to get back to my people. I won't be taken away again! I wouldn't die again!

Let me go!

I didn't care how weak I was, I tapped into myself and focused on everything I knew. This time, I wouldn't go without a fight.

Chapter Four
The New Strange

I reached through the mana that made me and gripped my only real Oracle spell. The power was as invigorating as it was draining as every spark of my mana flared to life at my command word.

Forbid! You will not touch me! I screamed with all my power as the spell's effect flooded my very being. As quickly as I felt its power, it rushed out from me and collided with whatever held me. All the while, I continued to scream the command. *You will not touch me!*

The mouth continued to stay shut around me as it trotted along as my power flowed out.

You will not touch me!

Its jaw didn't slack in the slightest, and it continued to hold me as I tried to impart my will onto the world.

You will not touch me!

Again and again, I repeated myself, forcing more and more of my power into it until the spell's cooldown began, but nothing happened. Whatever held me was too strong for me to Forbid. A strange mix of fear and annoyance washed over me as I processed my current problem.

I was helpless again.

As my mana depleted, my perception failed me, and my vision faded into outlines and shadows. All I could sense was the air around me, the mouth that nibbled me closer and closer to what I was sure was my death, and all I could see was tongue, saliva, and teeth. I did not like feeling like a piece of fruit.

I've never been so angry in all my life or death. I could almost feel my fists clenching in rage, and my ears folding back against my skull.

Every strand of fur on my body bristled as they stood on end, ready for combat. I wanted to attack. I wanted to tear at it. I wanted to kill it. Being handled so easily, moved without my will, forced to where others wanted me, and by a dumb animal no less! It all felt wrong, so very wrong, and I finally snapped the final string of sanity I had left.

No one tried to eat me without my permission!

I snarled in my mind's eye at the creature. I still may have felt weak from mana loss, but anger wouldn't allow me to stay that way. It fueled me enough to sharpen my weakened senses. I couldn't stop now. Another cantrip, I needed something offensive! Spark maybe? I hadn't mastered it into a Node, but I knew the form well enough to try. I tried to remember the Pattern for it, but something even stranger than meeting the goddess happened.

A voice resounded through the shell of my body and into my very soul like nothing I'd heard or felt in all my life or death. "If you can understand me, please stop that. You're going to kill yourself, young Core. If you exhaust your mana while you're this young, you'll cease to be, but if you want to truly die, by all means, keep trying."

Suddenly, the teeth were gone, and I felt the world drop around me. The creature had let go, I realized in the same moment as my momentum picked up! Whatever it was, it's master must have realized I wasn't a treat and made the creature spit me out.

Hooray for being a choking hazard!

Then, I saw the creature clearly for the first time and screamed. "Ah! Giant fox!"

Fear made you forget you couldn't talk. It really took all the fun out of things.

Strangely, the giant fox screamed back. I'd heard foxes in distress before, but this was even worse. It was like nothing I'd ever heard before.

Then I screamed.

Then it screamed.

Then I screamed again.

I'm embarrassed to say I don't know for how long this went on for, but eventually, I realized that the creature was as surprised at me as I was at it. As if we understood one another, the screaming stopped, and we were left staring at one another.

Carefully, it nudged me with its nose. I couldn't feel the nose, but if it was like all its kin, it would be cold. It was wet though, somehow, it left an imprint of its wet snout on the surface of my stone, making it a bit hard to see in that direction, which reminded me I could see in all directions.

I may have accepted this fate, but that didn't mean that I had to like everything about it. I waited for the creature's owner—the voice, presumably—to take it away, but after a few more seconds of it nudging me, I took matters into my own hands.

"Shoo! Go away," I projected. I couldn't really speak, but since it screamed at me too, I knew it could somehow hear me.

Then, it sat down on its haunches and cocked its head. That's when I noticed the entire world was huge. The trees were huge, the blades of grass were huge, everything was huge! It wasn't a giant fox. It was a normal fox, and I had just forgotten I was a fist-sized stone rather than a tall, luxuriously white-furred Foxkin.

Stupid adventurers.

It was a strange fox though. Its fur was pure white like mine. Unlike a normal fox, it also had a pair of golden amber eyes and two tails.

But soon you'll have all the help you need.

"Did the Goddess Vul send you?" I ventured.

I was talking to a fox. I mean, it was a special fox. It had two tails and that meant it wasn't normal, right? I doubted that the goddess would employ your average animal, and since I couldn't see or even sense another creature, I tried again when it didn't give me any kind of acknowledgment. "Can you hear me? Nod if you can hear me."

I was proven right about the normal part at least. Nearly the moment after I thought the words at it, the creature's tails shot up, and its head nodded once forward. Well, at least it understood me.

"I did, young Core! You can call me Vix!"

With those simple words, I stopped everything. Everything in my brain came to a screeching halt as an animal spoke to me. No, not just spoke to me, spoke inside my head at me.

I was not ready for this.

31

I'd been raised around feral foxes. We used them for hunting on a regular basis. I knew what they'd sounded like, but the voice... the voice of this one wasn't like anything I'd ever heard before. It was like an entire children's chorus at once doing a slightly delayed round of howling song. Every word had a song-like quality despite our earlier screaming. I kind of liked it if I was being honest.

As I considered what to do next, I thought about the day's events. I'd been murdered, trapped in a soulstone, finally met my patron deity, and agreed to become a Dungeon to better my own people. No, a talking fox didn't even really register on my new level of strange. The only thing that really registered was the word it used to address me.

Core.

The goddess said I was going to become a Dungeon, so why didn't it call me that or better, my name?

What was a Core?

The question didn't have a time to manifest as the creature's jaws closed around me. I don't want to say I panicked, but I managed to not throw mana at it—umm, Vix—like I had before. As the teeth gingerly closed around me, I felt a distinct happiness from the fox. In fact, I think it was doing a happy little dance now that it had me. I didn't have much more time left to think before it spoke again. The words were slightly garbled around my stone, but I could still make them out. More like they were sent directly to my mind rather than spoken to me.

"You are a Core! Didn't the goddess already go over all this?"

Wait... could Vix hear me thinking?

"Yes, I did. I can hear any of Goddess Vul's Oracles if I'm near enough."

Well, that was interesting.

The two-tailed fox considered my words before deciding to speak. "I've come to help you. My lady called me, and I have arrived! Though, you've been asleep for some time. I'm so sorry it's been so long, but I couldn't wake you."

I stopped trying to think and instead tried to imagine myself speaking. It was odd, but it felt better than just thinking to myself. Bitterness dripped from my voice like a poison as I replied. "You know, I could have used you two earlier when they smashed my head in like a melon."

I might not have been able to see Vix's ears or tail, but the almost overly-perky tones of its melodious voice melted into a deep sadness as it spoke again. "Well, I didn't know," Vix replied defensively. "Besides, I can't change the past, Master Core. If it's any consolation, I have been keeping watch around the forest while you've been asleep. You are one of the Foxkin, right?"

"I was," I corrected, feeling the acute lack of ears, fur, tail, or any sort of a body right now.

"You still are," Vix explained as it picked back up its happy trot. "In a way, you always will be. Your soul will always be a Foxkin. A soul only changes if there's some dark influence or corruptive magics used on it." That... wasn't comforting. "If it's any consolation, the entire sulk of your family and surrounding clans have been looking for you for over a month now."

For the second or third time that day, I was at a loss. It just wasn't worth keeping track anymore.

I felt like I would shatter at its words. If I had a heart, it would have sunken in my chest and broken. I was silent for a long time before my mind finally couldn't contain it anymore. "Over a month! How could it have been over a month? It just happened a few hours ago! I was in a puddle of bloody mud for the Pantheon's sake! They couldn't have died more than a few hours ago."

Then again, I hadn't seen any bodies when I woke up. Where were the bodies if they died? More troubling, where had the blood come from then?

"Umm, you've been unconscious for a long time," Vix began after a few moments more of thought. "I've only came to find you when my mistress told me to. I can't explain the blood though," and if it had read my thoughts, "or the missing bodies." That was reassuring in no sort of way, but the two-tailed fox quickly changed the topic. "Now, you're the first one I've met, but Cores tend to awaken slowly to their power, and you're already overusing it. If you keep doing that, it's going to put you into a dormant state. It's kind of like being in a coma if you're alive. Have you used yourself much since awakening?"

33

I wanted to shake my head, but when I realized it was pointless, I simply said, "Not really. I tried to counter a spell earlier, but that was just a few minutes ago"

Guilt laced Vix's voice this time. "It was a tracing spell attuned to Cores like yourself. I… might have over done it."

That was an understatement even from my smaller perspective.

Well, at least Vix didn't mind admitting when it screwed up. I couldn't stop myself from thinking something very rude, but I tried to drown it out by speaking over it. "It wasn't a great test."

"Could have been worse," Vix explained as it pulled me closer. "Now I need to figure a few things out. Do you know if any kind of restriction has been placed on you since you've died?"

Of course, restriction was a very broad word. I was just sucked into a soulstone, but other than that I had no idea what that was.

Sensing my confusion, my new friend fox continued its chorus of conversation. "A spell to put you to sleep or control your abilities?"

"Maybe? I fell asleep after that damned mage put me in here."

I bobbed in its mouth as Vix gave a nod, and its voice began to feel much more sympathetic. "It happens more often than you might think, but you are a happy accident."

"Oh boy, just like what my parents told me," I groaned. This was not a good day, or a good month if the voice was telling the truth.

"Um, yes."

At least I could still make 'people' uncomfortable with my humor. That did make me feel a little more alive.

"You have a divine blessing, so your soul is stronger than most. Knowing magic made it even more resilient to decay and corruption as you used and trained it. If you hadn't been captured, your spirit would have easily endured until your chose to leave this plane. You might even have become something greater, as some spirits occasion-ally do. However, when that mage bound your soul in here…" for emphasis, the fox lifted a paw, showed its claws, and brought it down onto me to tap on what I assumed was my face for emphasis. Of course, I felt nothing, but I did pick up a very distinct 'tinking' sound. "… your destiny was set as soon as the spell was cast. He had no idea what he had created."

The goddess did, but I wasn't going to point that out.

"An angry Foxkin isn't the obvious outcome of wrongfully murdering someone?" I growled. How many times would I wish for my teeth, my face, or anything to help me show anything. How did other races manage?

"That," it almost giggled, "and a Dungeon Core."

There was that word again. I paused taking it in and considering it. I knew what a Dungeon was now, but a Dungeon Core? "And that is…"

The voice sang again with more than a modicum of disbelief in its song this time. "As the name implies, it the Core of magic that's the heart of any true Dungeon."

"Thank you, Clan Leader Obvious the Great." I grinned inwardly as it seemed taken aback.

"You… haven't heard of Dungeon Cores before?"

I sent it the feeling of a shrug to see if it would have the same effect as my words, and to my surprise, it worked.

"And the Goddess didn't say anything about it?"

This time I shook my head.

"I see. Well, I guess there are very few proper Dungeons in any of the Beastkin lands." The beast sighed before continuing, "We have much work to do, don't we?"

"Apparently." Though what work to be done wasn't very appealing. I had my agenda. "It would help if I understood half of what you were talking about though."

"Of course." Vix cleared its throat. Its annoyance began to fade away as it began. "You are a rare creature. You are special. You are a Dungeon Core, and you are now one of the most important people your race has ever produced. Congratulations on that. Though your loss is great, your gains can be so much greater as part of this new life, and I am here to guide you to The Academy to embrace your destiny."

An academy? That was something I knew about. Humans went to academies. They were giant schools where they would learn everything from basic knowledge to more advanced concepts like runic magic and magical item crafting. It was a place where plenty of learning went on, tests were had, and titles were given…

35

And that sounded like work...

Chapter Five
Snap, Crack, Pop

There was only one thing I could do to waylay Vix's line of thought. "I have questions!"

At that, Vix sighed and set me on the ground. "We would move faster if we just went, and you let me do my job, but fine. Let's have your questions."

"What's the academy? Why can't I walk? Why can't I move? How come as a ghost I can't leave the stone now that it's not under a mage's control. Why is —"

Vix grew annoyed very quickly and put me back into its mouth, squeezing very gently on my shell. Not to hurt me, I think, but to get me to stop. "You talk like an annoying child! One question! One! Then we're leaving."

Sket. Alright, what would serve me best to know? "Why can I sense everything around me?" I quickly made an amendment, "Well, everything except you."

Even though it was technically two questions, they had the same outcome and Vix humored me. It laughed its disturbingly multi-faceted laugh and took a breath. Feeling my annoyance simmer, it stopped suddenly. "You're serious?" My thoughts began to boil as an answer, and Vix recoiled. "You can see me, tap into your Nexus for mana, cast rudimentary spells without a Node for it, and mark territory, but you don't know what your Dungeon Nexus Nodes do?"

I got the distinct impression I should be insulted, but I really, really was curious. When I was alive, and apparently now, I still had a Nexus, but no one had two Nexi. Was that even the plural? "Look, for me, it's been a day or two at most, and all my senses feel weird now. I need to understand everything to survive. I'd love to move too, but one thing at a time."

I felt something strange envelop me as I finished speaking and by instinct threw mana at it. It was starting to be a bad habit. Even if it was kind of fun to see the reactions to it around me, it left me feeling dangerously weak.

Vix just let loose a disappointed sigh. "Could you stop that? It's very annoying."

I had to admit, it was fun annoying the fox, but if I had been in my old body, I doubt I could have sat up with how weak I felt. "Would you warn me then before you cast a spell on me?"

"I'm not trying to cast anything," Vix replied defensively as its tails rustled in annoyance. "I'm trying to form a link from my power to yours. Seeing, speaking, feeling, hearing, and anything else a Core does comes from its refinement or mana reserves. You're reserves are low, no larger than when you were alive, and this stone..." I felt a quick prick of mana, but Vix ignored my annoyance and continued. "Is a very low grade soulstone. Your Nodes aren't properly developed because of it. Besides that, most Dungeon Cores begin with a Rank E mana reservoir, but with all the imperfections in this Core, you barely register as a Rank F. Just being around an SS Ranked Core like Ansith could kill you by accident."

That scared me.

Rank F was used to classify anything helpless that couldn't process or collect any of the ambient mana needed for basic bodily functions. Regular animals were even at least Rank E. Regular animals also had basic Nodes for survival, and Vix was saying mine were damaged.

That was a death sentence...

Again...

I focused and looked inward for the first time at my Nexus since my death. Strangely, everything was there that should be. I had my Nodes still connected and holding my concentration of Celestial mana like it should. It was still Rank D. I could feel it. It was nowhere near Rank F, but as I kept looking, I couldn't deny something felt wrong. There was more mana, a strange mana separate from my own that was draining from the imperfections in the stone itself. As I studied it further, I noticed my own Nexus was surrounded by five other Nodes, five other cracked Nodes. The cracks prevented the Nexus from doing its job and the mana it held was leaking like water through a cracked bucket, and worse, it wasn't replenishing itself.

I'd used that mana to counter the spell and to lash out at Vix. Twice.

A cold fear crept through my entire form as I realized just how dangerous the situation I was in was. I'd nearly killed myself with sheer stupidity, but did I do all this damage? How had I managed to nearly destroy this other Nexus? Where had it come from?

Either not sensing or ignoring my fear, Vix continued. "If we are going to take you to learn and serve your people, you need mana, and you need to have those Nodes repaired. Accept my help."

I hesitated. My soul was mine, I didn't want Vix getting its mana all entwined with mine. I didn't want to think what would happen if Vix did something it shouldn't. Then again, it was the goddess's envoy. At Vix's annoyed look, I realized my mistake. It wasn't a normal animal, just another part of my new normal. That didn't mean I had to like it though.

Of course, Vix knew all of that, and seemingly more. "Well, you can accept my help, or you can die from mana leakage, or I can leave you back in that crater of yours for some adventurer to find. Maybe you'll figure out how to repair yourself, survive, and figure everything out on your own, or maybe some lucky adventurer will cut you into a nice stone for a staff or a necklace. I hear opal is all the rage for Clerics and mages of the light."

Being cut and shaped? That... didn't sound pleasant either. Then again, none of it sounded like a good option, so did I really have a choice?

For a long while, I stared at the Nodes, trying to decipher the skills I had passively learned, but they were too badly damaged. If I tried to use any of them, they'd probably shatter and kill me all the faster.

I hesitated longer than I wanted to admit, but after deciding that having my soul repaired by a goddess's envoy was better than dying or being made into a fancy necklace, I finally answered. "Will it hurt?"

"Does using magic hurt?"

That was a stupid question, but I guess my question was stupid in its own right for someone like Vix. "No…"

"Then trust me, it won't."

With that, Vix tried again and extended another tendril of mana towards me. It was an odd thing. Now that I was focusing on it, I could see the mana in a way I hadn't ever seen before. It was a beautiful collection of off-reds, tinged at the edges with the shades of a hundred different oranges and pinks, like those of a sunset over the Wildwood in the early winter months. Encasing it all was the gleaming, glossy white of Vix's fur and the gold of its eyes. The power felt welcoming this time, homey, and more familiar rather than invading, so I opened myself to it…

"Okay, I've established a link!"

And… that felt like a mistake.

The acceptance of Vix's mana had opened a floodgate into me. The power rushed in, denser and stronger than I could have produced myself even when I'd been alive. It surged and thrashed as my essence fought to absorb it, and I was forced into my own soul.

I was a passive observer, no more able to control the mana than I was able to control a flood as it overflowed past my soul's capacity and into the strange Secondary Nexus. When it reached the first Node in a shallow tendril, I could sense Vix inside my head again, but I couldn't see it this time. My entire world was the rushing mana and Vix's voice as I watched the Nexus strain under the assault.

"Don't worry. I know what's wrong! The goddess told me this might happen. I am helping attune your soul to your Core."

That was easy for it to say. Vix's mana wasn't in danger of exploding its Nexus. The envoy's mana flowed towards that same Node and pushed, the mana flowing into the cracks, over the Node, and engulfing it. Then…

Crack!

I heard it before I felt it, and it hurt! It actually, really hurt! That lying bastard. It hurt so badly that I could actually feel my outer shell beginning to break under the stress of the new power. Whatever Vix thought it was supposed to feel like, I doubted this was it.

Too bad I couldn't scream.

The power flowed from one Node to the next, doing the same thing as it had the first time. As soon as the second of the five Nodes were engulfed, I heard and felt it again.

Crack!

More pain came with the next crack as the churning mana whirled around my original Nexus. Everything that was me was focused on redirecting or assimilating the power, but it felt so pointless. My soul was a hurricane beyond any control. Thunder and lightning echoed in myself as mana clashed against an opposing tide. I tried to control it. I tried to cycle it out of myself, and when that failed, I tried to reform it, but it wasn't enough as the third Node came under the same attack.

Crack!

This was worse than dying! I tried to do something with the excess, but any Node I tried to use just collapsed back into its network under the overflow of Vix's influence. Raw power just kept coming, overwhelming me until fear gripped me hard enough that it felt like a solid entity as my fourth Node was engulfed.

Crack!

I couldn't take it anymore. Mana kept coming and coming, stretching my reserves, cracking my Node's careful network, and finally breaking the last defenses I had been keeping up, forcing me further and further under its deluge. I was drowning in Vix's vast ocean despite being able to breathe. With no other options and no power of my own to oppose it, I finally gave up and fell under the current of power with a final thought. *Why me?*

Crack!

Pop!

Chapter Six

A Body of Proof

Pop?

The small sound was almost enough to make me laugh. That was anticlimactic.

As my fear ebbed, I released my grip on the ground—

Wait...

Hands? I looked down at them in wonder. They weren't perfect, but they weren't spectral either. They were mine, just more white-ish in appearance now, except for my fur. Parts of it had been streaked with violet, with the color fading out as it spread up towards my shoulders. Even with that strange violet, something else had changed. As I moved my new digits and examined my tinted furs, I could tell there was another difference too. My new body was just reflective enough to catch the light and throw it like I was made from glass. In fact, it was almost exactly as reflective as the soulstone I'd been imprisoned in. Everything about me gleamed in the setting sunlight, showing all sorts of colors dancing within—

Wait...

By the divine Pantheon, I could see like a normal Foxkin again! I reached for my ears and touched them, no doubt grinning wide and large like a child. I could see, I could feel, and I had my ears! Checking myself from tip to tail, I had legs too! They weren't hard to miss with the lack of clothing I had, but I had my tail, too, and other... important things. My fur kept me from feeling the worse of it, so I felt oh so wonderfully alive in the cool air. It was amazing in a way only someone that had it all, lost it, and regained it could know.

I was alive, and I was me again.

The feeling was wonderful in more ways than I could describe. I looked from my hands to the world around me and took it all in. I could feel the beautiful, cold winds of winter that brought the snows. I could feel the earth under me, and I could hear the howling storm approaching. The pop I heard didn't matter anymore. I didn't care what it meant. I was back!

I dropped all sense of pride and cried. I balled like a newborn child that wanted their mother. It was deep, true sobbing that could never be mimicked by an ungrateful creature. After my pitiful joyful reunion with the world I turned to thank Vix, only for my vision to move back into my Nexus as if my sight had a will of its own.

"Don't be alarmed," Vix echoed in my mind. "I'm just directing your sight to your Nexus."

At least I got a warning this time.

As I looked inward, I could see the first Node was fully restored now thanks to Vix's mana and efforts, and the second, third, fourth, and fifth. Never had I heard of magic that could repair Nodes once they'd broken, and hearing about a Node breaking was rare in itself.

"Holy sket."

One by one, my eyes scanned the Nodes, focusing long enough to take in what they were, and take it in I did. In all its glory, I read my new Class information:

Dungeon Core
Mastered Skills: 5 of 5
Secondary Skills: 0
Dungeon Core Rank D9
0/9 requirements met to reach Rank C
Dungeon Core Nexus Size 1
Dungeon Core Material - Opal/Amethyst
Mana Types - Celestial/Umbral/Unknown
Mana Reserves:
Celestial - 100/100
Umbral - 10/10
Unknown - 500/500
Class Passive for Mastery:
Dungeon Mana Reservoir: Mana Reservoir grows based on use.

Influence
Primary Class Node - Active/Passive Ability - Dungeon Core
Evolution Potential - None
Active Effect: Spread your Influence by spending mana to claim an unclaimed area or fight another Influence. Influence spread is equal to Size, Rank, and mana spent. Claimed areas generate mana equal to the power and density of aether present in the material claimed. Material touched by your Influence within your Influence gives off a faint light related to your primary mana type. Influence cannot be used to claim living things or sufficiently powerful constructs.
Passive Effect: When mana reaches critical levels within your Core and cycling has been sustained for a substantial time, the effect of cycling mana within the Core will become a passive effect based on your prior skill use.
Passive Effect: Fabrication and Absorption can only be used within an area of Influence.

Fabrication
Primary Class Node - Active Ability - Dungeon Core
Evolution Potential - None
Cost: Scales with complexity
Effect: Spend mana to create or recreate items from Patterns that you have absorbed via absorption, created, or have sufficient knowledge of to attempt to recreate it from memory. Cost is directly related to the power, complexity, and Rank of the item created.
Creation is limited to items within two Ranks of your current Dungeon Core Class.
Rank D Attributes Locked:
Item Fusion is current locked. Requirement Rank D2 - Core Size 2

Absorption
Primary Class Node - Active Ability - Dungeon Core
Evolution Potential - None
Cost: None
Effect: Absorb a non-living creature or item to learn its Pattern to recreate it. Upon absorbing an item, gain mana equal to the

complexity of the item. Items can be absorbed repeatedly to improve the detail of the Pattern or gain mana.

Manifestation
Primary Class Node - Active Ability - Dungeon Core
Evolution Potential - None
Cost: Scales with power
Effect: Use mana to create an inhabitable simulacrum based on a predetermined, personal image. The simulacrum's power is equal to the size, rank, and mana spent to create it. The Rank and mana of the simulacrum cannot surpass the non-Dungeon Nexus of the intended controller, though excess mana can be stored in the body to maintain it for independent operation. Cost to maintain the simulacrum is equal to its power.

Dungeon Memory
Primary Class Node - Passive Ability - Dungeon Core
Evolution Potential - None
Cost: N/A
Passive Effect: Stores and recalls the Patterns, mana requirements, ranks, abilities, and other attributes of any item, creature, or material absorbed by your Absorption ability. Patterns are separated between Pattern Memory, the Index, and Creature Memory, the Bestiary.
Rank D Attributes Locked:
Bestiary is current locked. Requirement Rank D7 - Core Size 2
Codex is currently locked. Requirement Rank D7 - Core Size 2

I was silent for a long moment as I came out of my Nexus trance, and it wasn't just because I had no sket-ing idea what to even say to Vix. I had a mastered class, and what a class it was! Even with all the power the Skill Nodes held, I was somehow still a D rank. I could even tell how much mana I had access to. If I was reading that description right, however, I was aetherically as weak as a child, but I had a class with abilities so powerful I could literally do anything!

Was this some kind of joke?

Vix didn't seem to think so as it looked me over with an approving nod. "I was worried it wouldn't work."

I felt a passing anger, but let it drift down the river as I said what was really on my mind. "What happened?"

Vix mentally sent me a smile. "Your Dungeon skills have awakened, my young Core."

"Please, call me Rem from now on," I said, as that term didn't really seem to fit anymore. "And I'm not a Core anymore," If I'd ever really been one, I helpfully pointed out. "As you can see, I'm a Foxkin, tip to tail."

I wanted to hug that tail as it twitched behind me. Opal and violet or not, it was still me again!

At my words, Vix looked annoyed and began to approach with a look of intent in its eyes. If you've ever seen a cute little fox try to be intimidating, you'll appreciate it was very, very hard to achieve. I will say that I was surprised when a pair of white and gold tendrils erupted from its back like tentacles of light and began to allow her, yes for it was undeniably a her now, to fly to eye level.

One of those tendrils broke from their floating, wing-like Pattern to move towards my face. First instinct told me to bite, but then again, I was smart enough to know that biting someone that worked for the goddess Vul would probably be organized into the category of bad ideas. I braced myself, waiting for some attack or some other triggering power to overwhelm me, but as the glowing limb of light touched my forehead that didn't happen.

Tink.

There was no pain. No blood. No… anything really. I didn't even feel the impact of her finger of magic against my forehead. All that I heard was that very un-fleshy noise of crystal. I must not have responded as she wanted, so Vix did it again, a few times in quick succession.

Tink. Tink. Tink. Tink.

Finally, it clicked, or rather, it tinked. There was something there.

Tink. Tink.

"Quit it," I protested and raised my hands to feel at my forehead.

The soulstone that had been my prison was now jutting out from my forehead! Tracing the object, I could feel a thumb sized chunk jutting out from my head. I couldn't see it, but I could feel it if I

46

thought about it. The rest of the stone was still there, buried just beneath the surface. Nothing had changed in it except for its location. The thought of the rest of it inside my skull was slightly disturbing. "The Mists?"

"You've Manifested. It's quite different from a true resurrection," Vix, oh so helpfully, explained as I continued to examine the stone with a finger or two. "With my help and the repairs to your skill Nodes—you're welcome by the way, Rem—your soul has infused itself with enough mana to exist outside the Core for now. Normally, only C or higher rank Cores can do this themselves outside of their or another Dungeon, or anywhere really in the West, without help. There are a few other locations it can be done easily, but anywhere else it's very taxing without sufficient natural mana. From what I've seen so far, you're not losing too much mana right now, so sustaining your form shouldn't be too hard once you've figured everything else out."

I tapped the stone in my forehead again a few more times for emphasis and sighed as the sound resounded through the air and my form.

Tink. Tink. Tink.

I had a fleeting idea that I could run back to the clans and assure them that the stories of my demise were greatly exaggerated, but with Vix's explanation, and another quick review of my Manifestation skill, there was going to be no running back to the clan for me.

Besides, they'd probably think I was a ghost at this point and try to free me from this mortal coil.

I relaxed a bit. Standing up, I focused on feeling my personal reserve of mana like I'd done a million times before. Sure, my Dungeon Core Nodes were there, but what about my Oracle ones? What if they'd cracked, or worse shattered, too? Thankfully, each of the Nodes were wholly undamaged. If I were being honest with myself, I was surprised to see that it and my Nodes were intact. My mana was even full too, just waiting for me to need it.

What I saw and felt, however, was nothing compared to what Vix had been using to sustain me. My Oracle Nexus was just a small drop in a sea of donated mana, outranking my power at least four to one.

Without her, I'd just be a rock again, and I couldn't go back to that with so much potential at my fingertips. "So, what do I do now?"

It wasn't even a question. "Well, you made a promise to the Goddess. She delivered, and now it's your turn to do your part for your people."

At least that seemed reasonable. I had given my word I'd help, and I wouldn't break it now after Vix had already done so much for me. Her power was a good deterrent, too. I didn't doubt for a moment that she could undo what she did in the first place. Not that she'd need to, but that kind of power gave someone pause. I gave her my best grin as my hands went behind my head and massaged the back of my neck. "Should have figured as much."

She smiled. "I'm glad you're not trying to run."

"Perish the thought!" I said, feigning some level of hurt, still unsure whether or not Vix could read my thoughts at that distance, contact or not. "Can you give me a moment?"

"Of course, Rem, but just a moment."

With her permission, I took one last look around. This was my home... I... I wasn't ready to leave. I hesitated, looking everywhere but at her. The crater she picked me up from looked so small a few feet away from where she'd dropped me and I'd Manifested. The tree leaves that still clung to the branches were starting to burn with the reds and golds of the fall. The grasses were still so green underfoot, and over there far to the west would have been the clan. If I kept going, there'd be a lake, and even further would be the edge of the Wildwood. I kept my attention to the forest, finding things to study or recalling memories, delaying my new question, but finally, I only had one thing to look to, Vix, and I felt my heart ache.

The goddess had said I'd serve my people, my purpose, as a Dungeon for the Foxkin, but... "Can I come back here when I'm done?"

I hadn't realized until that moment just how unfox-like her face was. Sure, it had a muzzle, wet nose, and all the other foxy accents, but her face was able to move in ways I'd never seen the animal do in the wild. I could have sworn that her face softened into something like a sympathetic smile, lips curling up and all. "The Goddess has plans for you, Rem." At those words, my heart fell. Vix was quicker though, and scooped it right back up to where she and I both felt it belonged. "She wouldn't have it any other way."

I may not have known the full extent of Vul's plans, but it was enough. I let out a soft sigh. My tail and ears must have gone with my breath though. Either that, or she could read my face better than my mind.

"Where a Core is created is usually where they return to. Your power has already touched this area. After your first few days of training, you'll return and make it truly your own, Young Core."

"Rem," I corrected her absently, trying to take everything in one last time. "Call me Rem."

"Alright, Rem then, so, shall we go?"

Hearing my name again made me smile. It reminded me of who I was more than what I had become. I had a family out there, and they were strong. When I became their trial, when I was a Dungeon proper, they might come to me to better the clan. When they did, they might see me, they might recognize me, and I might hear stories then of the person I was. Then maybe, just maybe, I could make a connection to the clan again. Maybe I could find some semblance of a family again. Maybe even friends?

It wasn't much to go on with my beck and call of a god, but it was a plan.

My smile turned just a bit wider at the idea. It wasn't as bit as a happy smile might be like all the times when I played pranks on Saria. It wasn't by far a sad one either. I'd like to think it was a purposed smile of determination. The expression was tinged with the weight of knowledge and challenge as I repeated my mantra again piece by piece, amending each one in my mind.

I am Rem.
I have a family.
I have friends.
I will not give up on them because they never gave up on me.
Whether they know me again or not, I will be their strength.
Finally, I gave Vix my answer. "Yeah, let's go, Vix."

Vix's face would have been horrifying if I hadn't been expecting that strange, feline smile again. "Good. Then we need to move."

"How far are we going?" I asked.

The smile faded from Vix's face at that, and I felt a bit of worry. "It's a long trip to the academy, Rem. Weeks, maybe even a month on foot in good weather." She gave me the smallest of smiles. "But we are not traveling on foot."

"That's good."

"Do not be alarmed," Vix assured me as her tails began to move like the floating tendrils.

Suddenly, I did not like that smile. "What do—"

In the span of a breath, Vix's tails shot forward and pressed against my forehead's stone, and the roaring tide of mana I'd become so accustomed to cut itself off from me. An instant later, my reservoir ran down to a comparable puddle, and my new body collapsed back into its container with a very distinct *pop* before I was just a soulstone… No, just a Dungeon Core once more.

Well, that was rude.

Chapter Seven

Opening Ceremonies

My new body might have had its perks, like being able to bring my soul back from the dead, but there was one major drawback. Not the constant need for mana to sustain myself, nor even the stone jutting out of my forehead. My major annoyance came from something much simpler than that.

I did not like popping like a soap bubble when I ran out of mana!

Manifesting felt like my old self. I had all my old senses, and I could even feel the old ticks I'd developed in my muscles when I felt happy, sad, or excited. That just made being popped back into the stone all the worse. It was just a cruel reminder of what I wasn't anymore. At least Vix had seemed sorry about it or at least tried to be understanding about it as I seethed and bristled, but her explanation was good enough that I couldn't argue.

"I can't fly with a Foxkin five times my weight even if I have Goddess Vul's blessings."

I grumbled, but my complaints were pointless. It wasn't like I could Manifest by myself yet. She said I'd have to be Rank C, and I was plenty of experience away from being able to expand my reservoir to hold that much mana. At least as an Oracle I was just a few Nodes away. As a Dungeon Core, I had no idea what I was doing. Sure, I could gather mana like a kleptomaniac could grab coin, but most skills needed to be taught to be used effectively. I very much lacked that training, so as it stood, I didn't have the reserves or the environmental support for it. Besides even if I did, Vix would just drop me anyways. Where would I be then? A hunk of broken crystal on the ground probably.

So, for now it was back to the bubble vision and foot wide sphere of knowledge-gaining. I could still sense things I touched or that entered my limited Influence, and that was interesting in itself. I learned a lot in a short time. Clouds were water, apparently, in a different form; who knew? Even with my newfound ability to break down simple things into parts, I still couldn't sense what made Vix. To my senses, my Influence and Absorption skills mostly, she was a puzzle. Thinking back to how my Influence skill worked, it was probably because she was a living thing or a construct powerful enough to resist me. I doubted it was that hard at my level of power.

I knew she could read my thoughts, but I was glad this time there wasn't an answer. Maybe flying took a lot more focus than I thought? I know I wouldn't want to plummet like a rock out of the sky. I might even enjoy her flying me around if it wasn't for the complete lack of any other sensory information and the eternal view of the inside of her mouth.

***

Are we there yet? I projected to my carrier.

It felt like we'd been in the air for days, weeks even, but that could have just been my boredom talking. All I'd sensed for the entire trip was the never-changing composition of air around me, the clouds of water we passed through, and the pressure of the hand moving me back and forth while holding itself around my shell of crystal.

Days in the air to think about myself were leaving me more like myself, so banter it was.

"For the tenth time today, Rem. No, we are not there yet."

And for the tenth time today, I didn't like the answer. *Bored.*

"It'll be —"

Bored!

Her sigh of annoyance was just a small tick of victory for the old me. In retrospect, maybe I deserved what happened next.

She opened her mouth wide and dropped me.

I couldn't feel the drop itself at first, but I could feel the pressure of her teeth loosen around me. A second later, the air was rushing past me, and my sensory input was growing by the second as everything rushed by me faster and faster. At first, I laughed and hollered with the thrill, but I quickly realized that was not the right response and screamed. Not that she could hear me without touching me, but I kept screaming as my velocity increased.

Then, the familiar view, tongue, pointy teeth, and all, returned.

Vix had, thankfully, reclaimed me from my free-fall, and I felt air rushing in the other direction. Despite the speed and pressure, there was something new in the air that chilled my soul. Vix was laughing at me.

How dare she!

I was hurt and felt just slightly betrayed as she asked, "Are you still bored, Rem?"

I couldn't even pretend as I felt the humor in her sing-song voice and projected a smile, knowing a good prank when I felt one. "Nope."

Unlike Saria though, I was smart enough not to provoke the prankster again for the rest of the trip. Once we landed though, all bets would be off.

One good turn deserved another, after all.

***

Vix spoke to me again; it felt like it'd been another day, and we'd landed again. Over the trip, she'd landed a few times to rest and eat, but instantly, I could tell that this place was different. There was a thickness to the air, a heaviness lingered around everything that I could feel even within my soulstone prison.

It felt like… me.

It was a raw power I knew well enough by now since I'd become it. The air was rich with mana ripe for the harvest. I'd never felt so much of it, so purely before. I tried to draw it in from around me, and it came to call. The mana-rich world around me didn't even lessen as I pulled at it and focused on the same feeling I had before when I had

Manifested the last time, when it had been forced, but Vix interrupted the process, tapping on me with a series of melodious tinks.

"Not yet, Rem." Her tone wasn't harsh, but it was enough to know I was being scolded. I wanted to be me again. I knew Vix could feel that, and she elaborated. "You've not Manifested on your own yet, so listen carefully. You had a powerful sense of self when I repaired your Node. With a little prompting, it was easy to bring you out as you saw yourself. Don't lose that image, Rem. That is your key to Manifestation. It'll also let you skip the Core of Yourself class."

Class? Her sense of humor was odd enough that I wasn't sure whether or not she was serious, but this place was supposed to be an academy after all. Of course there would be classes on how to use our skills. Why wouldn't there be? I was pulled from my thoughts as Vix continued to lecture me.

"Are you listening?"

"Of course," I assured her.

"Good. Now as you pull in mana from the aether, there are two parts to triggering Manifestation. First, you need to picture yourself preferably dressed. Otherwise, you'll be in the nude again, and I don't need to see that again."

Ah yes, I'd almost forgotten in my excitement that I was naked before, and that nudity was frowned upon if you weren't a child in normal society. If this place was going to teach me what I needed to know, I guess I should want to make a good first impression. If they wanted to see the real me though—

She tapped on my surface again with a little more force than necessary. "No."

"But I'm beautiful!" I protested.

"No, Rem."

"Fine." Stupid thought reading.

Letting go of the minor annoyance I had towards her, I did as Vix explained. I'd triggered plenty of Nodes before and used plenty of skills. Dungeon Core skills were no different than that. In all honesty, it was pretty simple. In my mind's eye, I brought up a picture of myself like I would a spell form I was trying to cast. Taller than most, I was always the kind to stand out, even without my white coloring. That part was easy. From there, my image got more specific.

I was Foxkin with shaggy fur atop my head, two pointed ears that erupted from the chaos, and well-treated fur across everywhere to protect me from the elements. I had two each legs and arms, both with well-tended claw like nails at the end of my hands, a reliable, long tail, some muscle here and there... All of that and more came together to make me who I was. With that clear self-image, I held it in myself firmly in mind, and I began pulling in mana from the air around me. Then I stopped and let it go.

Oh yeah, clothes were important. I'd almost forgotten.

I started again when my entire self-image was dressed, wearing a pair of comfortable pants and an equally comfortable shirt. I had a curious thought when I added that. Would the material be comfortable, or would it be just made to be comfortable? The thought faded as I focused on the next step.

Unlike when Vix forged a connection, the power of magic wasn't a storm inside me. Instead, the power began flowing into my reserve at an accelerated rate until it began to overflow into the Dungeon Core Nexus that my first Nexus was nested in. It was like trying to contain a river in a bucket. Slower than last time, I felt my power grow, and I focused it into the Manifestation skill Node. This time there wasn't any cracking, thankfully. More and more power flowed into the Node, and the image I held in my mind's eye began to glow. More mana brought a stronger glow, so I did what any curious mage would. I forced every ounce of the flowing power into the image to see what would happen.

Then, the skill triggered.

Pop!

Everything went dark. I tried to open my eyes, and, thankfully, they responded. Light painted the world in all its beauty as I took in the fact that I had eyes again.

Eyes? Definitely. Check.

I looked over myself as a whole and smiled. Arms, legs, and... training robes? I didn't want robes! I wanted a shirt and pants. I had enough of those things from my childhood! Eh, either way, they were clothes all the same, so check. My tail swished, my ears twitched, and my smile continued to grow. Tail and ears, check. One thing was off though. Even though I pictured myself with my natural tones, everything about me was an opalescent coloring. There was an odd exception to my fur still too. After another examination, I realized that every patch of fur from my ears to my tail had a slight, but still visible, purplish undertone to the rainbow opalescence rather than the strange, solid streaks of color from before. A result of the soulstone maybe?

At the thought, I ran a finger over the piece of stone lodged in my head. It didn't feel as jagged this time. In fact, flakes of opal and amethyst broke off and fell from my forehead like a weird, valuable form of dandruff. This was a bit strange even for my new normal.

"I like it," Vix said as she landed, then wasted no time trotting around to examine the clothes from all sides. "Many choose to make themselves armor, but I wouldn't worry too much about that. Brain can always beat brawn."

Just another question for another day, I thought to myself. "Where is here exactly?"

There were six identical buildings that I could see, each of which could easily house twenty or thirty people. The grounds were a well-tended collection of lawns and walkways that reminded me more of an estate than anything else. Most impressively, at the center of it all, there was a large building almost like the castles I had read about. It had only four walls, connecting up three of six soaring towers, leaving room for gates between the remaining spaces to outline all six spires and create a continuous wall. Each tower had a pointed peak that glimmered with a spectrum of a different color: red, green, blue, silver, gold, and purple. There was more at the center, but I couldn't make it out from where I was. Everything about the place was beautiful, but I couldn't help feeling that the forest had this place beat in natural beauty.

When I'd finally taken it all in, Vix took to the air again and floated just few steps away from me. With her mental talents showing her full range of emotions and, to my surprise, cheering noises, she announced our location with more flare than a clan flagger. "Welcome to Ansith's Academy for Dungeon Training and Combat, Rem. Until you are deemed worthy to graduate, this will be your Dungeon away from Dungeon!"

Dungeon away from Dungeon? That didn't sound right. "Don't you mean home away from home?"

"Nope!" Vix chirped.

I was starting to realize why some of the races hated our sense of humor. Nevertheless, I took in the name of the place, smiling just a little bit. "Fancy title." The thought was passing as I looked around. It was a nice enough place, but it didn't feel like home even if I could Manifest, so I guess Vix's saying worked a little bit better. "So, this is the academy you told me about?" She nodded, and I continued. "So, I'm supposed to learn how to be a Dungeon Core here?" Again, she nodded. "It's not quite what I expected."

Vix shrugged. There wasn't any annoyance there, just… statement. "The Goddess works in mysterious ways."

Mists! Was that ever true. Having my head smashed in like a melon and becoming a Dungeon was a very convoluted way of getting me to help my people. She could have just asked like a normal person.

Vix frowned, and silently I hoped she wasn't trying to read my thoughts again. "Now, I don't know much about how these places work, my understanding is that most academies and universities take up entire cities, but to keep the mana density high enough to simulate a Dungeon environment, have multiple iterations of instanced realities, and just to make things easier to manage in general, Ansith had to sacrifice the overall size of the surface area for efficiency."

Ah, so Ansith is a person. The name scratched at the back of my head as important as I tried to pry out more information. "And Ansith is…"

"The headmaster," Vix quipped, finishing my sentence without a moment's hesitation. "Ansith the First is the first Dungeon Core of the sentient races. He is the first Dungeon Core to interact with the races peacefully, and he is the authority on teaching the sapient Cores how to properly run their Dungeons in a way that won't get them killed or worse. There's not much else I can say on the matter of the dwarf."

Yeah… this sounded like work, but if it would let me help my people, I had to at least try to learn, right? "Sounds fun."

"Some of it will be, many Cores find that building their home is an enjoyable, rewarding experience. Some enjoy learning and fusing monsters and beasts to protect themselves. Some love to toy with the skills and items they unlock as they rank up. Some…" she hesitated once more. A sign that I learned meant she was picking her words carefully again. "Some of your new race simply enjoy the thrill of the hunt."

That didn't bode well. At least, it didn't from the little I knew already of my new people. "The hunt?"

Vix was hesitant, but she was interrupted as some sort of chime rang through the area. It was a sharp, clear noise that got our attention, and it hurt! Though the noise, a monotone, mechanical voice screeched out through the air from everywhere in the most unpleasant of ways. "Welcome, Cores of the Fall, the final member of your class has arrived at last. Please report for sorting at the academy stage in the center of the elemental annexes."

My ears rang and folded back as far as they could as they tried to lessen the burden on my poor senses. I could make out what was said, but gods, goddesses, and all the Pantheon alive and dead, that hurt! Was that going to happen every time someone here said something? All I could hear for another long moment was the ringing of the words.

Vix, while her ears were still folded back and her every expression spoke of the same pain as mine, bit the leg of my robes and pulled me forward. She must have said something, but I couldn't hear her. Whatever spell they used to transmit sound was not designed for my kind. As she floated to eye level and pointed towards the large building at the center with one of her ghostly mana tendrils, I understood her meaning well enough.

You need to go there. There, Rem. Go there. Gooooo Thereeeee.

I was pretty sure that's what she said to the letter.

With a new mission, I said my thanks and gave her a smile, though it may have been more of a scream. From how she looked at me after I finished, I doubted it was a normal tone. Screaming at someone with a smile might get someone that look too. She gave me a weak, pitying wave, and vanished. This time, I heard her clearly within my head.

"Rem, do us proud."

58

Why hadn't she done that in the first place?

I shrugged and did my best not to feel intimated by those words, trying my best not to let the weight of them show. I gave her a small wave, and to my great surprise, she vanished as if she'd never been, fading back into the background of the world like dispersing wisps of smoke. A small pang in my chest told me the truth of the matter, I'd miss her too, just like I missed so many others.

Steeling my resolve, I began to make my way towards the area beyond the gate of the towers.

As I moved, I began to notice I wasn't the only one. From the outskirts of seemingly nowhere and from the six, large buildings that dotted the perimeter, people I quickly identified as other Cores began to appear. There were five, maybe six others in the various colors of the mana spectrum. All of them seemed to be monotone in their hues though. The closest to me was a short man, maybe three feet tall at most and entirely brown. Brown hair, brown beard, brown skin, and a brown, roughhewn stone sticking out of his left palm. He also had full brown plate armor covering nearly every surface of his form. The helmet was pulled back, and instead of just resting behind the head, it unfolded into something almost like a metallic small cape behind him. I won't lie. I stared. I'd never seen anything so delicate meant for combat.

I wanted to ask him about it, but there wasn't much I could say for my interspecies relations. I vaguely recalled being told that I shouldn't interact with anyone from outside the clans at the risk of causing an interspecies incident, but the thought was weak. It was probably just my own imagination really. Were we even different races anymore? Vix had collectively called us Dungeon Cores, but would we even speak the same language? The announcement asked for Cores, too, not beastkin, humans, elves, korgans, dwarves, and whatever lesser races that had been discovered since my last lessons. The idea of causing an incident faded even further towards being an afterthought as I looked at another of the travelers. As my gaze landed on another Core, I grinned. This one was a lot easier on my eyes.

She was all purple or some kind of deep, dark blue. This one was closer to my height, if not taller, with obviously pointed ears. If she had worn furs, she might have passed as one of the clan if they'd been any tighter against what passed on us as skin. She wore a simple dress that accented her form well. Though there wasn't much to show. Sure, she had hips and bust in spades, boarding on excess, but it wasn't anything special beyond that.

Strangely, the look suited her. As if she were just full of quirks; I couldn't see her Core. It must have been somewhere under her dress. I shook my head, ending a distracting thought and looked back towards my ever-growing goal.

In the distance, I could see a pair of red figures moving from another building, a yellow one dashing from place to place like autumn leaves, and a few other colors as well, and a thought struck me. Elves weren't blue, dwarves weren't brown, well, not that shade of brown anyways, and neither race had a reflective sheen to their skin. The demi-human's stone was the same color as the rest of him, too.

At that, something that should have been obvious came to mind. Maybe Cores could only manifest as the color of our Dungeon Core?

It made sense, so if I took that a step further that would mean their colors could signify elemental affinity maybe? It could be, but I'd always felt Earth magic was green in my mind when it'd been used to mend me. Maybe the others next to me were specialized? Maybe specialized magic was a different color than generalized spells? It would be an interesting idea in itself as I looked back to the buxom elf. Maybe she had used Water magic then or maybe some kind of Umbral spells before she died? Then another thought interrupted the others. Were they all dead like me? Some sort of accidents that got them trapped inside soulstones or worse? Did something else happen to make them this way? What did they remember?

Speculations concerning the others consumed me until I was well onto the campus. It was strange. I didn't feel my muscles twinge, I didn't feel exhaustion, I just felt sustained and content. As I focused on the feeling, I noticed my body was still using mana, albeit at a slower rate. It was like I was using the mana around me to take the strain of activity away. It would make sense, but how far could mana stretch with so many of us using it?

60

The closer I got, the more mono-hued individuals I began to notice. We were a broken, flowing rainbow of confusion that only grew larger and more chaotically fractured as we approached and passed through the gates. By the time we'd gathered, there were at least twenty of us, and no two were the same. I saw no other Foxkin, let alone any of the other Beastkin clans among us. By this time, I had to fall in line as we finished our approach.

Three by three, we filed almost silently into the courtyard without the towers and walls. There, we approached something I hadn't made out from the other side, a large stone stage that came up to my neck as I got near the front. For about half of the group, it was much larger than they were. That in itself put a smirk on my face. There were advantages to height sometimes, and I always felt safer when I could see everything. My satisfaction didn't last all that long as the stage began to retract into the ground, becoming no higher than the lowest head, with plenty of room for people to surround the stage on all sides.

With an audible pop, a burly dwarf appeared at the center of the stage. The figure was shorter than I expected, and, factoring in the ornate, diamond-tipped staff he wielded, he was still at least a head and a half shorter than I was. He didn't wear robes or armor like the rest of us either. The dwarf wore what could best be described as a regal looking jacket, pair of pants, and a shirt with far too many buttons for my liking. His beard looked well-kept, trailing to his waist and braided at the left and right edges of his face. A third, tightly kept braid lowered itself from his chin and rested against his chest. Compared to the other two, it was longer and much more intricate. It also had a piece of jewelry the likes of which I'd never seen. In the center of that thick, fancy beard braid, the largest diamond I had ever seen glistened like a thief's dream. At the sight, I brushed against my own stone, slightly jealous of the man. It was just one of many things that set him apart from the rest of us.

The dwarf looked around, eying the crowds, his attention darting from face to face as if confirming his own ideas. He opened his arms wide and smiled as he addressed the gathered peoples in a billowing baritone. His staff clacked loudly on the ground as he picked it up and

61

drove it down. "Welcome, one and all, god, goddess, and even fate-touched, to my humble academy!"

His academy? This was Ansith?

Well, at least Ansith had style.

Chapter Eight

Ansith the First

In all respects, Ansith the First was probably the most impressive dwarf I'd ever seen. Being that I'd only met two dwarves now, the armored brown dwarf and him, that still wasn't saying much. Outside of the fact he was the headmaster of this place, there were other, smaller things that made him impressive in my eyes.

Ansith had a strangely normal color-tone rather than our mono-hues. His clothes, his hair, his staff, all of it looked normal, like he was just another Dwarf that was about to go to his place of work in one of their universities or something. We couldn't do that as far as I knew. I'd tried, but all I could manage was give my skin the color of my stone. Was it an ability that was locked somewhere?

The Nodes did seem to have locked abilities...

Despite knowing that he was in charge of the academy, Ansith was probably the least imposing creature I'd ever met with his short, but stout, stature. I was never good at reading other's magic, something that came at higher Oracle ranks naturally, but if he were the leader here, he had to have power. According to Vix, he kept this entire school mana rich and... what did she say, in instanced realities? That couldn't be easy. Simple items with dimensional properties...?

My trail of thought was diverted like someone had yanked my tail as my attention was turned completely to the man on stage.

Apparently, he had been waiting for that as he stood patiently, smiling out at the now silent crowd as he stroked that magnificent beard of his, gently fingering the stone in his center braid as he came across it.

"Thank you for your undivided attention." My face felt hot at the accusation, but I said nothing as he continued. "As no doubt many of you have been informed, either by a patron of the Pantheon or by one of the Parapet, you are all the latest in a long line of a magical race known as Dungeon Cores. In you, lies the future of the world as you are destined to build your Dungeons to train adventurers and yourself for the good of the world at large. We have a large class this call and such variety." The man pointed as he began naming, "Five Fire Cores; Four Earth Core; six Water Cores; three Air Cores; and—"

His gaze fell upon me like a hungry wolverine on a rodent.

"A Celestial-hybrid Core!" He stepped closer as his excitement began to build to a more than noticeable level. It made me a little uneasy as he bound to my side of the stage like a kit on their Naming day and knelt down to examine my forehead with a bit too much intent in his eyes. As he did, he spoke with an excitement that matched my vision. "A rainbow opal filtration matrix? Interesting choice of stone." His hand found my chin and moved it from one side to the other in a way that made resistance futile. "Not as efficient as diamond or starstone for a Celestial soulstone though." His finger ran along my forehead diagonally as if tracing something as he continued to speak. "Hmm, Celestial mana and Water?" He moved back a bit and tapped my Core stone with the bottom of his staff. I waited for the sound to echo through me again, but I perked up a bit when I didn't feel anything or hear the same tink as before. Weird. "No... Celestial with an unnaturally fostered Umbral impurity in the stone as... hmm... a binding agent? Amethyst, maybe midnight fluorite, so as to not interfere with the rainbow? A refinement line to prevent the soul from shifting to another elemental alignment? A means for extraction and reuse of the finished stone? Hmm... very curious, I'll have to do more research."

As though his examinations meant nothing, he got back up and continued his speech as if he had never been interrupted in the first place.

I felt slightly offended.

"Heedless of your alignment, your training will all begin the same. As we speak, my elemental annex towers are examining your alignments, your strengths, and your weaknesses and logging them to compare against previous students to determine the best course to take for your development." As he finished walking back to the center of the stage, he turned on his heel and faced the majority of the crowd again. As he did, a red-hued Ansith appeared to step out of his back to face away the opposite direction! If that wasn't enough, two more Ansiths, one yellow, one blue, appeared to cover the final direction. It was surprising and just a bit impressive. "If you had a class you trained in life or if you mastered any Nodes, they may have carried over into your new form and influence your power. If you were a man or woman that could practice magic while you were alive, you will have a distinct advantage in the coming days. Even if you couldn't cast a lick of magic in your previous life, you may find yourself casting spells now that you've discovered your elemental alignment."

Oh, I loved being right about things. It made me feel all warm and fuzzy inside.

"Your base classes will be the same. Some of you will be mages, some will be warriors, and still others will be rogues or thieving Dungeons. Until I deem you ready for more advanced coursework, you will all be attending what I like to call Dungeon Building one-o-one." Ansith paused at that moment for effect, expecting some kind of reaction. Of course, there was none. If there was a joke or something we were supposed to understand, it landed like a brick. Not the least bit phased, the man laughed at a joke only he understood before he continued. "No doubt, you've already seen your new Nexus and its Nodes. Yes, they are mastered. You have the power of a Dungeon at your command now, but that's like giving a bastard sword to a toddler and telling him to go show it to his friends. Without proper instruction, someone's going to get hurt."

I wondered if that analogy came from personal experience. Dwarves were some of the most intellectual people in the world, but that didn't mean they always used common sense. At least, so I've heard. I knew that some were a bit more eccentric than others, too, and I was fostering a growing feeling Ansith might just be more on that eccentric side.

"Here, you will be learning how to spread your Influence, build your base of operations with style, and how to unlock and craft new Patterns of creation. These Patterns will be everything from the summoned minions you create to defend yourself to the treasures you'll craft to lure in adventurers to test yourself against. I will provide you with the basics, my staff will give you the best lessons they can, but the rest of it will be up to you."

I felt drawn into his rhetoric, but I didn't understand a lot of it. Patterns? Bases? Influence? Treasure? I know my abilities talked about Patterns and Influence. I liked treasure, and I figured our base would be our Dungeon, but one part did catch my attention more than the rest though, adventurers. Adventurers like the ones that had killed me? I could test myself against them?

Could I humiliate them?

I had to admit that did sound fun, a lot of fun actually. So much so that I began to gleefully rub my hands together before my attention snapped like a whip back to the dwarf who had raised his staff.

"You'll also learn more efficient and guided ways to Manifest your simulacrum away from the campus here to fight those that would do you harm more directly."

And... he lost me again.

The prospect of fighting unknown forces sounded much less entertaining, and my tail fell in disapproval. I was strictly against violence when it was directed at me. At others, sure! Why not? At me, that was a different story.

My attention turned back to Ansith as his tone changed. In an instant, the friendly educator was gone, replaced by a commanding, battle-hardened general, someone that demanded respect out of experience rather than duty.

"The wild Dungeons that are left will search you out as soon as they begin to sense your growing power. They will seek to devour you to add your power to their own, so it is up to us to grow stronger and end them before they end us. Long have we kept our watch over the sapient races and kept the number of wild monsters in check. Not a single calamity-level threat has occurred in the last four hundred and ninety-nine years thanks to our divinely granted assistance!" Cheers went up at that, but he had lost me again. As the tide of applause dimmed, his voice drew me back in. "Whether the sapient races appreciate us or not, we must do what we must to ensure that everyone survives! No race will be left behind!"

I may not have known what a calamity-level threat was, but things were starting to make sense as the new information mingled with the old. Even among my people, legends told stories of great heroes protecting cities and villages, of epic battles between monster lords and their hordes, and then they just seemed to stop. Monster numbers began to decline long before I was born, and the areas where they were strongest on the continent were too dangerous for anything less than a raiding party full of master-class warriors and mages to fight. Was that because those were protected by wild Dungeons or maybe even other Cores like me?

I had so many questions, but I'd not get any answers today as the dwarf had stopped talking. Had I missed something again? I waited anxiously as I'd been lectured already for my deficit of attention, hoping I hadn't missed something important. Thankfully, his silence didn't last long enough to make me into stew.

"Some of you may be allies, some of you may become enemies, but while you are here, you will abide by my rules. They are simple, but essential to the way the academy is run." Holding up his opposite hand, he raised up a single finger to begin. "First: while you are here, you cannot shatter each other. Here, the death of your Manifestation is just an inconvenience, a loss of mana that's easily rectified for the sake of knowledge." A second finger rose. "Second: in the real world, the world beyond this campus, you must always be ready to fight to the death. When someone enters your Dungeon, it is kill or be killed." His third finger rose after a small murmur from the crowd. "Third: you will bring no harm to this campus. I have not had a class so large in the past hundred years, and I would like it to stay that way. I see a lot of potential in you all, and I would hate to see it shattered before it's had a chance to shine." His fourth finger rose, leaving only his thumb still folded back. "Lastly, you will not rise up to destroy any of the civilized races, or I will personally raise an army to destroy you."

That last one seemed a bit ominous as far as I was concerned. Why would I want to destroy an entire race? Replaying his rules in my mind, I realized that wasn't the only issue that seemed ominous. The entire setup seemed more like the rules of the jungle rather than the rules of a school. I was no stranger to death, but the idea that people would actively hunt me didn't sit right.

As the crowd seemed to work over the same ideas in hushed tones, Ansith looked satisfied with the majority of the responses—or lack thereof—from the crowd, and turned to the back of the stage as he finished his thought. "Now, find a room in one of the six dorms; once you are settled in, your schedule of classes will arrive. As I said before, they will be tailored to your strengths and weaknesses, so be on time." His lips twisted into a smile before he finished. "As long as you work hard and advance in rank, I won't have to break you. Dismissed!"

The last word was punctuated by the headmaster popping back out of existence in a haze of color. I noticed this time that there was no Core left behind as he did. Had he manifested without a Core, taken it with him, or was it hidden somewhere nearby? Then again, Vix had said this was his Dungeon, so maybe he could Manifest anywhere he saw fit in his territory.

Again, a smile found itself a home on my face. A pleasurable idea had grown at the thought of what Ansith had just done. Soon, the entire Wildwood would be my territory. When that finally happened, I would go home again, whether they recognized me or not.

With a newfound purpose, I got lost for a moment in daydreams. By the time I came back to reality, the group was already starting to disperse as Ansith had willed. Picking the shorter of the two lines, I followed the rest of the manifested Cores out from center of the academy, and—

"Hey, silver fox guy. Wait up!"

—had myself distracted by a lovely, feminine voice. In truth, other than Ansith, it was probably the first Dungeon Core's voice I'd heard clearly since I arrived. With a smile on my face, I turned to face a rather attractive creature.

Hello. I thought to myself as I took her in. It may not have been the most appropriate first thought, but I could still appreciate how someone looked.

The other Dungeon Core was slightly shorter than myself and was running to catch up with me and waving. She wasn't the deep blue elf from before. Instead, she was an amber-colored Core Manifestation. She was, however, an elf, maybe, to judge by her ears. They weren't as long as those on the woman I'd seen earlier. The longer I studied my new companion and the closer she got, however, the more it appeared that she was not quite... right.

Her ears were almost stubby in compare to the other elf and uneven, and one of her eyes was hidden from the smoothness of her features under a stray tuft of her hair. Her arms were a little too long, and her legs were a little too short. She was still buxom, but the size didn't seem to fit her or the strange garb she wore. It looked like a single piece of fabric wrapped around her again and again until the dress covered everything important. I could see her stone though. It was sticking out from the fabric on her stomach and vanished a little bit more as she bent forward as if the part that had stuck out had never existed. It seemed Manifestation couldn't block a Core's visibility. Interesting.

"Hello." It was a simple word from me, but it seemed to surprise her that I said even that much.

As she reached me, she stopped and panted. Another strange thing seeing as I hadn't felt a single weakness like a strain or needing to draw breath yet. She already seemed a bit off, but a curious odd.

"Finally!" she bemoaned as she caught her breath. "No one's even given me the time of day since I got here."

I shrugged as my tail swished idly behind me. "They're probably worried about what Ansith said and how he implied some of us would fight each other without the rules." Though we'd all just been given that speech. If she'd been here longer, maybe they were just all jerks. I felt a slight twitch at the implications of the rules. I wasn't worried about the girl lashing out and trying to kill me, but just the idea that someone here might want to do so put me on edge all the same. "I'm Rem."

Her eye, as she did only have one, I realized as her hair moved with her rising brow, grew hilariously big at that. "You have a name? I don't have a name. Bastion said some people wouldn't yet. Do you have yours because you're a Celestial Core or because you just look like you're perfect?"

Well, that was unexpected. I smiled a bit at the compliment. I was indeed perfect, and it was nice to be recognized as such. Though, something else she'd said caught my attention.

"Bastion?"

The amber Core gave me the slightest nod before elaborating. "She's one of the Parapet, one of Ansith's people, the one who found me." As she spoke, I could see the fire sparking behind her eyes. It must have been a good memory, or maybe she was just happy to share something with me I didn't already know. "Bastion was so kind to me, even if I tried to kill her when we first met."

If their first meeting was anything like when I had my meeting with Vix, I could understand trying to fight back. I caught her staring at me, and I knew my thoughts had wandered into the woods again. I smiled, returning my attention to her, and when she was sure she had it, the amber Core continued.

"Bastion scared me when I first saw her, and I tried to blow her away. She wasn't having it though. Bastion just patted it out with a hand, picked me up, and began to explain everything."

As she went on, the Core described the member of the Parapet as she had seen her. Bastion of the Parapet looked like a humanoid woman, but that's where the similarities stopped. She had exposed skin only on her back. The rest of her was covered in shiny, red chitin armor. The member of the Parapet also had four extra eyes all around her head to limit her blind spots and huge, ant-like pincers jutting out from around her mouth that could fold back into tusks. If that wasn't scary enough, Bastion had magic, stingers on the back of her hands, and could fly.

As she went into how Bastion had stung a wild monster to death, I came to the conclusions that I did not want to meet one of the Parapet walking through a dark forest. They sounded as frightening as they were amazing.

The Core was smiling though, so that was good. "Now, you never answered me, Rem. How do you know your name?"

I tried to think of a better answer, but there wasn't really much I could say.

"I just do," I admitted, breaking the illusion of my perfection. "I've known it since I was just a kit." Then, almost wistfully, I added, "I don't think I could ever forget it."

"You're lucky then." The amber Core was silent for a few more moments before she nodded as her mind took an easier path. "Bastion brought me here and helped me Manifest about a day or two ago." Her face fell a bit at that. It was much more expressive than I was used to, and sadness was painted across its every feature. "Apparently, I didn't have a clear picture of myself and my memories were a part of me that didn't make the transfer."

I visibly winced at that. I could feel my ears turn and my face scrunch just a bit at her loss. Losing everything? Your personal image, your memories, just about everything that made you you? That sounded like a fate worse than death itself, but she was still here, still trying. That in itself made me respect the woman like I would an injured warrior. They'd lose arms, legs, tails, ears, and still continue to work for the clans without a word about their injury. Well, without words except for jokes and pranks on occasion, aimed at visitors. It took so much more than strength to move on from such an injury like those. It took the will to live and find meaning.

I saw her face fall, and I knew I'd offended her with my reaction, or maybe she'd said something and my mind was wandering again. I gave her a deep bow and sighed. "I'm sorry. I was just thinking about how I would deal with that kind of loss."

The amber Core seemed surprised. "No, I'm sorry. I thought you were done with me already," she elaborated waving her hands to dismiss my worry. She was a strange one, that was for sure. "Bastion helped me a lot by describing the other races. It's how I had a few ideas about what to make for myself, and well…"

Now that I could study her a bit more closely, it made sense. She had the features of nearly every race: elvish ears, a dwarven hair style, a human frame and height, and something under the fabric of her shirt on her back, one of the avian Beastkin maybe? Clearly though, she didn't like it. That much even a blind beggar could tell. However, this... now, this was a battle that any of my clan's men would have known how to help with if they were worth their salt.

"You look fine," I assured her with the warmest smile I could muster. "A little mismatched here and there, but I've seen worse far worse. I once saw a human that had magically grown a tail, ears, and tried to join our tribe. She stuck out like a sore thumb in so, so many ways."

At least, I thought I knew what to say. Saria never really liked when I tried to compliment her, but then again, she didn't like anything I did overtly.

"Thanks." As her lips curled upwards, I smiled. At least that had been enough to make her grin, even if I had made up the anecdote. "Bastion called me Amber Core, and said I'd get a name during my first classes."

Classes where you learn about yourself? Inwardly, I groaned. Please let Vix have been joking... "Let me guess, Core of Yourself?"

"Yeah! She said I'd learn to fix things, get a name, and figure everything out." And there went all pretense of the joke. Well, if others needed it, let them have it. She smiled, waiting for my attention to come back to her before she continued. "Until then, you can call me Amber Core, too."

"How about just Amber?" I offered, not wanting to presume. "It's a bit easier to say."

Another smile, and her head bobbed happily. "Works for me. Where are you going, Rem? It would be nice to know someone where I'm staying."

An interesting prospect, and it seemed innocent enough. The girl didn't seem to have a mean bone in her body. Figuratively and literally seeing as none of us had anything except mana. At her question, I stopped for a moment. Where was I going? "I don't know. Just wherever my feet take me, I guess."

She nodded as if processing the idea. If she had the same common knowledge retained that I did, I knew what would be coming next. "Beastkin aren't for stone buildings or the indoors, are they?"

Where'd she learn that?

"We like buildings just fine," I said, slightly irritated. "Other races just don't understand the values of sleeping under the stars on a warm night. I can't count the number of times I ran away from home to watch the stars and moons. I—" I had to stop. Why was I getting mad at her? She'd literally lost her entire mind except for, it seemed, randomly scattered stereotypes about the races and basic knowledge.

As if processing my sudden stop, Amber nodded knowingly. Her voice was almost tender as she spoke, as if she were checking on a fresh wound and was worried it might reopen. "I haven't gotten to talk much. I remember some things, ordinary stuff. Other things just appear in my memory like sparks and disconnects. I didn't mean to offend you. I just… it's confusing for me and no one wants to talk to me about it. Now that Bastion's gone, no one understands —"

They probably did, but perhaps didn't want to see in her what they just narrowly avoided for themselves. Instinct took over, and I couldn't help myself. I hugged her, wrapping my arms around her and pulling her into the imagined warmth of my comfortable robe. My heart pulled for her in a way that I wouldn't have known before I'd died. I knew loss, but I couldn't imagine losing everything. This poor girl didn't even know how she looked, who she was, her people, or even her name, but that was enough. She knew enough to know that she once had it. In some ways, that was worse than never knowing you had it at all.

In the clans, actions spoke louder than words, so I said nothing and let my ears and tail fall to show mourning for her loss. She didn't even try to fight my hold and wrapped her arms around me, digging her face into the top of my robe and the fur below it.

The rest of the Manifested Cores continued to pass us by as I held her, while she sobbed openly. A few looked at us in confusion or at least at me with that expression, and a familiar finger showed them my thoughts about their look.

I wasn't like them, but then again, neither was she. I was a Foxkin among those that thought lowly of us, and she had lost everything they still took for granted. We were a pair of imperfections among the others. Like me, she couldn't tear up or cry, but the action alone seemed to help her as the minutes dragged on.

Finally, she loosened her grip and looked up at me. Her face was a sad kind of happy as she smiled at me. "Thank you."

I just gave her a small smile and began to walk again. This time, the opposite of the way I had begun. "I think I'm going to keep going to the other side of the campus. It seemed as though everyone was going to the same buildings, and I'd rather have my space away from them." As I began to walk, I expected her to follow immediately, but she didn't. I didn't hear her footfalls following. Did she not understand we were friends now? The other races were strange when it came to relationships, so I turned and was blunt with her. "You're welcome to join me. I'm sure there will be plenty of rooms."

For a moment more, she hesitated.

"Right." She wiped at nonexistent tears and smiled as she caught up with me. There was little to talk about, but the silence was nice. A part of me felt a little more alive though. A new friend always had a way of doing that for me.

I wondered if she liked medusa frogs?

I hesitated at the thought and looked down at my crystalline body. I should probably find out if she could throw first.

Chapter Nine

An Eventful Morning

For the most part, it was an uneventful rest of the day.

Without incident, we reached the furthest dorm, the one marked by what I assumed was Celestial mana, and I wasn't surprised that we were the only occupants. With closer homes available, why go further than you needed to? In my case, I wasn't comfortable yet with what I was, and I didn't like the way the others seemed to treat those that were different. Amber, well, she wanted a friend nearby. Since I was the only one available, it made sense for her to go where I went.

It was a large, mostly unadorned dorm on the inside. Polished white marble floors flecked with gold inlay marked the entryway and every hall with five rooms on the first floor, but ground level was never a good choice. Instinct drove the choice of my room as I went to the second floor, and Amber followed without a complaint. She asked why, but all I could really do was shrug as I answered.

"You always want to have higher ground in case of an attack."

In the Wildwood, the dangerous creatures prowled the grounds, but the most dangerous waited in the lower branches, and to be counted as one of them was safety in a new environment. Well, that or under them, but there wasn't a basement door that I could find, and I wanted to be able to escape if the need arose.

She didn't argue with my reasoning.

We examined the rooms together, but by the third room, we realized that all of them were the same. Each room had the same pieces: some kind of ward at the entry and at each possible exit and a large window facing either towards the campus or out towards a large forest of evergreen trees spread out like an ocean. They all had the same furniture too: a desk; a chair; a bed; and a closet with nothing inside but more empty space. The only real differences came with how the items were placed. All the ones at the back were mirrors of those at the front. Maybe it was the other way around? Either way, it didn't matter how homey the dorm was meant to feel, it did not give me a sense of ease. I felt a lot better knowing someone was watching my back, and I'm sure she felt the same.

According to Ansith, we couldn't get hurt here but that didn't stop my fur from standing on end at the emptiness. I didn't like being alone when I could help it. Whether it was my instincts or not, I just knew I shouldn't be isolated. It wasn't right to be alone in the world. If it hadn't been for Amber, I might have broken down and moved into a dorm with the others.

Thankfully, it didn't come to that.

In the end, we took rooms across from each other on the top floor at the far end of the hall away from the stairs. I may have been fine sharing rooms, but this time it was Amber who said that her 'instincts' told her otherwise. I hoped it hadn't been from some of that 'common knowledge' about my people she knew. Some races had very wrong ideas about who we were and what we did. At least, that's what my 'common knowledge' told me, and I had a feeling mine was a lot more reliable than hers.

Closing the door behind me, a thought occurred to me. Why did I need a bed? I wasn't tired, and, in reality, I didn't feel like I needed sleep. If my perception of time was right, I hadn't slept in days. In fact, the last time that I remembered falling asleep, it had been for a long time and because of something Cecil had done to me.

Yeah, I wasn't going to risk sleep again.

Instead, I pulled up the chair and sat by the window. I didn't need to sit, but still, it was a small action that made me feel more like my old self. The night was my time to think.

For the rest of the night, I sat watching the animals of the night skirt by the tree line. I watched as if it were my job the fascinating blur of creatures bobbing in and out of the campus's ghostly night-light of a barrier. Odd sounds of even odder creatures pierced the silence, even this far up, like a discordant song of the hunt.

As the night went on, I caught a few clear glimpses in the moonlight of what looked like wolves yet with the features of spiders. They had spindly legs that carried them through the trees, but were much meatier than your average spider. I felt my fur stand again as they crossed into the campus, but they were quickly deterred by a dim glow as a group of warriors with long spears appeared from the air itself. This encounter happened three times that night, and the more glimpses I caught, the more I noticed that the warriors on the outermost edge of the clearing looked suspiciously ant-like.

Other than that, it was overall an uneventful night.

***

Hours after the sun had risen, I heard a knock on my door. Not knocking, a *knock*. A singular, powerful bang that probably would have broken down doors where I had come from. Not that we were poor craftsmen, but it sounded more like an attack rather than a gesture. I hadn't bothered to lock the door knowing that there was only one other person that knew where I was, so it was either Amber or Ansith. Neither of whom I wanted to anger. "Come in."

There was no response except for that the banging got louder at my words.

"Come in, it's open!" I barked back a bit louder.

And of course, they didn't. Instead of acting like a civilized creature, the banging just got louder still and more frequent with every second.

To the Mists with you, Amber! I thought clearly as I tried to figure out why she wouldn't answer me. Was this another of those racial differences? Did she think that Foxkin didn't like talking though doors?

For a moment, I felt bad, knowing that was unfair. She didn't know any better, so I grumbled and walked over. I knew that I was yelling. I knew that I was loud enough that the entire floor should have heard me. Did her ears not work this morning? It was a distinct possibility.

With an air of annoyance, I flung open the door to stare at… what was decidedly not an amber-colored, one-eyed woman. To my surprise and slight annoyance, it was a hovering scroll. With the door open, it hung in the air like it was suspended by invisible strings. Cautiously, I felt out above and below it for any support. I was used to seeing magic communications in action, but the spell I was familiar with just delivered a letter to a specified location. It took too much mana and was far too inefficient to target people. The scroll must have taken offence at what I was doing, and it took action, hurling itself into my chest.

Yep, could still feel pain.

I stumbled back catching the letter and cupping it against my stomach. It was about as disorienting as a gut punch normally was, but instead of keeling over and vomiting all over the floor, it just felt a little draining on my mana. I noticed one waiting patiently in front of Amber's door as well and felt slightly annoyed.

"You've got a letter, Amber," I called out, leaving my door open as I moved to sit on the bed. That way, I could face anyone that came through the door. "If I were you, I wouldn't keep it waiting."

I heard her door open and a thank you before it closed again. Oh, yeah. Wait for her with the patience of a paladin. Stupid scroll.

Opening it up, the rollers at each end dissolved back into whatever had created them, leaving me with two separate pages. The first was a letter with my name scrolled on the top line. A quick glance at the second sheet told me that it was much shorter. I focused on the letter. It was written in an impressive deep blue ink, but more than once, I had to read that opening line. It felt good to see someone else use my name.

Good morning, Rem,
I am Ansith the First, and I will be one of your tutors for your time here. Because of your level of control over your simulacrum and the training your goddess has already gifted you with, you will be given permission to skip the introductory classes including Core of Yourself. I must explain that you have already attained a sense of self equal to that of a D ranked Core. As such, you may hear cracking or see parts of your Core flake away in the coming days. This is normal. As Cores refine themselves into the higher

ranks, our density increases, and the Core becomes more compact and re-fined. When this first happened to me, I thought I'd made a miscalcula-tion. It turned out for the best though. I have to laugh still that as we grow more compact our size ratio increases. I will never truly understand extra-dimensional magic. Also, from here on, your Nodes will be learning as your ranks increase. Your mental direction will determine how your Nodes progress. Mastery is only the beginning, my young Foxkin.

Now, you must be wondering why I reached out to you with this letter. Perhaps you have already figured it out. You are a Celestial-Umbral Core. Your power is unique among this cohort. Your elemental affinities are for the stars and the primal forces of nature and will require a different ap-proach to that of divine magic. As such, your schedule will reflect this. Eventually, you will learn to mimic other forces, but you must master your own first. Your potential for creation will also be greater than even my own if you foster it correctly.

I must stress these next words, Rem, and I will stress them again when we meet in person for your lessons. Do not be tempted into selfishness by the power that you have. It leads to corruption and death. I can only guess at your end goals once you reach the upper tiers, but you wouldn't be here if they weren't noble. Nobility is what I expect from a god-touched Oracle and the first Dungeon of the Wildwood. Focus on your kin, become a chal-lenge, become a rite of passage, and make your people better for your death. There is no victory in destroying what you have lost or what is not out of reach. It is what truly separates us from becoming monsters.

I will see you soon for your first lessons once you pass the first classes.
Ansith the First, Headmaster

I let out a soft whistle as I finished and read the letter again. It was impressive to say the least and a bit more than I expected from Ansith. He seemed so methodical and technical, but at the same time, his sense of humor was about as complex as a wasp's reasons for stinging some-one.

The second paper was a bit more simple, thankfully. My schedule of classes:

Mundus:
Core of Yourself - Morning chime - Excused
Manifestation - Midday chime - Excused
Influence and Fabrication - Late Afternoon chime - Academy Hall,
Center Stage

Tiera:
Influence and Fabrication - Academy Hall, Center Stage

Wispa:
Influence and Fabrication - Field Work

Thuren:
Influence and Fabrication - Field Work

Freiag:
Influence and Fabrication - Field Work

Sol/Lune:
No Class—Independent Study

Schedule will update as necessary

I looked over the schedule and shrugged. Well, at least I was already excused from a pair of boring sounding classes. Questions always kept pestering me though. How did the others Manifest? I was sure I'd seen at least twenty Cores. Did they all just... do it? If I looked closer, would they all have been like Amber was? Were they all as imperfect, strange, and lost? Did they even know they were? It wasn't like there were mirrors around.

All this and more plagued my mind until a yell broke my concentration.

"Late!" Amber screamed more to herself than at me as the door slammed behind her. "Late, late, late!"

The self-deprecating cries continued down the hall until she slammed into the wall near the stairwell. I knew it shouldn't hurt, but

I winced all the same and went to help her. That's when I noticed something different about her this time. One leg was shorter than the other, significantly shorter. Her arms were a normal size this time, but the rest of her seemed slightly off proportion. Her ears being the most notable as the tips of them trailed behind her back like a pair of braids. Helping Amber up was easy, and I tried not to draw attention to her problems.

"Good morning."

She nearly snapped my head off. "I need to get to class, Rem! I'm late! I need to fix this!"

It must have been the Core of Yourself class she was talking about. "Where is it?"

Amber opened her scroll and looked at the listing. "Academy Hall—Aero Tower, Floor One, Room Four."

Academy Hall was easy, the tower... well, I'd figure that out when we got there. It was probably the tower with the yellowish glow at the peak though.

I helped Amber to her foot and noticed another change. She was a head shorter than me now, nearly the size of a dwarf. She was wobbly on her one good foot and whimpered. She wanted help, but she didn't want to ask for me. I was starting to get the impression that this wasn't the first time she'd tried to fix things. So I picked her up and began to move.

As we moved, I didn't ask how things came to be this morning, but she was more than forthcoming without my prompting.

"I tried to fix myself," she began. "I saw so many other people with perfect bodies. I know I should have waited, but I kept popping myself and manifesting again, hoping I'd get it right."

"Still can't figure yourself out?"

She shook her head, and her ears wiggled like a pair of elven worms. "It's hard when you don't know who you were."

I could only imagine and said as much, but she frowned.

"It's like I know how every species is supposed to look and act, but I don't understand it. I know, but I don't know how they would be for me. I think it's messing my image up."

As we continued to descend the stairs to the first floor, I nodded. "At least you got your clothes right. It could have been embarrassing if I had to carry you into class like this naked. Way too much to explain on the first night." It was a friendly tease, no worse than I would have teased Saria, but her amber hue darkened a bit.

Oops.

I wasn't aware we could blush with our projected forms, or was she a special case because she felt she had to when she pictured herself? Maybe I should stick around for that class.

"It took two hours to get this far again," she explained. "I wish Bastion had been more specific on how to do it."

I still had to ask her about Bastion's directions. Maybe they'd be helpful to me, too, but I didn't feel like this was the right time to do it. As we left the building, the fresh air rushed past me. It was a windy morning today. In the distance, the trees swayed to the unseen force, making a soft rustling through the quiet campus.

"Hold on," I warned her.

She gripped me enough that I felt the pressure and asked the obvious question. "Why?"

I grinned as I shifted my stance. If there was one thing a Foxkin was good at besides playing tricks, it was running. She was no heavier than a pillow, and my speed was no worse for wear as the academy grounds rushed below us to the satisfying sound of my feet crunching the grass underfoot and then padding along the paved stone. My ears folded back, my tail swished happily in the breeze, and Amber held on for dear life as I bounded forward. It was easy to ignore her cries when the wind was blocking out everything.

I moved faster and faster; faster than I ever had. I could feel my mana pool starting to drain as it began to flow through me to sustain my motion. That was interesting. How far could I push myself beyond my limits with magic fueling every inch of my body?

The back gate of the academy was approaching faster than I was comfortable with and I tried to stop like I normally would. That was a mistake. My change in speed was too much, and I couldn't decelerate before my legs decided it was time to stop moving. In an unholy, unceremonious heap, we tumbled to the ground and rolled through the gate like a couple of tumbleweeds.

As we came to a stop, Amber was looking down on me as a few other manifested Cores did the same. I grinned and put my hands behind my head as I looked up at her.

She flushed again and fell to one side as her lopsided form lost what balance it had. I sighed, missing the perfect opportunity to tease her again and opted to pick her up instead. I regretted it.

EEEEEEEEEEEEEEEEEE

A chime sounded through the campus, gathering the attention of everyone and my ears rang again. It was so much worse here. The high-pitched noise sent my hands flying to cover my ears the best they could before I dropped Amber and fell to my knees. For the duration of the tone, I was deaf to the world around me. It felt like my ears were going to explode from the noise, and I gritted my teeth the best I could before it finally stopped.

As I got my bearings again, I noticed there were a few eyes still on me, but only one pair seemed to be really concerned: Amber hobbled over towards me. I rubbed my ears back and continued till the pain was at the back of my head. "Sorry."

"Are you okay, Rem?" Amber asked as she got up from where she rolled to.

"Fine, just those noises hurt," I explained. She gave me a quizzical look, and I added, "We have sensitive ears."

She seemed to space for a moment before nodding and watching me carefully as I got back to my feet. I bent down, picked her back up, and continued to push our way to where the rest of the yellowish Cores were going.

My original guess seemed to be right as we entered the yellow-tinged Aero Tower. I felt out of place among so many of the other Cores. The original few from our twenty were there, but there were more than that. There were maybe triple our original group in here. Bustling through the halls, yellow people of all shapes and sizes moved from the hall and into classrooms, but I pushed ahead, finding the room Amber had indicated. I opened the door, and was face to face with a yellow-tinged copy of Ansith. Everything about him was like

83

any of the other Cores in the room. His suit, his skin, his hair, all a tinge and shades of yellow like fine desert sand. I'm not too proud to admit that I almost dropped Amber again right there and then.

I didn't though. That should count for something.

"Rem," he said as his greeting before turning to the Core I carried. "Amber Core, you are right on time. Please, take a..." he hesitated noticing the disproportion of her features before turning back to address me. "Please help her to a seat, please."

Taking the instruction as a chance to be nosy, I led Amber to her seat and studied the others in the room. One student had an extra set of arms, another had no hair—which, by the way she kept rubbing at it, it wasn't by choice—another's problem was as clear as the lack of a nose on her face, and still another didn't have a chest. There was a literal hole where his heart, lungs, and other organs should have been. His clothing didn't even cover it. A final Core was missing her eyes. By comparison, Amber really had her sket together.

After I dropped her off, the yellow Ansith gave me a warm smile and a slight bow. "She will be able to make it back to her room under her own power by the time we are done. Thank you for your support."

I nodded and took that as it was: an exit. "I'll see you after you're done."

Amber nodded, gave me a weak smile, and I left. As the door shut behind me, I felt uneasy all of a sudden. I was alone again. I had an entire day before my class was supposed to start. It wasn't that hard to remember where the center stage was, but I didn't want to be anywhere nearby when the chime went off again.

A pang forced me to stop though. Where would I go? There was nothing around the campus. I wanted to talk to Amber, but that wasn't possible. Vix had vanished into the aether like a morning fog, so there wasn't a point in looking for her. I didn't know anyone well enough to risk pulling a prank on a stranger either. Instead of worrying about going anywhere else, I put my back to the wall and just sat down to wait.

Chapter Ten
Self-Reflection

I had a longer wait than I expected. It wasn't bad though. I felt less jumpy after the first half hour. Without anyone else around, the halls were as quiet as the forest on a winter morning, so it gave me time to think. There was no second tone inside the building, thankfully, but it was a few hours before the class was over. This gave me time to think. I wanted company, but Ansith had specifically said we Cores may well be enemies after this was all over. I couldn't really trust anyone, but Amber felt different.

I couldn't explain why, but she didn't seem hostile. She didn't feel like she had an ounce of anger, malice, or spite in her entire body. Well, other than what was directed back at herself. She really didn't like being 'wrong.' I was a little smug about the fact I had it so easy, but she made me realize how stupid that had been. I was a day or two ahead at most. Looking inward just to confirm it once again, I still had my connections to magic as well, so I could probably cast spells in a Manifested form too. Why hadn't I tried that yet? I mean, I had used Forbid, but that was different to a cantrip.

I felt an affinity to Will-of-the-Wisp. It was a versatile, simple cantrip that let me control a small ball of light as an extension of myself. It could be as big as my head or as small as the tip of my finger, so it had plenty of uses. Not to mention, I had pulled so many pranks with this spell alone that using the Node's spellform was second nature to me: I imagined the size of the spell; the color; and the duration that I needed it for; then pushed mana into the idea and as surely as I knew the ears on my head, a tiny orb of light would shimmer into existence.

Following my own directions, I smiled as an opal orb of light glimmered at the tip of my finger. The small ball of light glowed brightly with undertones of the rainbow and hints of purple. As I took my hand away to study it more closely, it continued to float at eye level.

Opal, I thought to myself with a moment of recognition. *I wanted green.*

Dismissing the spell, I touched the Node's power again, rebuilt the form as I wanted it in my mind's eye, and focused specifically on the color this time.

Green, I thought forcefully. *I want a green light.*

As strongly as I could, I willed the spell into existence again, and again the spell was the glimmering rainbow white of an opal. In all my seasons, I'd never had trouble with a single aspect of the spell since I created the Node and mastered it. Why was it giving me trouble all of a sudden? I looked inward, checking the spell despite the fact I already knew it by heart.

Will-of-the-Wisp
Secondary Node - Spell - Cantrip
Evolution Potential - Flexible
Cost: 5+
Effect: Spend mana to create a sphere of light in the color of your choice. Cost of this spell changes based on size, intended duration, distance from user, and color of the sphere.

Everything was in order, and the Node was the same rough crystal it always had been as it kept its place within my Oracle Nexus. The effect was the same, the cost was the same, but I still couldn't change the color. Maybe it was just me? Increasing my focus, I tried again.

And again.

And again.

For three more attempts, I tried to get any color other than the opalescent white for the spell. First, I tried green again, then blue, and I even thought I could try purple to get something different since it was part of my stone's coloring. Despite my best efforts those three more times, nothing came into existence but the little pearl of light.

A few more experiments with my other spells gave the same result, indirect or not. Mend gave off an opal glow as it examined the material before dispelling itself, Stabilize Wounded did the same before it fizzled out. I thought about using my command word again, but I wouldn't see any effect without another living thing for it to command; I assumed it too would cast an opal light around the target of my words. The only spell I had that didn't give off the same aura was invisibility, and if it had, the spell would have been useless.

Before I had any more time to experiment, the door opened, and I shot up from my sitting position. Real or manifested, the last thing I needed was someone to step on my tail.

The Cores leaving the classroom were not the same people that had gone in. All of them were complete, flawless-looking individuals now. No missing eyes, torso pieces, or arms, they all seemed whole. It must have been a good lesson to have them all find themselves. There was one person I was more eager to see though than any of the others, but she wasn't coming out. As no more Cores came from within, I waited a bit longer to see if maybe she had stayed behind to thank the sandy Ansith.

Instead, Amber was alone inside. She was very different than the first time I'd seen her. She was in proportion this time. A bit shorter than at our first meeting, but taller than our latest encounter. I couldn't put my finger on it, but something was still off. Maybe it was because her ears were a bit too small, her hands… No… Maybe it was because she looked exactly like a better-chested version of me.

"I hate this."

There were empty seats all around her, and even the instructor had vanished. It was just Amber and I. Usually, I knew what to say when Saria was mad at me or doubting herself, but I was looking at myself, and I was a little biased.

"I dunno. You pull it off better than I could," I mused aloud. At least her voice hadn't changed. That would have been weird.

"I spent three hours trying to fix myself. This isn't funny!" She snapped loud enough to make both our ears fold back. "Ow."

A few moments later, our ears were sticking back up. "You get used to it."

"I'll never get used to it," Amber groaned as her ears fell. She held the sides of her head and put her head down onto the desk. "I tried to focus on me, but all I could focus on was how easy you made it look, and I ended up like this."

"There are worse things to look like," I countered. "I'm sure you'll find yourself. If you want to look like me though, I might imagine a different face. It's a little strange looking at me."

She groaned at that and didn't lift herself up. "Everyone got it by the end of the class. I know who I want to be, but for some reason, it doesn't want to stick when I try."

Sitting back, I tried to relax as I listened to her. "Well, what do you want to be?"

She didn't even hesitate. "I want to be strong and help prepare my people for whatever's coming. I want to do well by them. I want to do them proud even if they don't know who I am, but how can I be that for them if I don't know who they are?"

"And Ansith couldn't tell you anything?"

"Only what Bastion did," Amber explained. "They found me out in the middle of nowhere. No villages, no other bodies, just me in this rock." She grumbled again. "At least I have a personality."

"Positivity is everywhere here," I joked. Her head shot right back up and she glared at me. I don't think I've ever looked that annoyed with myself. Slightly uncomfortable. "You've got a good thing to start with. Why not just build your image around that?

"You don't think I tried?" She nearly shouted, but her voice wavered, remembering the sensitivity of our ears. "I don't even know where to begin."

"Well, did you like the long hair you saw or my short hair?"

I would never get used to seeing my face scrunching to think about hair. "Long. It doesn't feel right short like this. How do you even like this?" She gave a slight tug on the short hair as emphasis.

"Having fur to keep the back of my neck warm helps." I grinned a bit, rubbing the mentioned spot fondly. "What body felt right?"

"Slender," came another quick response as she looked down. "Every time I kept these though. I liked them, and they feel familiar,

88

but I feel like I shouldn't be this curvy. Especially not after seeing how Bari looked."

"Bari?"

"Another pure Air Core. She looked like an hourglass!" Her hands went out as far as they could in front of herself. "She was huge!"

I snickered again. Yep, I remembered seeing her on the way out. "I think I saw her on the parade of perfection. It looked hilarious!"

She snickered back. "Yeah. Bet she can only walk because we don't have weight."

Progress is being made, I thought to myself and continued with her self-assessment. "I've always seen you with elven ears. What about those?"

Another nod. "Yeah, they're another thing I like. Maybe I was an elf?"

"Or an elf lover," I pointed out, even if elves weren't the only race with pointed ears. She could have just as easily been a dryad or another of the nature-born races like them. "Or maybe elves killed you and that's your way of reminding yourself."

She sat quietly for a few minutes as she thought through the implications. "Maybe," Amber said thoughtfully as she touched the tips of the fox ears at the top of her head. She must have squeezed a little too hard and winced, dropping her hand away as if she'd been bitten. "But they feel right to have. These are too sensitive."

Couldn't argue with that logic. She wasn't wrong. Amber was trying to find herself, so whatever felt right to her should be what she went with. "So, you want to be a slender, small chested woman with eleven ears and long hair?"

She shrugged. "Yeah, that sounds about right."

"I bet that'd look nice." I grinned at the implication and was rewarded with a slight darkening of her amber hues.

"It would. Wrapped in my dress, I'd look amazing. I'd be perfect."

Gotcha. "Sounds like you know yourself."

She stopped and looked at me. I grinned as what I did processed. I bet she thought we were just discussing our thoughts on the feminine form. She seemed surprised but smiled all the same. "I guess a bit better, yeah."

89

"Care to try again?"

She sighed. "Two-hundredth-thirty-sixth time is the charm, right?"

"Maybe the thirty-seventh time," I grinned, trying to get her goat. As much as I loved having goats, this one wasn't mine to keep. "Just do me a favor." She cocked an eyebrow. Now that I was used to feeling. I'm glad that it looked just as inquisitive as I'd hoped. "If you come back as me again, try to get some hips too. I wanna see what a full feminine Rem would look like."

She snickered. "Be careful what you wish for, so don't be too disappointed if you're looking at all this again." She motioned across her body one last time then popped out of existence a moment later. Her Core fell to the chair with a small, crystalline clunk.

For a while, she just sat in the chair of her desk unmoving. Just looking at her there like your average rock, I had an unmistakable urge to poke the Core that sat before me, but something told me that it'd be wrong, a violation of her trust in me. I don't know why, but it rang as deeply for me as my magic did. Instead, I took in what she was. Her Core was as rough as mine, a bit chunky with rough edges and sharp points, but she was unnaturally smooth across the middle bulge of stone. I wished I knew more about Cores to know something about her power just from a look, but I didn't have time to dwell on it. Amber began to hum ever so quietly and glow brighter. Her glowing shimmer grew brighter and brighter until a moment later when she popped back into existence. When I could see again, I knew she'd gotten somewhere.

Amber wasn't what you might call beautiful, but she had a natural attractiveness about her. She was indeed slender, but it wasn't without strength. She looked like a deer ready to run through the forest with the way her muscles seemed to blend into her frame. She wasn't as busty as any of the female Cores that left, but I doubt she noticed or cared. It suited her the way she curved under her dress wrap. Her hair was indeed longer too, it stretched down to her kneecaps at least in flowing, amber locks. Before I could say anything, she leapt at me and tackled me into a hug.

"Thank you! Thank you! Thank you! Thank you!" she repeated again and again before I started tuning her out.

90

I couldn't help but laugh as she finally stopped thanking me a few minutes later. "I can't believe that actually worked."

She sat back up and looked perturbed. "Ansith just kept going on about finding your inner self and cast Clarity on the group to make some of our old personal memories sharper." Her face fell at the thought and sighed. Personally, I would have loved some sharpness to what I remembered, but I doubted it did what I thought it would. "Most of them instantly remembered their forms clear as day, popped, and their forms fell into place so they could start working on their class Nexus. I didn't have the memories they did. I kept struggling, and he just kept casting different memory sharpening cantrips on me. It just kept failing, and I kept getting so frustrated that I just defaulted to the only Core form I was really familiar with."

"I wouldn't say you're familiar with it." Another grin crept across my face.

Her stern expression told me I shouldn't continue that line of joking. "He thought that since I had a form, it was fine to use and continued the lesson as I tried more and more to get the form I wanted. It was humiliating to keep popping like that. I could do everything with Manifestation properly, but I just couldn't be me."

"At least you're comfortable now." As she watched me, I considered how well I might have done in her place. Could I have had half the willpower she did to continue? Could I have been as brave as she was? I couldn't help but think about how deeply I took my good luck for granted. It could just as easily have been me sitting across from someone else getting help.

I gave her an approving nod. She looked better now, more like herself, and I smiled as she perked back up. "Oh! So what name did you choose?"

The flush of amber gold returned to her cheeks as she sighed. "Amber." She gave me a stern glare before she added. "No, it's not because of you. Nothing else felt right."

I got up and offered her a hand as a grin plastered across my face. "Well, Amber. Let me be the first to say hello again."

She took my hand and smiled. "Hello to you too, Rem."

91

Chapter Eleven
Building Ideas

I wanted to stay in the tower until after the tone, but Amber wouldn't have it. We needed to be near the front so we didn't miss anything, or something like that. I didn't really want to leave, so I toned her out a bit. It wasn't going to work though. Despite my protests and before I could whine further, Amber grabbed my hand and dragged me out into the warmth and light. I had been inside so long it felt like the sun would burn away my flesh in mere moments.

Thankfully, I didn't have any for it to take, so it just glinted off me. I may have complained about being made completely of opal, but I was pretty at least.

Out in the common of the campus were more Cores than I thought there could be in the school. Milling about inside the building were at least a hundred Cores of various ages, sizes, and species. I knew I didn't see anyone the previous night or on the way to Amber's first class, so where were they all before? In fact, where were they now? I had seen plenty of Air Cores in the tower and they couldn't all have still been inside. After trying to puzzle the question out to its end, I couldn't find the answer. I just had to write their vanishing off as a coincidence. One mystery later, I was sure there were many more Cores here than I thought.

EEEEEEEEEEEEEEEEEEE

My ears split a moment later, and I fell to the ground. I hadn't been ready that time. I managed to cover my ears as I lay in a ball on the ground, but the sound still rang through my hands as clearly and as easily as if they hadn't been there. I really needed a way to deal with that.

After Amber helped me to my feet, we reached the stage. Only the original twenty or so of us from yesterday were there, so there wasn't really any competition for spots as we took a position directly in front of the doors to the Aero Tower.

Amber began speaking about what she had learned in class while I took note of my surroundings. The stage marked the center area of the campus with all of the towers facing with their doors towards it. There was another structure I noticed in the center of the stage. There was a small indentation with a glimmering, perfect cut diamond as big as my fist. For Clerics and Oracles alone, that stone would have been invaluable. At a high enough class, I bet it could be used for a trans-migration spell or a few resurrection spells! It looked perfect. Then again, I bet my former self could have used my current nature for a few grand spells too.

Then it hit me as Ansith materialized in all of his natural glory. That was probably Ansith's Core. I was looking at what must be one of the most powerful Dungeon Cores in existence. If he was as power-ful as I imagined, I should be more scared than awed. If Ansith was able to create this mana-rich environment by himself and provide enough mana to manifest every Core on campus and still have enough to protect this area, his power must be devastatingly strong. If Vix was right, which I had no reason to doubt, and he was an SS Rank, he might even rival weaker gods if he pooled his resources!

I looked at him with a newfound respect at that. He chose to teach, to nurture those of his race, if we could be called a race, and seemed to be peaceful enough.

"Greetings, Cores!" Ansith beamed as he looked across the small selected crowd. "I see you've all found yourselves a body that feels right to you, and names to fit your form if you wanted to abandon your old ways. It took some of your longer than others, but you did it." I swear he looked at us directly and smiled a bit wider. "I must apologize though, some of my aspects are less... nurturing than others. They take after their elements I'm afraid. My aspect of Fire is a bit hot-headed without my Water aspect to cool his fire, and my Air aspect is a bit flimsy without the Earthen aspect to prop up his ability to teach."

"Well, at least he has a reason for being a sket teacher," I whispered to Amber, who, to her credit, did her best not to snicker.

He cleared his throat, drawing everyone's attention back to center stage before he began to speak again. "This is a special class only for fresh Cores. This is the only time a skill is directly taught, and it's probably your most useful skill as a Dungeon Core, next to designing and summoning your own defenses, so listen well. Welcome to Influence and Fabrication. I will also assure you that your schedule is not wrong. You will be here for the next few days perfecting your abilities to do so. By the time we are done, you will know all of your new Nodes inside and out."

Sket. Well, at least I didn't have to eat, sleep, or answer the calls of nature.

There was a brief rumble through the audience as one voice from our left spoke up. It was the deep blue Core I'd seen before with the too perfect body. "When will we sleep?"

Ansith's expression darkened at that. "If you have not figured out yet that you neither need to sleep or eat, you have larger issues than I can attend to at this moment. If you are sleeping, you are mana deficient and will die without tending. Have you slept since you arrived?"

The woman nodded meekly.

"Mera, go to the Aqua Tower and seek out my aspect on the top floor. He will evaluate your treatment. Participation today will be excused as your reckless use of mana might kill you." When she didn't immediately turn tail, the air echoed with his annoyance. "Go!"

I'd never seen a creature move so fast in my entire life.

With her gone, Ansith's demeanor completely changed. Once again, not a care in the world bothered him as he returned to his jovial expression. He almost sounded aloof as he continued his lesson. "Now, in this lecture, I'll be discussing the basics of how to build your territory and your Dungeon of trials for adventurers and for your own protection. As some of you may have noticed, you have mastered the Dungeon Core class and the Nodes associated with it. There is a reason for this, I assure you. Being a proper Dungeon is a simple, but lengthy process, and your skills aren't something you really have to learn, they simply are. All Dungeon Cores have the same base abilities.

You can learn various subsets or additional skills, but all Dungeons are masters of their class. If you haven't looked at your schedules yet, which I can't understand why you wouldn't have by this point, you can see that this class will take up the majority of your first week. It is important to note that you will be draining and building your reserves as we go. By the time we are done, you should have at least double your current mana capacity and plenty of power to influence the world around you with it. If you're lucky, you'll also fulfill most of the requirements needed to surpass the D Ranks, and unlock some new tricks and skills along the way."

Double mana capacity and new skills? I liked the sound of that, and from the look of the others around me, they seemed just as entranced by the power they were about to be given. It couldn't be that easy though. No one just gave someone the power of a god and said have fun with it, goddess-declared or not.

"There's a fine balance to the power you're going to wield. This isn't natural for our races, and we can lose ourselves to it. We do not have pixies, fae, nor wisps or spirits bonded to us to enhance and guide our growth. At higher Ranks, we can Bond with elemental essence to help enhance and refine our power, but they are still simply an extension of ourselves. We have to function as individuals rather than pairs, and some can't deal with the isolation. I've had to quell more than one Dungeon going rogue in hopes of finding their own shortcut to power." His expression darkened for a moment as he thought aloud. "I will not lose another student to the corruption that plagues the wilds of the east."

I liked the sound of that less. Bonding was something the Beastkin did, but it was for marriage and family, not for power, and we certainly didn't get stronger for it. If anything, we were weaker as we felt each other's pain as much as we felt their joy. Next to me, Amber seemed to be having the same thought. That was curious in itself, but my thoughts about it passed as our teacher moved about the stage, speaking to all corners in equal measure.

"Every piece of knowledge they have is obtained cheaply through stolen lives and power; we can gain the same through work or training. Though I admit, I have not found the secret to breaking through to the SSS ranking of power like they have, but I will find it in time. Five hundred and one is the charm as far as I'm concerned. However, we do have Manifestation, something that they do not, which allows us to use the powers and skills from when we once lived. As such, we can work as a team to defeat them rather than sending out wave after wave of minions to do so, and for every wild Core we smash, for every Dungeon we clear, we can gain a fraction of their knowledge and power."

It was so much to take in. I wanted to ask more, but it seemed like I was already behind. Everyone's silence and attention seemed to speak volumes. They all seemed to know what these Dungeons were already and why they needed to be defeated so desperately. Were my people so far out of the loop, or was it simply more of a 'civilized' kind problem? Either way, I was here now, so I might as well learn as much as I could. Amber could fill me in later with her common knowledge about things, I hoped.

"I digress though. Currently, we are not here to wage war, we are here to learn. Today, I will be giving your imagination wings to build and create as you've never done before. This requires two parts, Influence and Fabrication, as the class is entitled. I will now be sending you back to your origin point to begin."

Before I could even ask how, I had popped again and was lying against the soft forest floor once more.

What was with people doing this to me?

Chapter Twelve

The First Steps

This was exactly what I didn't want. I didn't want to lose control of my senses, I didn't want to be trapped back in my Core, and I didn't like being teleported without consent! Was it so hard just to warn people they were going to be teleported? Was it that hard? I mean really!

I didn't like being in my Core. It added layers of senses I wasn't sure I was happy with. I could see in all directions without fail. I could sense all the little things as well. I could feel the make-up of the dirt under me, the leaves nearby poking into the edges of my sphere of understanding, and the fresh, living grass at the edges of the crater I rested in. I felt stronger than last time, but even as I tried, I wasn't powerful enough to manifest.

I was stuck, but thankfully, I wasn't alone.

Can everyone hear me? Ansith's voice echoed inside my soul. *If you can, just project your thoughts back towards me as if you were talking to me face to face.*

I can hear you, I projected back as I had done in the past. Was it really only a day ago? It felt like weeks since I'd been trapped like this.

There was a sudden pressure in my soul as I felt someone prodding, trying to find something. I was worried until a voice answered me back. *Sorry about that, but that's good, Rem. I'm Ansith's Celestial aspect. You may call me Ansith.* I got the distinct feeling that the aspect was making another joke, and when I didn't chuckle, there was a long pause before he began again. *As you're the only Core currently in the class attuned to my alignment, and Umberal isn't quite suited for teaching you yet, I will be your personal tutor for the next few days. Do you have any questions before we get started?*

A personal tutor was nice. That meant I could move more or less at my own pace though I wondered what he meant by 'Umberal isn't quite suited for teaching you'. I couldn't help but fell a pang of guilt at being so lucky, as I thought about what Amber must be dealing with. Then again, her mood had brightened greatly at the creation of her new body.

More than you could possibly imagine.

Ansith's aspect snorted and laughed. It was mildly disturbing feeling another's laugh inside your soul. *Rem, I've been alive for over five hundred years. I've had more answers than you could possibly have questions!*

I sent him the feeling of a smile along with my reply. *I don't know anything about these wild Dungeons you keep talking about. I don't know what the corruptions in the east are either. I want to humiliate adventurers though. I have to repay them for making me like this.*

There was a pause before Ansith spoke again. It almost felt like he was giving me a once over as the pressure passed over my Core's spirit again.

Revenge doesn't suit a Celestial such as yourself, Rem, but what you do after our training is none of my concern as long as you don't affect the school negatively or start a purge of Dungeons here in the west. However, if you'd like to keep coming back to learn, vacation, or even teach if the mood strikes you, you're going to have to play nice. We can have a private lesson later about the nature of Dungeons though. This is not the time for it, as it won't help you accomplish your classroom goal.

If anything, at least I could say that Celestial Ansith was a reasonable person. I may not have wanted to play nice, but at least he gave me just enough reason to try. The possibility of losing a centuries old line of knowledge and a possible escape from a bad situation was quite the incentive.

Alright. I can accept that. How do we start?

For a moment, there was silence as Ansith contemplated the question. *Well, the first thing is to spread your Influence to the area around you. It's a simple process, Rem, though it isn't quite the same as using a normal skill. It works like how you would purge mana as an Oracle. There is a key difference though. As you expel mana where there's no competition, the area around you will become attuned to your Core. As your mana permeates the soil, you can control it as you see fit. You can even devour it into your Core to return a fraction of the depleted mana and create cave systems, rooms, or simply to deepen your Dungeon's floors: though at your current power level, controlling multiple levels of mana, minions, and functions would be very difficult. Devouring anything permeated by your mana also has a bonus. It teaches you everything about the object, so rather than what just makes it up, you'd know how to arrange your mana to create copies of it. Fabrication is a skill we'll discuss later though.*

It was a lot to take in, but I thought I got it all as I repeated my side of the story. *So, I want to use Influence to push as much mana out of myself as I can to claim the area, then keep doing it until I've got a larger area of control.*

Ansith beamed. *I'm glad you understand the basics! After that, I want you to move yourself as far underground as you can. The deeper the better. When you're, oh, let's say a hundred yards underground, I want you to create a chamber for yourself, a cave of the toughest rock you can find. Fifty feet by fifty feet if you can manage. Once you've completed that, we'll continue.*

I wanted to argue, but Ansith's presence was gone before I could ask how would I know when I was that deep? So, I had to improvise. I knew my vision was about a foot in every direction, so I'd have to push myself and my Influence down... I sighed to myself as the calculation came to me. I'd have to do it about three hundred times to get as far down as he wanted.

Sket.

***

42... 43... 44...

Yep. Digging myself a deeper hole was about as much fun literally as it had been figuratively. Every three feet, I had to stop and wait almost ten minutes before my mana recovered enough to continue. On the bright side, I was leaving quite the path of my Influence. There wasn't much else interesting though. Since I didn't want to leave a hole, I willed the earth to move me deeper like how I'd swallow food. It was weird to say the least.

I could still sort of see in my sphere of Influence, there was just nothing but dirt in all directions. Decayed leaves, dead insects, living insects and more were everywhere as I went deeper. Foot by foot, I continued to go deeper as I absorbed and replaced the more interesting bits I found.

***

120... 121... 122...

Yep, still not that fun.

The deeper I went, the more I learned though, so there was that. I learned about different kinds of stones, some trace metals like copper and iron that I didn't know existed this close to the surface, and soil compositions that got more unique the deeper I went. I didn't devour everything since it would be even more taxing to return the soil I took, but I did take nibbles here and there whenever I ran across something new. I even found gemstones! Granted, even I knew what quartz was already, but it was nice to have something shiny. In what training I remembered, quartz was the base material in many of the simple magic tools the clans used, so if what Ansith said was true, I could replicate it without end. That meant I had a great set of starting materials to build with.

***

280... 281... 282...

Bored couldn't even begin to describe me anymore. Bored was what I felt, but it was much greater than that now.

I was Boredom incarnate.

Behold, my amazing ability to control dirt and push myself deeper into the bowels of the forest. Watch as I devour peat, animal bones, rocks, and dirt. Be astounded as I drop foot by foot into the solid dirt. Well, drop was still inaccurate for the most part. There were times when I made drops just so things would be different, but then I had to waste more time filling it back in.

I really led an exciting life now, didn't I?

***

298... 299... 300!

Finally, I came to rest in a spot of soil no different than the one I had left. The only difference was this was **the** spot. This was supposed to be the center of my new empire of dirt and darkness. I beamed, through it was hard to tell in the all-consuming dirt of the earth, but now it was time to actually do something!

The most basic lesson a mage learned was to push their mana out of their reserve and into spell work. Different mages did things differently, so I didn't know how runesmiths or enchanters managed compared to an Oracle or a Dungeon Core. Ansith simply described it was emptying my reserve and letting it refill, so it seemed even easier than casting a spell.

I let my mind relax as I felt for my mana within my soul. Reaching around my Nodes, I gripped at the power and willed it to flow through my crystalline body. Normally, I would focus on the form and direction, and the mana would flow through my hands or voice to create an effect thanks to the associated Node. With this Core method, I was able to cut out the middle man and let it ooze out all around me. As quickly as I had started, my reserves were already at half capacity. I nearly flinched when I realized that and stopped the flow. If I lost my mana, wouldn't I die? Ansith hadn't been direct about it, but Vix had been pretty clear young Cores like me died pretty often from mana loss.

Strangely, I didn't feel sick or weaker this time.

As I explored that idea, I looked back inside and realized something very important. Somehow, I had unconsciously set what I determined as my mind and my Nodes outside of the normal flow of power and protected it within its own little bubble. All around me, the mana swelled and twisted like a whirlpool around a kraken, but I was safe.

101

This new revelation gave me a sense of smug satisfaction as I pushed myself to the limits. Every few minutes, I would push my Influence further and further into the steadily growing sphere around me, and as it swelled, so did my ability to see.

For the first time, I was glad that I didn't have my normal sight. It would have been useless down here. It was curious seeing the earth and moving my sight through it like a ghost. I knew I wasn't moving, but I could travel and explore my Influence up to the very edges now. I could move mana within it as easily as I pleased. It was like swimming in a giant lake that would go where I wanted once my Influence was everywhere.

It wasn't as easy as Ansith made it sound though.

Sometimes, materials resisted my Influence, so more of myself needed to be focused into that region. Sometimes, it ended badly. The first time I was slowed, I was being actively resisted. Something fought my power despite it being surrounded by my mana on all sides. The area it was in was hollow, so I simply pushed the dirt in around it until it vanished. Only after I controlled the area did I realize I'd just crushed a family of some variation of ground squirrel. A deep squirrel, my senses told me. It had sight similar to mine but more refined, a sort of aetheric echo location. With the death of that creature, I felt its power added to my own and I knew everything about it inside and out just like Ansith had promised.

The kill taught me a lot. In the end, it made me stronger. I knew this would come in handy, but I wished I hadn't needed to kill it. Eh, I'd get over it though. I doubted it would be the last thing I'd have to kill.

***

A second curious thing began to happen as I reached maybe forty feet in all directions. As my Influence became something of an ocean compared to what I was used to, mana began to return to me faster and faster the closer I was to the center of the sphere. It was as if the mana I created was flowing back and making the spot denser near my Core.

At the very center, it was nearly as thick as the academy was, but the depth of my mana density was nothing compared to the school. Worse, it weakened drastically the further out from the center that I pushed. When I started, I could feel myself thickly permeating everything like a rainstorm in the aftermath of a drought: everything wanted to take my power. After a few hours, the mana seeped back towards the center of myself and only left enough of a mark to show it was mine and to allow me to use it. My mana seeped back and pooled at my Core until the density was too high and the dense pool grew wider.

So, I began to slow down. I cycled my power, pushing the density out as it came back, cycling it through the soil and reinforcing it with more and more of myself until it was as dense as I could make it. Then, I poured more, letting it spill over and naturally expand my Influence. It was much, much slower going, but the results were longer lasting.

Soon, I had a thick density that I couldn't even dent if I tried. I just kept pouring more and more power into it. In the center of the pool, my mana didn't even seem to budge as I just kept cycling it through. I tried to slowly press against my maximum, but at the rate it kept coming in, it would have shattered me. So I kept using my skill again and again. I pushed and I pushed mana from myself until I felt a change. The skill felt so easy now, like it wasn't even there. I didn't even feel the mana coming and going. Had I broken the Node?

Curious, I checked the skill.

Influence
Primary Class Node - Active/Passive Ability - Dungeon Core
Evolution Potential - None
Active Effect: Spread your Influence by spending mana to claim an unclaimed area or fight another Influence. Influence spread is equal to Size, Rank, and mana spent. Claimed areas generate mana equal to the power and density of aether present in the material claimed. Material touched by your Influence within your Influence gives off a faint light related to your primary mana type. Influence cannot be used to claim sentient or sufficiently powerful living things.
Passive Effect: When mana reaches critical levels within your Core and cycling has been sustained for a substantial time, the effect of cycling mana within the Core will become a passive effect.

Passive Effect: Fabrication and Absorption can only be used within an area of Influence.

Huh, so that's what that meant. I'd done it so often that cycling the mana had become passive. I didn't know whether this would spread my Influence or simply pool the mana where I was and increase the density, so I kept the flow of power going through me and the entire area I now controlled.

It had to be hours before I finally had the control I needed, but time passed as if it were nothing. And on the very dot when the density and control were where I wanted them, a voice echoed in my soul once more.

Good, good! I didn't expect for you to figure it out so quickly.

To my credit, I didn't scream. I wanted to jump, but that was hard, as I was just a stone. Ansith paused though, giving time to process that yes, he was still watching me from days away.

Most Cores just keep dumping mana at the edges of their control and expecting results. You're a natural draw for mana, and your own power is no exception to this. Thanks to the passive effect of Influence, the longer you are here, the denser the mana will become: as long as nothing is using it. As a part of nature now, you will draw in all natural mana towards your own and convert it to what I like to call Dungeon mana. This can be further converted by you into Celestial or, if you will it, Umbral in emergencies for your spells and automatically convert for crafting once you've learned a Pattern, though it will take a higher toll. In a rare case such as your own, you'll even be able to create divine relics when you reach the higher Ranks thanks to your connection to Goddess Vul.

I'd never heard of Dungeon mana, and the only extra type I remember seeing in the Dungeon Core Nexus was Unknown, but I knew everything about divine power. For a moment, I wondered how he knew my connection was to Vul, but being as she was the patron goddess of the Foxkin, it probably was just an educated guess. Despite the slight hiccup, I couldn't help my soul from glowing happily within my crystal. I loved feeling special and smug. Spug-ish, some might say. The kinds of magic I would wield from those kinds of power were —

You aren't done yet though, so quit that, Rem. You have the sphere, now you need to convert the soil and stone into a room.

In my daydreaming, I'd almost forgotten there was more to it than just cycling mana endlessly. *And I just convert it?* Then I remembered the Nodes I had now. *Do I use Absorption?*

Ansith's aspect projected the mentality of a shrug. *Sure. Give it a try.*

That didn't sound so sure. In fact, it sounded like he was expecting me to do that. I knew when a teacher was goading me. He thought I'd learn something from it. Sket! I was missing something.

And there goes that smugness, Ansith beamed.

Mists. What was I missing though? He all but confirmed his teaching moment, but what else was there to do? I thought it out for a few moments, and decided to focus my attention at the top of my sphere. He probably thought I was going to start at the bottom and fall on my tail or something.

So, I began to devour the rock and soil that made up the sphere. The first problem became apparent immediately. The more I ate, the more mana I had. The more mana I had, the slower I worked since I could only cycle my mana so quickly. I could feel Ansith's beaming smugness in my little kernel of self inside the stone, so I snapped.

What's so funny! Quickly, my little outburst was followed by, *Ow!*

It felt like someone smacked me on the ear. It was strange enough to describe to myself in this form. I didn't have an ear, I didn't have nerves, but I felt the pain clear as day. *You are, Rem. It's a simple law of magical conversion. Sure, you can devour it, slow your progression, and lose a little bit of mana in the process, but you can also directly convert it into something else that you know. It'll save you time. Remember what I wanted the shell of your room to be?*

Dense stone, I responded almost automatically.

The densest you found. Whatever material you shift it into, keep pressing mana into it like you did to create your dense mana bubble of Influence and see what happens.

I took a moment and reviewed the other Node related to Influence:

Fabrication
Primary Class Node - Active Ability - Dungeon Core
Evolution Potential - None
Cost: Scales with complexity

Effect: Spend mana to create or recreate items from Patterns that you have absorbed via absorption, created, or have sufficient knowledge to attempt to recreate from memory. Cost is directly related to the power, complexity, and Rank of the item created.
Creation is limited to items within two Ranks of your current Dungeon Core Class.

It seemed easy enough, but I guessed better. I knew how to simply replace what I took with dirt or stone, but I didn't know how to convert minerals. *Fabrication says that it's used to create items. How do I convert?*

Ansith sighed. *It's similar to how you manifest but unique. This is the act of Fabrication at the base level. Instead of creating yourself, you'll focus on the mana in the material you want to convert and then pour mana into the Pattern of the item you wish to create with it. The materials will be unique from each other and your power will be drained by the amount you need to create the material. Since you have such a dense area and plenty of thick, packed soil, it shouldn't be too hard to create your shell, and this will serve a dual purpose. For this exercise, build the Pattern out to line the entire area, and fill it in slowly or you might have to start all over.*

Working the words over in my head a few times before I started, I decided that the concept was simple enough. In theory, it was just like working an area of effect spell, except on a larger scale. I imagined the shell for my new room, and, to my surprise, the idea I had for the sphere glowed like a ghostly haze through the stone exactly as I imagined it.

I liked it!

With the image in place, I focused on the dirt inside of the shell's ghostly image. Instead of absorbing it like I had been doing, I began to push everything into it, and the mana-saturated soil responded. A dense granite was my idea to start with. It was durable and somewhat colorful, so it was a natural choice. From tip to floor, I held the image and pushed. It was harder to create than it was to break something down, but I adapted quickly. Slowly, the dirt around me began to retract and vanish as a layer of stone began to form. I could feel it distinctly growing from the dirt. This was my creation, this was part of me. It wasn't just Influence anymore. I kept pouring and pouring power into it and noticed the density of the area lowering as I did. So, I slowed further without stopping the process to the point that it became painfully slow.

In all, it took over three hours to fill in the granite shell. Soon, it became easier. Tedious, but easier. As the last of the shell was filled in, I noticed that I was on the floor of a perfectly hollow, rounded sphere of granite. I was devoid of mana and wary, but I beamed proudly at my new rock.

I should have known by now that I wouldn't be the only one.

Chapter Thirteen

The Signature Beast

Well, well! Not bad at all, Rem.

There was no irony in his voice, and for some reason, it made me beam just a little more. *I try.*

Ansith seemed to be concentrating on the entire area for the next few minutes as he checked the completeness of the shell. It was strange being able to feel him prod at my work. It wasn't like when he checked out my soul or connected to me, more like what I imagined poking a water skin would feel like if I were the skin. My Influence flexed without breaking at least five times before his attention turned back to me.

Now, before anything else, what have you noticed about your mana, Rem?

Looking at my reserve, empty was a thought of the past. A lot had changed while I'd been working!

Dungeon Core Rank D4
Mastered Skills: 5 of 5
Secondary Skills: 0
5/9 requirements met to reach Rank C
      Absorb a new raw material
      Reach Nexus Size 2
      Absorb a new Bestiary Component
      Trigger a passive cycling of Influence
      Fabricate your Heart Chamber
Dungeon Core Nexus Size 2
Dungeon Core Material - Opal/Amethyst
Mana Types - Celestial/Umbral/Dungeon
Mana Reserves:

Celestial - 250/250
Umbral - 20/20
Dungeon - 1000/1000
Class Passive for Mastery:
Dungeon Mana Reservoir: Mana Reservoir grows based on use.

New Dungeon Core Augments unlocked at Nexus Size 2
    Bestiary Unlocked
    Codex Unlocked

By the Pantheon! I had increased my mana reservoirs by over six hundred points, increased three Ranks, and increased my Nexus Size. Whatever that meant. I was too excited to care! It couldn't be this easy. There was no possible way I'd doubled my mana capacity in the span of… well… how long had it been? I'd lost track of time long, long ago. I was left without words as I lay on my new polished stone floor.

I had absorbed the mana and converted the materials until nothing was left, but the room's ambient mana was rising. The density was growing in the sphere, higher and higher until it was thick with it, and despite the passive cycling ability of Influence, I could feel the power was being forcibly returned and cycled away from me.

Where's all this mana coming from?

Ansith had his turn to beam. *I said it would serve a dual purpose, didn't I? Dungeon Cores have a unique property when they create their Dungeon walls. The walls create and radiate the power I referred to earlier, Dungeon mana. Not only that, but they are one of the sole sources of filtration that can continuously convert the mana of nature into a power that only you can use; this slows another Dungeon's invasion, and prevents leakage without your direction. It overwrites the natural mana production in this area and is twice as potent as ambient mana because of its specific nature. You can convert it back into normal mana for your spells, but that will be more of a last resort or when you're on a hunt.*

As interesting as that was, I was three hundred feet underground in a sphere of Dungeon granite. What was left? More importantly, how much power could I still gain three hundred feet underground in a sphere of Dungeon granite?

Now, I know what you're thinking. What's left? Ansith chimed in. I swear the man could read my thoughts directly even when I wasn't trying to talk to him. *Well, this will serve as your heart room. From here, you'll produce mana to power yourself and experiment. It will also serve as your building point where your Dungeon will begin. As you so helpfully counted out, you have a hundred yards, or three hundred feet, to play with before you reach the surface. At an average of fifteen-foot ceilings, you have a lot of room to work with before we open your trials. Your next task though isn't about expansion. You'll have plenty of time for that later on. It's about Fabrication. Before we leave here, you're to have a signature creature to act as your Core's Guardian when you're away from your Dungeon.* Something dropped onto the ground and echoed a few feet away from me as he spoke. *These scrolls detail the entire process. Consider these your first tests, Rem. Ta-ta.*

Wait! But he was already gone from my senses. Damn him. How was I supposed to read scrolls when I couldn't... even... unroll.

If there was a reward for missing answers that should have been obvious, I would have won all of them at this point. I had power and a constant flow of mana like nothing I'd ever experienced. A single, blazing thought filled my mind as the Dungeon mana flowed into my idea and triggered Manifestation, and I popped back into existence soon after.

Sure enough from tail to tip, the power of the Dungeon mana was still dense enough for my Core to cycle and use, but something was different this time. I felt... lighter somehow. I couldn't put my finger on why until I looked down at my feet. My Core was still on the ground, and I was elsewhere. I could still feel it tethered to me, but it felt odd. It was fueling me still, but I wasn't there. If I focused, I could feel a small part of myself still within the stone, the part of me that was controlling this part and governing the distribution of the necessary power from my pool, but it was seamless if I didn't focus too hard on the connection.

Eagerly, I bent down and opened the scrolls. The first one I opened was a glimmering Pattern of white etched into a circle, but nothing else was there. The second, was a set of directions. Directions however, was a very loose term.

How to Create a Signature Creature—The Minion

Step One: Learn about a species by Absorbing a sufficient amount of its organic matter

Step Two: Using Patterns and the Bestiary as guides, combine aspects of different creatures by assigning their attributes to a base form.

Step Three: Flow the appropriate elemental and/or Dungeon mana into the construct to bring it to life.

Note One: Fabricate and consult your Dungeon Bestiary for more information on a given creature by finding its entry and focusing on it. This will tell you what you know and can use.

Note Two: The mana used in the construction process will give the creature an elemental alignment and skew its abilities as it grows stronger. For this purpose, Dungeon mana is considered a neutral alignment and recommended as a starting point for all experimentations. After a Pattern is created, it will be stored in the Bestiary or Codex, and your Dungeon mana will filter itself into the proper alignments during the creation process.

Okay, that was simple enough. I already had absorbed one creature, the deep squirrel, but I doubted that would be enough. I turned my attention to the second scroll and was horrified to see that without my attention a corpse had appeared in the glowing runic circle, the corpse of a small, furry, orange creature. A small, furry, curled up ball of fox fur.

He hadn't…

I held my breath as I bent down to look at the creature. Ansith wouldn't kill a Foxkin in cold blood for me to toy with, would he?

Upon closer inspection, I let out a sigh of relief. It wasn't a kit of some lost Foxkin mother; it was just a dead fox.

It took a few moments for me to recover from the shock of seeing the small orange creature. It was just a beast though. My clan raised them for hunting and kept the smarter ones as pets, but still, seeing a dead one wasn't exactly a welcome sight.

It's just organic matter, I told myself. It's not alive, you didn't kill it, just absorb the organic matter. The sooner I did that, the better I'd feel.

At least, I hoped I would.

Just like I had with the stone, I pushed mana through the body, saturating it with my power, making it just another extension of my Influence. Unlike the squirrel, the corpse of the fox didn't resist the mana filling every inch of its form. Then, I willed the mana through my Absorption Node to break the item down and bring it back into the folds of my power. The entire deed was done in less than a handful of seconds.

The creature's attributes instantly were second nature to me. Interesting enough, it had died of a poison that still pulsed through its system. The fox's lungs were weakened, the muscles were ravaged, and the wounds around each bite mark, six of them in all, were beginning to become necrotic. As I focused, details of the poison became clear and a new attribute was added in addition to the tally: Corrupted Acanthophis Venom.

I also absorbed the scroll the body was on for good measure and was rewarded with a storage rune script as well along with paper, polished wood, and silver ink! I knew I wasn't special and that the others would be doing the same thing, but with everything else I had gathered. I was really beginning to feel excited about the things I could start to accomplish.

Focusing on the Bestiary, I set about my first real task. As I brought the idea to the forefront of my thinking, I expected the information to be something I could sort through in my mental space. It was, but there was more to it than that. I could get what I assumed to be Patterns to appear, but not what I needed.

I needed the Bestiary.

As I focused, some Dungeon mana flowed into the idea and a book slammed to the floor. It was how I always imagined books should be. The binding and covers were strong with softly glowing white script that read: *Rem - Dungeon Bestiary*. I didn't even bother to sit before I cracked the book open. It wasn't a thick tome by any stretch, but it had a lot more within it than I thought! Each species of insect I killed and the creatures I absorbed were documented in excruciating detail marked off by sections. In the end, I decided to start with the base form as the note suggested.

Flipping to Section One, I had the choices of 'small beast' and 'insect'. There were no pictures, but as soon as I focused on the entry marked small beast, a new list appeared and the other faded from view.

I grinned at my new magical friend and focused on the entry marked 'small canine'. Immediately, the outline of a fox hovered just above the pages in a wispy white outline. The fox's form looked about as substantial as if it were made of fog, just like the sphere I built had been before I fed mana into it, but it still blocked my view of the pages. I discovered quickly that I could move the image around the room and change its size as I worked. Moving it about five feet away, I made it slightly larger and then changed from the base form page to that for attributes.

As soon as I did, a number appeared above the fox, zero out of three. The creature's legs, head, back, and tail were all a more substantial white at this point, so I took that as an indication of where I could modify it. The book was very Core friendly, it seemed.

Attributes were more interesting than I thought. I had everything from wings and chitin, to horns, poison, and the aetheric echo location ability, so I began to experiment. The first thing I added was insect chitin focusing on its head and back. The fox's form instantly grew a sleek shell of white, like a helmet over its head and across its back. The number next to it increased from zero to two as the change finished, and a new note appeared under the creature: Light Armor.

I still had one point, and plenty of options for what to use, but one had vanished from my choices: Corrupted Acanthophis Venom. In fact, it was nearly completely gone from the list, barely visible. Did that mean I needed more points to be able to use it, or had the armored fox just become incompatible with it? Either way, I settled on another skill from the list, Aetheric Location. I didn't need to focus on any one part in particular for this. Instead, the creature's tail grew longer and longer and puffed out. That was not what I expected.

With that done, I took a hard look at the creature. It was interesting, almost regal looking in its smooth white armor and overly puffy tail. To my surprise, new information appeared as I stared at it.

Compatible Pattern finished.
New page has been added to Rem - Dungeon Bestiary: Aether Fox.
Armored Aether Fox
Health: Healthy
Intelligence: Feral - Clever
Growth Potential: Medium
Compatible Mana Types: All
Evolution Potential: Unknown - Experiment with different types of mana to populate this information.
Survivability Rating: Unknown - Experiment with different types of mana to populate this information.
Mana attributes: Unknown - Experiment with different types of mana to populate this information.
Mutation Chance: Unknown - Experiment with different types of mana to populate this information.

Well, that was interesting. I didn't expect to get information on it like that. Thankfully, as I read the information, the terminology made sense: health was how healthy the creature was; intelligence was how a creature thought; growth potential measured how fast something could grow or how far, *et cetera*. Honestly, I would have thought that I'd have to watch it fight or something. It felt like a clean process, something that I had a distinct feeling wasn't how the Dungeons Ansith seemed to be preparing us to fight did things. I couldn't imagine some dark, evil force holding out a book and playing at put the attributes on the body. It was enough to make me laugh. I liked the process and what I had created, so I began to filter Dungeon mana into it.

It took less than a minute before the foggy form of the armored aether fox came into being. It had a distinctly gray appearance. The fox had stone gray fur; reflective, but still gray armor that curved with its spine; and black, piercing eyes. It looked around, seemingly confused by the new environment then laid its eyes on me. The creature's tail fell a bit, but wagged as it sat down, looking to me with a radiating reverence as it wrapped its long tail around itself.

As I focused on it, the same information from the page came up around it in ethereal lettering.

Armored Aether Fox
Cost: 50 Dungeon Mana
Challenge Rating: E5
Healthy
Intelligence: Feral
Growth Potential: Medium
Survivability Rating: E
Mana attributes: Lesser Dungeon Born
Reward Seed: Natural

So, Dungeon mana gave it the attribute Dungeon born, whatever that meant. Materializing my personal Bestiary again, I found new sections in the index titled Mana Attributes and Reward Seeds. With a smile, I turned to the first new section to find just one entry.

Lesser Dungeon Born
Attribute Type: Passive
A minion brought to life via Dungeon mana or Influence. It cannot survive outside of the mana rich Dungeon environment and has no will of its own outside of its own survivability. The minion leaves behind no corpse upon death and instead converts its bodily mana into its assigned reward seed.

Next came the reward seed section. Eagerly I turned to it, and found a simple entry.

Natural
Reward Seed Type: Common
This is the default reward for all creatures created by any Dungeon. A natural reward seed materializes rewards from the mana expelled at death based on the natural composition of the creature killed and the mana put into its creation.

Well, what had I expected from something called a natural reward seed? A fox to drop a sword when it was killed? That thought, however, brought about a new idea.

What would happen if I created a fox with my Celestial mana?

The idea piqued my interest, so I attempted to pour mana into my image of the armored aether fox. The creature popped into existence with a shimmering glow of life.

Instead of the gray tones of the original, this one was nearly pure white. The creature's shell mimicked my own coloring and the soft glow of my Influence, while at the same time it gave a slight contrast between the two tones. Its tail wasn't nearly as puffy though. Moreover, it had grown a pair of small horns on the top of its head. Its eyes weren't a solid black either. Instead, the eyes of the creature glowed a brilliant golden glow. Something was off this time. I felt... weaker somehow. The only thing I'd done was spend my Celestial mana, so I checked my reserve.

Celestial - 100/250

That one creature had cost me one-hundred and fifty of my two hundred and fifty mana. Could this creature really be so different to the Dungeon mana variant? Maybe I didn't feel the same strain from the Dungeon mana base because I had so much coming in? Costly, but I couldn't argue with the results as the new fox bounded around the room, barking wildly for its companion to join in the fun.

I tried to focus on it to get the same information as from the other creature, but it just kept moving like a child with too much sugar from sweets coursing through its veins. I began to get frustrated and lost it.

"Stop it, you stupid thing!"

Immediately, it stopped dead in its tracks, and I mean a dead stop. The new creature stopped moving its feet so fast that it tumbled forward and rolled up the wall before falling back onto the floor. I felt bad for a moment, but it sat back up seemingly no worse for wear.

With the creature still at last, I focused on it again:

Armored Celestial Fox
Cost: 150 Celestial Mana
Challenge Rating: D9
Hearty
Intelligence: Clever, Curious, Hyperactive
Growth Potential: Average
Survivability Rating: D

Mana attributes: Blink, Limited, Lesser Dungeon Born
Reward Seed: Natural

The Celestial variant seemed much more powerful, but it had a few different attributes as well. So, I looked them up to find out if that drain was worth it.

Blink
Attribute Type: Active
Cool down: 30 Seconds
As a naturally nimble creature, a Celestial variant can spend Celestial mana to use the ability 'blink'. This ability allows the creature to arrive faster at its destination or to avoid an attack.

Limited
Attribute Type: Passive
Due to the constrains of power needed for such a minion, a minion with the limited attribute can only exist at a rate of one per room, per rank above F.
Current rank: D4
Current Limit: 2 per floor

It was an interesting creature for sure, and the fox was nearly shaking to the teeth from its inability to move. With a gesture, I let it move again, and it was all the happier for it.

One step left, Rem! A familiar voice rang out.

"Damn it!" I screamed. I had forgotten Ansith was watching me. Stupid disembodied voice, couldn't he have cleared his throat or something? "You'll give me a heart attack."

You don't have a heart, Rem. Ansith reminded me. *You've made an interesting minion there. A bit basic, but its unique mana attributes will serve you well in the future. I'll be honest, I thought it might explode on you. Celestial mana can be a little tricky.*

"Thanks," I said bitterly at the thought of being blown up and dying again. "So, am I done?"

Nope! It's time for your final part of creating a signature beast. In the wild, these are called Dungeon bosses since they guard the way to the next floor of a Dungeon. We simply call them our Guardians. It will serve as your last line of defense and will always be your strongest creature on the floor. Are you ready?

Did I really have a choice? I thought to myself. "Ready as I'll ever be."

Good. Now all you have to do is think about your creature and signify you want it to become your Guardian. Then, push as much mana as you can of your own into it, and the change in intent along with the rush of mana will fuel an evolution! I've never seen a Celestial evolution, so this should be fun.

I was glad he was having fun, and, I had to admit, there was some visceral pleasure in creating life. It wasn't as much fun as I had hoped, but still, it was something to be in awe of. Hopefully, this would be the last real issue I'd have with learning my skills.

"Come here, pup," I called to the hyperactive creature, and it came to heel with all the grace I'd expect from a toddler. It bounded into my chest, knocked me down, and sat proudly on my chest as if it'd done me a great service.

I sighed, pointed to the ground in front of me, and the fox moved. Focusing on the Armored Celestial Fox, I began to convert my Dungeon mana and push it into my target. I could feel my power waning as the Dungeon mana rapidly changed and was absorbed by my target. The original armored fox vanished as the environment's density dropped, but my fox began to grow.

Where it was once about the size of a normal fox, it grew to twice that. The armor expanded backwards and out, growing across legs, and its long tail became a row of chitinous plates looking almost like a lizard's tail, but it somehow still retained its width. It howled as the light around it grew denser and denser, and its features began to obscure. The outer edges of my sphere were as easily seen as if it were day by the time I felt like I was at the limit of my power, then...

Pop.

Chapter Fourteen
The Right to Survive

Suddenly, I was aware of everything around me again. The realization that I had pushed myself too hard wasn't lost on myself. If I had been out in the real world, I would have probably been dead. Thankfully, I was safe underground in a thick sphere of stone with Dungeon mana all around me. In the time I had been out, the mana density had returned, and I felt like my new-old self again. With some focus and a pop, I returned to my preferred form of limited vision and unlimited potential.

Giving myself a once over, I was satisfied with my appearance and began to look around. Where was that fox?

My thought's path completely went into the woods as I looked at what had once been my Armored Celestial Fox. It sat proudly, waiting for me, as I let the information flow:

Unnamed Guardian
Cost: 250 Celestial Mana
Challenge Rating: D
Very Healthy, Inquisitive, Loyal
Intelligence: Clever - Autonomous
Growth Potential: Complete
Survivability Rating: D
Mana attributes: Celestial Phase Armor, Blink, Floor Guardian
Reward Seed: Unassigned, Natural

The words weren't lost on me. Most importantly, I needed to learn what those attributes were, so I opened the book to the section marked mana attributes. It had grown by a few entries.

Celestial Phase Armor
Attribute Type: Active - Single Use
Normally, natural armor cannot be removed from the body. In this case, the minion can shed its armor and increase its speed for a cost without taking damage to its health. As a Celestial variant, the armor will reduce all incoming elemental damage by twenty-five percent. Celestial and Umbral spells will have full effectiveness.

Floor Guardian
Attribute Type: Passive
This minion acts as a defense to the Dungeon floor it is assigned to and is limited to acting in that room alone unless otherwise directed. The Guardian cannot be directly controlled by the Dungeon's Core and recalls all important experiences in its life, even after death, to improve its abilities.
Only a single Floor Guardian may exist in a Dungeon per floor.
Floor Guardians may not be repeated within a Dungeon.

Now those were interesting. The terms under Floor Guardian were a bit confusing. What was a Dungeon floor? Direct control? Assigned rooms?

I sighed, I'm sure there would be a lesson about all that coming up once things were a bit more progressed. There was one thing I needed to do though as I studied the creature. It wasn't an Armored Celestial Fox anymore, so according to its own entry, I had to name it. What would be a good name for such an imposing creature though? It sat looking at me, tilting its head to one side as it studied me, waiting for my decision. So, I made one.

"Tenko." The name was the first in my mind, but I hadn't been the one to create it. It was the name of the last Oracle of the Foxkin before me. Tenko of the Heaven's Tail was his full name, but Tenko would serve my Guardian well enough until he earned a title of his own. With that, I watched as the new bit of information updated his status before my eyes.

Tenko
Guardian Beast - Armored Celestial Fox
Titles - None
Cost: 250 Celestial Mana
Challenge Rating: D
Very Healthy, Inquisitive, Loyal
Intelligence: Clever - Autonomous
Growth Potential: Complete
Survivability Rating: D
Mana attributes: Celestial Phase Armor, Blink, Floor Guardian
Reward Seed: Unassigned, Natural

Tenko nodded its head, accepting the name before coming to stand at my side. He reached to nearly my shoulder now, but he was gentle enough that I didn't worry about him accidentally rolling onto me or ripping my arm out of my socket.

Ansith beamed from his unseen vantage point and took the chance to throw me a bone. *Excellent! Your Guardian is exactly what I'd hoped for from you. Now, for the fun part.*

Fun part? I didn't like the sound of that as I looked around. "Should I be worried?"

Yes, Rem. You should.

Sket.

Whatever was happening, I didn't like it. First something cut my mana and then these... things arrived. Their hollow faces and empty eyes carved from colored stone made my fur stand on end. Where'd they even come from?

I didn't like the way that they were staring at me or how their eyes began to glow with all the colors of the rainbow. I didn't like the way that their bodies joined in the glowing. I didn't like the look of their blocky, dwarven armor or their bulky limbs, and I really, really didn't like how their heads twisted on their shoulders in a full rotation before they began moving towards me.

Really, I just didn't like them at all.

"What did I ever do to you!" I yelled into the multicolored light.

I knew he was there, listening and watching me. He had invaded my sphere and locked me away with six chest-high golems. They glowed with the six colors of the academy, and I only knew one person that could use six kinds of mana. So, it really wasn't that hard to guess what they were: Ansith's minions.

Tenko responded to my emotions without an order and fell into a position to cover me. The Guardian moved to block their advance, snarled, and bared his teeth at the constructions that clanked as real as any metal towards me.

Of course, Ansith didn't respond, and the creatures continued their approach towards me with a mindless determination. I fell back on my magical training almost immediately and began to channel my mana into my cantrips. Will-of-the-Wisps flashed to life all around the area, throwing a pearly light that made the cavernous area more easy to navigate. My power may have mostly filled the sphere and given me a better awareness, but that didn't mean I wouldn't trip in the darkness.

Tenko took to the offensive a moment after the cantrip had been cast and with jaws wide open lunged for the purple construct. A moment later, my Guardian had clamped down on an aetheric arm and whipped its head to the side, violently sending the minion into the air, severing limb and body as it flew into another of the golems.

The four others were on him in a second, faster than their smaller bodies should have allowed. Fists moved with mechanical precision as they attacked Tenko's unprotected knees and belly. Each punch was enough to turn my stomach with the way the flesh gave way, and Tenko howled.

Then he was gone, his absence punctuated by a flash of light.

Five fully functioning minions, and one slightly less functional one whirled their heads around to look at me again, and their bodies followed after in their creepy, jerky movements. For some reason, I figured Ansith's creations wouldn't be so off. Even if they were slow, the further in they moved, the more Influence Ansith had in my sphere.

It was just another in a long line of things that I wasn't happy about.

I didn't have anything that could stop them, but I did have ways to survive. Focusing my mana again, I smiled as I saw the air around me ripple, and I vanished from sight. I moved towards where my Core lay on the ground, scooped it up, and focused as they twisted in all directions looking for me.

That was when Tenko Blinked back to reality. In another flash of light not a minute later, Tenko was back on the attack. Glimmering opal blood came from wounds at his side, but the time away had evidently given my Guardian time to think. His armored tail swept from behind him, flying forward into two of the closer golems, the blue and green ones, and sent them crashing against the wall. The blue shattered in a shower of mana, while the green was mutilated and mangled as its arm broke its fall.

The remaining four resumed their attack a moment later. The red golem held its hands forward and spewed fire as the yellow made a similar motion. I couldn't see anything at first, then the flames leapt to life and engulfed Tenko's entire body. He roared in pain, yipping as the one-armed golem ran into the fire. I had to help.

"You will not harm Tenko!" I commanded from the far end of the impromptu arena as I focused on the red golem. It was my only shot as I felt more of my Celestial mana drain, but it was worth it.

The red golem dropped its arms and the flames died. It wasn't enough though as I saw what the purple, the Umbral, golem had done. It was latched to Tenko's torso and driving its stubby arms into his hide again and again. It pulled on anything it found, which seemed to be plenty as the creature's pearly organs joined blood on the floor. I shivered, not wanting to see my Guardian dying, but I couldn't look away. If I did, they'd get closer. Realizing I wasn't using every tool at my disposal, I brought up the image of the Armored Aether Fox and poured mana into it over and over again.

Each time I did, another of the foxes came to life on the floor in front of me. The mana density of the room began to fall, but I couldn't stop. First there were five, then ten, fifteen, and by the time I was nearly depleted, I had an entire sulk of at least twenty of them at my call. With a draining reserve, I poured enough to summon a Celestial counterpart to join them. They weren't large, they weren't powerful, but they had numbers and, if the Bestiary was to be believed, they were smart enough to take advantage of that fact.

"Attack!" I ordered as the Celestial fox took the lead, charging ahead with all the energy its power could muster, with its kin following behind. "Free Tenko!"

The battle was brutal as the sulk fell upon the Umbral golem. The Celestial fox tore into the good arm of the creature while the rest tried to drag it free of Tenko. It didn't matter whether or not the arm was supposed to be metallic or stone, the aether foxes gnashed and tore at it as if it were flesh. Parts flew and disappeared as they worked together to take out the superior foe and retreat as Tenko reached his feet, shaky, but quickly healing.

During their rescue attempt, Ansith's golems weren't idle.

Between my cheer and the sounds of the fox sulk rallying, the Celestial golem finished its repairs on the Earth golem, and it was soon back in fighting shape. Of course, I didn't notice that until a jutting spear of stone erupted from Tenko's back. He howled helplessly as I watched just as helpless to assist as its form blinked again. I almost cheered his Blink until I saw a collection of Celestial mana stones and perfectly cut meat flop sickly onto the floor.

Tenko was gone.

The smell of spilled opal blood filled the air as the remaining foxes rushed to encircle the group of golems. They wanted blood for their fallen kin.

I wanted blood, too.

At my mental order, the sulk crashed into the six, biting and tearing, retreating from stronger strikes as elemental attacks peppered them. A rain of fire here, a gale-force wind there, a wave of shadow took others. No matter how hard they fought, the golems had the advantage of raw power, and my numbers could only do so much.

Damn it, I need to do something!

I couldn't summon Tenko again, or I'd leave myself vulnerable. I tried to summon more aether foxes, but none came to call. I tried to spread my Influence to reclaim ground, but I felt like I was in a bubble. All around me, I felt the same power I had on the school grounds.

Ansith's power.

The headmaster had taken nearly all of my mana and Influence from the area. I barely had enough to keep myself Manifest, let alone use any more spells to do much of anything. What did he have against me? I nearly screamed it again, but it was pointless.

All I could trust now were my sulk and me. Together, there were eleven of us and only five of them.

With that thought, I watched as the Fire golem fell, adjusting my count to four. My Celestial fox had gone for the neck and tore it asunder. It was a risky move, flying into the reach of golems, and he paid the price. The Umbral golem caught him midair and snapped him in half before he could Blink away. The sickening sound of bones and chitin cracking told me all I needed to know as I looked away and made another adjustment.

Nine.

Then, an idea struck me as three of my foxes took down their Umbral foe only to be run through with stone again.

Six.

They were ignoring me. Why were they ignoring me? Were the foxes that much more dangerous than I was? Then it hit me. Of course they were! Ansith knew I couldn't do much. He was probably watching all of us. He'd seen me use spells, testing my power. He knew I didn't have anything offensive, and that made me even more angry as two of the sulk fell, leaving jagged crystal and meat behind.

Wait...

An idea struck me and a dark thrill crept along my spine. Oh, it was a grand, stupid idea, but an idea worth trying as my familiar popping echoed across the chambers. Back in my Core, I focused. I could create anything with my mana.

Celestial - 100/250
Umbral - 20/20
Dungeon - 200/1000

Checking my numbers again, I was dangerously low, but that didn't mean I should just roll over and die. I wasn't going to go out without a fight, so I turned to my endgame. A short prayer later, and I pushed a new image through my Manifestation skill. One with a little more bite to it...

And it hurt.

My mana was cut off, and I was spending everything I had to the point that my very soul burned, spending itself in the process to create one final offensive.

Celestial - 30/250
Umbral - 20/20
Dungeon - 100/1000

More! I needed more mana! Everything I didn't need was dropped from the image to save on mana. Clothes? I didn't need clothes! Who needed clothes?

Celestial - 5/250
Umbral - 20/20
Dungeon - 100/1000

With everything cut to the bare necessities, I made the final push. In my mind's eye, the image grew stronger and stronger as the yelping of my minions grew weaker and weaker. A familiar power bloomed, a familiar pressure built up within the Node—

Pop!

And it was done.

I couldn't believe it.

It had taken every drop of my remaining power to do it, but it had worked! My body was the same, but I wasn't helpless anymore. On the back of my hands were a pair of opal, Celestial mana claws that stretched out over my fisted hands. I looked up just in time for another spear of stone to impale another of my minions.

Three.

There was no energy left in the last of my sulk. They were beaten, singed, and panting with their tails between their legs. They whined their injury, searching for help. They couldn't do it alone.

They needed their leader.

They needed me.

There wasn't even a second thought as I charged in. Without the constant flow of Dungeon mana, I couldn't help but feel the drain on my body as I moved, but as the claws dug into the Earth golem I ripped its head—sparking and beeping in protest—from its shoulders. It was only noise in my ears, as I felt a rush I hadn't felt before. I relished the feeling of revenge, of the death of my foe at my hands as a shower of Earth mana rippled around me like an avalanche of power.

The sulk regrouped to my side, tails level and their movements showing a renewed hope in the battle. Together, we stared down the final golem as it clicked and chimed its mechanical sounds. It made no move to attack. It waited, resigned to its fate as we struck as one with the sounds and fury of the forest. It was the noise of rushing air, of claws and teeth, and the power of a single entity striking out against its foe, shattering it like so much paper.

As the Celestial power of the golem faded away, we were alone again in the darkness as the Will-of-the-Wisps finally died. Slowly, I could feel my power and Influence begin to return. I absorbed the meat, the Celestial mana stone, and the assortment of mana-imbued dwarven parts that had dropped from Ansith's minions. Strangely, I couldn't absorb the mana. It dissipated as I learned about gears, golem Cores, and ocular sensors, but the broken-down items were enough to restore at least some of my power.

Celestial - 55/250
Umbral - 20/20
Dungeon - 500/1000

With the room cleaned of blood and invading Influence, I smoothed out the surface of my sphere.

Satisfied, I summoned the full sulk back one at a time, so as not to too greatly drain my power. I had to wait almost an hour before I felt enough power within my Nexus to convert it into Celestial mana without losing myself again, and then their heavenly brother joined us. As much as I wanted to, Tenko wouldn't be returning to us again just yet. He was strong, but I didn't have the luxury of excess power if Ansith was still going to attack me. I cycled my mana, pushing it into the stone, forcing it denser and denser until it would take no more, and feeling the returns of power grow as I stood there.

Hours passed as I stood watch, and it was starting to get boring. Every now and then, I would feel Ansith's presence attempt to invade once more, and every time I'd throw so much power at it that it surprised even me. I felt stronger, but if he really wanted to destroy me, why was he playing these games?

An explosion of power broke through my Influence a second later.

Why did I keep tempting fate?

Everyone prepped for our final stand, but it wasn't another golem. The old dwarven man himself stood there in his school attire with a smile of pure satisfaction on his face, clapping like a madman.

"Excellent! Excellent performance, Rem."

Chapter Fifteen
Results

I didn't trust him any further than I could throw him, and since I couldn't get anywhere near him, that should say loads about my faith in the dwarf at this point. Carefully, my Influence prodded at his position, searching for any weaknesses, but his power struck back, destroying my mana so completely that I couldn't even sense it vanish. It was there one moment, and gone the next. Whatever his game had been, Ansith wasn't playing around this time.

That... wasn't a great sign...

"I honestly didn't think you'd make it through the trial on your first try, Rem. You've reached D-Two in record time thanks to your little trick there. I wasn't going to teach manifesting weaponry for yourself until you'd mastered your own Dungeon, but you surprised me." He continued walking towards me as his thick shoes clicked with each step. "What made you think you could create other things besides yourself?"

I saw red.

"First off, what in the Mists and all the Pantheon did I do to deserve this!" I tried to say more, but I just ended up screaming incoherently. The sulk growled, yipping angerly at Ansith, but they didn't dare strike.

Ansith said nothing and simply stood, waiting for something.

Some time passed and my temper cooled before I could make full sentences again. "Why should I listen to a single, sket-stained thing you have to say?"

His expression darkened, but I didn't budge. Every single hair stood on end as I starred him down. It wouldn't do me any good if he decided I was being an ass and needed to die, but you didn't turn your eyes from trouble. You figured out how to get out of it unscathed.

For his credit, he didn't try to stomp me into a fine, crystalline powder. His brow did furrow a bit in annoyance though.

"You'll listen because you have potential. Do you know how many students were able to create their minions and defend themselves successfully?"

The words were ice in my veins as I processed them. Everyone had been tested like this. "How many?" I asked, my voice barely above a whisper as I began to worry.

"Seven…" Then, a moment later, "Excuse me, six were able to properly create their minions and fend off my attack." I was about to interrupt, but there was no need. "Yes, your friend was among them. I still can't fathom how she managed what she did, but she was a greater surprise than even you were. I was thoroughly impressed by her strategy and ingenuity."

"What did she do?" My attention had completely left my original questioning. Over fifteen of my class had been crushed by this man as a test, and I'd barely survived myself. However, Amber, the Core, with little to no manifestation talent or image of herself, had fought him back so completely that it had impressed him.

"That is for her to tell you, but I would advise both you and her against sharing too much. This was a test of survival, ingenuity, and pure willpower. This wasn't conducted out of malice." He must have seen the confusion in my face, because he continued to elaborate. "This was a test, Rem. If you'd have failed, you would have been mediated, not killed. All Cores need to learn to work their way out of a terrible situation. At least for now, it's better to learn how you work, rather than how the others do."

"And they say my kind are cryptic," I grumbled. Foxkin were taught to share our strengths among our kind so we could work more efficiently, but some of what he said made sense. My fellow students would have a certain amount of shared skills as Dungeons, but other skills would be unique with our backgrounds being very different from one another.

Of course, he ignored me, and the sage on the stage continued unabated. "Your Celestial mana, as you've seen, will grant creatures special abilities such as Blink and improve the flexibility of protection abilities. As you progress as an Oracle, your flexibility will grow even further with your spells, and you'll eventually be able to use your spells as attributes for your minions."

Now that sounded useful, but not useful enough for me to trust him completely. The information only made me believe that he needed us. It must have shown, so he followed up.

"You'll learn this isn't a life of luxury and power, Rem. As much as you can do, you're still limited by what is and isn't permitted by the rules of nature. However, your Core is growing stronger. Soon, you'll be rank C, and some more of your restrictions will be lifted. By Rank B, you'll be working on your own projects at your leisure while minions and elemental spirits maintain your Dungeon's day to day functions."

I simply nodded warily. "So, now what?"

"Now? Now, we head back to the academy! You still have much to learn, and I'm sure you'd like to practice your new-found skills in a more... open environment."

Looking around, I realized that a huge underground sphere wasn't the best option for what I needed. My foxes were nimble, but I wasn't sure everything that I made would be. I'd have to change things later. My tail twitched with possibilities. Maybe I could make a forest for them down here! That would be much more relaxing than stone, and I could...

I was lost in thought for longer than I cared to admit to myself, but when I came out of it Ansith was grinning at me. Before I could say a word, he began to laugh. His beard waggled and his stomach shook like a bowl of fresh strawberry preserve. "Now that is a look I remember fondly. All the possibilities and things I could create. It's what lead to the Parapet hive. Such a useful race. I modeled them after your Beastkin race actually, but used insects as a base. They're much stronger and resilient than I expected."

That explained so much.

Too much, actually, and the idea that a Dungeon could create an entire race was a bit frightening. From my attributes, I knew my creatures couldn't survive outside the Dungeon, but what stopped someone like Ansith from destroying the entire world with his creations?

Lastly, you will not rise up to destroy any of the civilized races.

We would.

Realization hit me like a sledgehammer to the skull. I had thought I had put it together earlier. I thought that we simply kept the monsters at bay and trained our races for combat, but that wasn't it. Ansith's Academy for Dungeon Training and Combat wasn't just a fancy name. It was literally what we were going to the school to learn. We were going to be fighting the source of the Dungeons, the very heart of what created the ancient beasts of war.

As the realization continued to dawn on me like the morning sun, I felt like an idiot. How could I have been so dumb not to realize the connections simmering around me. I had been so close to it.

We have long kept the number of wild monsters in check, and whether they appreciate us or not, we do what we must to survive.

He hadn't just meant we'd be fighting for our own survival or the survival of a single race. He meant we'd be fighting for the survival of everyone.

Recognition seemed to register in the dwarf's eyes, and his smile darkened just a bit. "So, you realize why we're necessary now?"

I nodded hesitantly. "I think I'm starting to."

"Scary thought, isn't it? If I abused my power, who would stop me? What could stop an endless force that can generate its own unique mana? What could an army do against a single person who can Manifest himself to fight endlessly. What happens when he gets bored and creates an army in mere moments to end the game?" The recognition only grew deeper as he continued. He didn't confirm what I already figured out. Instead, he simply turned away. "We have to save the world, Rem."

"Why us?" I managed after a few moments of contemplation that came up wanting. "Why are we special? What have we done to deserve this?"

Ansith sighed. "Nothing, Rem. We aren't special, we aren't deserving. We are simply the ones that got caught up in a game beyond our knowledge." He paused for a moment before reminding me of something simple. "I did this to myself, Rem, and I don't regret it." Ansith's words were heavy on my ears, but there was an even greater gravity. I could feel the chill of them in my entire body. "If I hadn't, there wouldn't be an east or a west anymore. There wouldn't be a Sundering, there wouldn't be continents. There would simply be Dungeons, corrupted land, and monster spawning grounds. Our races would be huddled like cattle and used for no better until Eventide was done with us."

Eventide. The name sounded familiar. It sounded like something I'd heard of in a dream and forgotten, and it itched the back of my mind.

I hated that.

"What's Eventide?"

A fire lit in Ansith's eyes then vanished as quickly as it came. "Someone that you should pray never to meet alone." His more chipper demeanor returned a moment later. "But, we've tarried too long here though, Rem. Your Core will stay here and cycle, creating and purifying the surrounding mana while helping to bolster your personal reserves. For now, let us return to the academy. They are waiting for us."

I opened my mouth to protest. I didn't want to leave my Core behind. It'd be like me leaving my brain somewhere else to wander off, but Ansith silenced me.

"Do not worry, Rem. Your Core is still connected to you and will be safe here. If any danger approaches, you'll be pulled back here. You could always pop as well, but then you'd have to wait until I came back to get you." He snickered. "Besides, removing your Core at this point would remove your Influence and you'd have to start all over. From now on, removing your Core is a last resort."

I hated when people made sense. He'd covered every possible reason I'd have to bring my Core with me. I still wanted to, but he had an answer for every objection. "Fine."

"Excellent!" Ansith grinned, raising his right hand into the air.

With a snap of his fingers, we were back on campus in front of the stage. Around me were the other Cores that had survived. Everyone looked more serious, darker somehow. They looked like the warriors who came back from a hunt and lost someone. Then again, we were the minority according to Ansith, the few survivors of his first test.

As I arrived, a familiar Core found her way to my side. Something had changed since the last time we'd all been together. I could feel them and their mana mingle with the air around us. Amber was familiar, almost warm compared to the others. It wasn't a bad sensation to feel brushing against me, but I'd never felt someone's mana before. The others were like a scent on the air. I could sense each to follow it if I needed, but I couldn't be quite sure which one belonged to who.

Amber took my hand, squeezing gently before letting it go. The act surprised me, but before I could reply, Ansith took the stage and addressed the noticeably smaller crowd.

"Congratulations, students! You have all passed our first true test."

"You're a monster!" one of the others, the Earthen dwarf Core I had seen on my way in, screamed. "You killed all those other people."

Everyone and everything went silent for a moment before Ansith took a direct route to the man in question. He stared long and hard at him before kneeling to nearly put his face in line with the other dwarf.

"I did not bring about their deaths, nor did I destroy them." His words were just slightly solemn, but they almost felt practiced. Then again, how old was he again? How many times had he done this? How many times had he had to explain to classes why their fellow classmates hadn't returned? "They weren't cut out for the battles that lay ahead, but I never said they were dead. Master Copperbrand. The other Cores who failed my test will simply be staying in their Dungeons to advance their control. When they're ready, they can try again and return to the campus, so I'll thank you not to not compare me to what you'll be fighting soon. I am not the monster you have to fear."

The brown dwarf's face seemed to relax at that. In fact, all of us released whatever weight we were carrying at that moment.

For my own credit, I took a deep breath as Ansith confirmed again that no one had died. It really was just a test. A scary, ill-defined test with vague methods, but a test all the same. His methods were harsh, but they did get results.

"So," Ansith continued when he was sure the other dwarf wasn't going to interrupt again, "If you have more to say, please wait to air your grievances with me in a more private setting. I do have an office for those kind of things." There was a devilish smile on his face as he got up and turned back to face the rest of us. "Now then, if there are no questions, you are all dismissed until next Mundus to recover and consider what you have done. Then, we'll work on becoming more familiar with your Bestiaries."

I didn't have any questions, neither did anyone else.

Ansith stood on the stage and smiled. "Dismissed!"

As Ansith's voice faded and he vanished back into the power of his Influence, we all filtered back to our dorms for a well-earned mental break. The wear of battle and the new burden of knowledge kept us silent, pondering the events of the day.

Chapter Sixteen

Recovery

The silence was nearly deafening as the normally chipper Amber said nothing. In the time I'd known her, there hadn't been more than a handful of minutes that she hadn't said anything. Even her breathing was quiet. Silently, we entered the dorm, moved to the top floor, and we opened our doors in tandem. I walked inside and turned to close the door.

Her words stopped me dead in my tracks.

"That was the most horrible thing I think I've ever felt."

At first, I didn't know what to say to her. I thought about those words and the weight they had for her. Was it any different for me? I'd never literally had to fight for my life before. Fight for seconds at a meal maybe, but never my right to survive.

"I had my head smashed in by people thinking I was a werewolf," I began simply, not trying to sugarcoat things. I knew I wasn't as perky as normal either, but it wasn't worth it right now. "I would have rather done that again."

As if remembering my own death was another of my oddities, Amber didn't let it show. She didn't wince as I expected either. Instead, she walked over and let herself in. I didn't try and stop her. Without more than the sounds of her feet creaking the floor, she sat on my bed. Not waiting to seem presumptuous, I moved the chair and sat myself across from her.

When I was seated, Amber let loose.

"I had so much fun at first with it at first. I could create things and bring them to life, then..." she paused, and I could see the battle replaying in her mind's eye. I could see her heart drop as she no doubt saw the same destruction I had. "They were mutilated around me. I'd never seen so much blood and gore in a single place before." She paused again, as if the memory physically hurt her to recall. "I only survived because Aja sacrificed herself to burn them all away."

Burned? Wasn't she an Air Core? She must have been a dual Core like I was! Interesting. Relishing the insight into a small secret, I brought my attention back to the name. "Aja? Is that the name of your Guardian or your minions?"

She gave a curt nod. "She's my Guardian, a three tailed elemental cat." A smile worthy of a feline crossed her face. "Apparently, I can use two elements and Dungeon mana, so I was able to make her do it too. She's amazing."

Why didn't I think of that? Not that I had any experience with Umbral mana or spells, but did I need to? Maybe I'd have to try that later. "That's a good idea."

"Ansith said I was impressive." Her voice trailed off a bit as she turned to look out the window. "I don't want to die again, but..." Her voice trailed off again. "I don't know if I can do what he wants, Rem."

I waited for a bit, seeing if there was more she wanted to say. When nothing came, I chose my words carefully. It had been a long time since I'd thought about it, but this was one thing that had, thankfully or not, stayed with me through my transition. "Among the Foxkin, I was supposed to be an Oracle. I didn't have a choice in the matter. My fur and hair were white as snow, even my eyes were silvery. From the day I was born I was trained to be a connection to the gods, but I didn't try like I should have. I didn't think I could live up to their standards. I wasn't some god-touched creature, I was just me. I was Rem. I didn't get to choose my path, my class, or even who I could be around when I was younger, so I used what I could to control my life. It was selfish. I realize that now, but I wouldn't let myself be defined by everyone else."

I spoke a bit more passionately than I meant, but it didn't matter. Amber's eyes just glazed over with a tinge of annoyance. "I don't understand."

I nodded and elaborated. "I didn't respond well to threats or insults. It took someone believing in me and giving me a goal to even want to become more than what I was." She didn't need to know I brought a lot of those on myself or that it took a beautiful woman giving me a chance at something more to get me moving in the right direction. She really didn't need to know that was what brought about my death either. "Go your own way and survive, Amber. Things will work out, and if you're not what he wants, be indispensable. Show him that your life has purpose and power."

She seemed to contemplate that for a few minutes while I had the distinct feeling of everything twitching in nervousness. I wasn't good at being a counselor. I was terrible with everyone else's problems, but she helped me play to one of my greatest strengths. I was good, no, excellent at lying when I had a seed of truth to go from. From a seed of truth, I could grow an entire orchard of lies. I could convince anyone of anything, and at the heart of the matter, that was kind of the same thing. Lying for a good reason was just as good as advice, right?

More time passed as she thought about it to the point that I was starting to feel uncomfortable. Her closed, amber eyes made me think she was sleeping, but as we both knew, we didn't need to sleep.

"I think I understand," Amber began somberly. "If I don't want to be what he wants, I need to be something unique, something that they need, something that they can't live without while still staying true to myself."

Eyebrows waggled as I smiled and added onto her remark. "The useful kind of unique."

She cracked a momentary smile and nodded. "I think I can do that."

"I think you can too." At least I didn't have to lie about that. I truly believed it. If Amber could impress Ansith, a five-hundred-year-old dwarf who had somehow birthed the Dungeon Core race for our kind and built an academy to house us, I was sure she could do great things.

She smiled a bit more. "Wherever I came from, we were wrong about your race."

My ears perked at that. It was an unexpected surprise, but now I was curious. "What did you expect?"

She blushed a deeper hue. "That you'd kill and eat me for being too weak."

I almost choked.

"What?" She made us sound like some kind of monsters or something. I knew some people thought that, but a race as a whole? We didn't kill eat the weak to raise the strong. I was a great example of that, even if I was god touched. "Where in the Mists did you get the idea that I'd want to kill and eat you?" I stopped for a moment as I let some steam out. "No, better question. If you were worried about that, why'd you come in here?"

Did she want to die?

She didn't answer right away, but if that was her thought. I could imagine. "I trusted my instinct about you. You've already shown me a lot of what I know about your race is wrong."

A sigh escaped before I could ask, "Do I want to know what else you've been told?"

The deeper blush told me the answer to that. "Not if you want to have any respect left for wherever I came from."

"To be fair, I don't have my respect for anyone or anything that's piled sket onto someone's plate and told them it was steak." She looked kind of confused, so I elaborated. "They made you eat shit without being able to question it?"

She nodded with acceptance. "I don't know what they had against your people, but I remember it clearly."

Sometimes, I took for granted that I remembered so much from my previous life. "Do you remember where you're from yet?"

"No more than the last time. Just the general area I was found in."

Can't win 'em all. I wouldn't be going to correct anything it seemed so I simply relaxed, but I couldn't be satisfied with just resting and focused on my Bestiary. It was harder away from my Core, but soon enough, the pages came into being with the same opal coloring it had the first time with the same lettering. "Wanna compare notes?"

She smiled and did the same.

The next hours that passed were strange. Amber and I compared pages from our Bestiaries, the attributes we'd discovered, the mana traits, and everything else we could think of to get more information.

To my surprise, she was already D1 and ready to break into the C Ranks. She didn't talk about her Manifested Class though, and I didn't pry.

I noticed the more we talked, the more information my Bestiary gained, so it had the dual pleasure of being useful and relaxing. I was only a bit disappointed as we went on since the entries I had gotten from her were different to those I'd expected.

Many of them came up faded in the book despite having the full description. My favorite was one of her mana attributes:

Explosive: Minions imbued with a combination of volatile essence have a tendency to be unstable. At a rate of fifty percent upon death, this instability is triggered and their bodies explode rather than leaving behind a loot seed manifestation. This explosion leaves burning aether strewn in an area equal to twice the creature's central radius determined from their center to either the tip of their tail, legs, or head.
Higher Ranked creatures can use this as an Active ability rather than a Passive skill.

Giving that to the foxes would have been devastating! Cruel, but devastating. Sadly, this was one of the ones that had additional text with it.

Explosive is limited to a minion of combination of natural Fire and Air essence. This cannot be emulated with Dungeon mana unless previously unlocked.

It was like having candy I couldn't eat. I almost stopped dead in my tracks at that thought. I was upset I couldn't blow something up? I'd never enjoyed blowing things up before. In fact, the noise hurt my ears quite badly the last time there had been explosions at the chemist's. Then again, there were a lot of strange things I wouldn't have done before. At least, I don't think I would. What was happening to me? The thought lingered far more than it should before Amber interrupted it.

"Hey!"

It was loud, but not enough for me to recoil, just startle a little bit.

"You there, Rem?"

My tail slumped behind me as I nodded. "Sorry. I was just chasing a dream." Again, her expression told me more than her lips. "Got distracted."

She nodded at that as a familiar noise broke the silence and echoed from my door.

Knock. Knock. Knock.

Pause.

Knock. Knock. Knock.

I looked to her, and she looked right back. We both knew no one else lived here. After a few moments, the knocking began again in the same rhythmic Pattern:

Knock. Knock. Knock.

Pause.

Knock. Knock. Knock.

My fur stood on end, every fiber of my being ready for the attack that was coming. I knew that knock. It was the knock of work, the knock of wood on wood, the knock of one of Ansith's scrolls.

I groaned and sent my Bestiary back into the aether before readying myself, but after spending so much time with Amber, things were finally starting to settle in the whirlwind of thoughts within my Core. Staring at the door, I started feeling silly. Maybe Ansith's first scroll had been my mistake. Maybe I'd opened the door when the spell told it to knock. Scrolls weren't alive. They didn't have agendas.

Maybe I was just a hopeful dreamer, but I got up and opened the door.

A moment later, I was staring at the rolled-up paper scroll.

Another moment later, and I was clutching my gut as the scroll collided with me, putting smalls cracks in my body and knocking me forward. I healed nearly instantly, but Amber was still on her feet to see what had happened. I appreciated the gesture, but what got me most was how Amber's scroll oh-so-lazily floated into the room and rested in her outstretched hand like a newborn kit cuddled up with its mother.

I was beginning to think they had something against me. Two out of two times can't be a coincidence.

"Are you okay, Rem?" Amber asked. Her laugh was barely held behind her smile, and I couldn't blame her.

Thankfully, the worst thing hurt was my pride. "Yeah. Stupid scrolls."

The scroll in my chest tried to pull back again, but my grip was tight. Amber's ruffled itself in annoyance at my words and I prepared for another attack, but it never came as Amber broke the seal and undid whatever spell animated it. "You shouldn't antagonize Ansith's constructs. I think they have some sort of hive mind memory linked to us."

Of course they did.

Wasting no more time on my opponent, I snapped its waxy life in two and felt its power wane as the scroll was undone. Neither of us had an additional letter this time, and the classlist was, of course, listed in a brilliant orange ink.

Class: Rank D - Post-Invasion Test
Mundus:
Creature Fabrication - Morning chime - Academy Hall, Center Stage
Tiera:
Creature Fabrication - Morning chime - Academy Hall, Center Stage
Wispa:
Dungeon Influence Expansion - Field Work
Thuren:
Novice Dungeon Level Design - Morning chime - Starlight Tower, Northern Spire - Rm 101
Novice Dungeon Trap Design - Afternoon chime - Starlight Tower, Northern Spire - Rm 105
Freiag:
Novice Dungeon Expansion - Field Work

Sol/Lune:
No Class—Independent Study

Schedule will update as necessary

Well at least that explained why we only got a week's schedule last time. Either we'd be ready to do more with our Dungeons or we'd be stuck repeating the lesson Ansith had been trying to teach us. At least there was a method to his madness.

I was about to absorb the paper to learn about the ink when Amber interrupted. "What's your schedule?" I read off the list and she nodded. "It's the same for me, but my design classes are in the Aero and Ember Towers."

"You have it twice?" I asked.

She shook her head. "No, the schedule has me in the Ember Tower for level design and the Aero Tower for Trap Design."

I nodded. It made a kind of sense. Fire was already dangerous, so why not use it for what it was meant for. If her Guardian Anja was already a Fire beast, why not build on it?

Seeing the list, I was thankful that we at least we had the weekend to recoup.

Chapter Seventeen

Cooperation

Mundus came on me like a morning fog, cold and nobody wanted it.

Since I didn't sleep, it was hard to keep the days straight. Amber was a help for this, but we only had so many things to talk about before I ran out of stories. When it was her turn, she felt awkward and changed the subject. Eventually, she was so self-conscious again that she didn't want to talk anymore.

I gave her space for most of Lune, but when Mundus came, she was right back at the door, knocking in a way that was distinct—thankfully—from the Mist-damned scrolls.

Talking to me through the door helped too.

"Rem, you ready to go?"

I opened the door, flashed her a smile, and stepped out into the hall at her side. "Always."

Her face betrayed her feelings as she smirked, but she said nothing as we walked down the hall, the stairs, and out of the building onto the campus again.

I'd done some exploring after we parted ways on Sol and during most of Lune, but the campus was pretty self-contained. It was like the barest bones of a city, but without any of the fun things to go along with it. There were no stores, no libraries, no games, and no people. This was one of the many reasons I just sat around the dorm, studying my Bestiary. I didn't even bother with the Codex. I didn't have any real use for the items yet until I learned how they fell into the grand scheme of things within the Dungeon.

We made more small talk on the way to the center stage. Amber told me about a few ideas she had involving exploding mountains, and

I talked about my idea for creating a forest for my Dungeon. She listened as intently as I did, and we arrived at the stage before either of us were ready to stop talking.

The others were already there waiting before the chime rang. Something I was once again, unprepared for as it screeched through the air.

EEEEEEEEEEEEEEEEEEEEEEEEEEEEEEEEEEEEEEEEEEEEEEEEEE

I managed to not lose my footing as my ears folded back, my hands moved to cover them, and I tried humming a tune that the bards used to sing before the Harvest Day celebration.

It didn't work.

My ears felt ready to melt off the sides of my head and my skull hummed with pain. As always though, as quickly as it started, the pain and the noise were gone.

I really had to talk to Ansith about his treatment of the Foxkin on this campus, about his treatment of me. I hated that noise. I still wasn't sure if it was just a problem for me, but there was a strong indication this was the case from the way everyone looked at me afterwards.

Ansith appeared a moment later in his usual prismatic appearance, looking no worse for wear for all his recent efforts. Defeating nearly fourteen or so other Dungeons at once must have just been practice at his Rank. Though to be fair, I didn't feel any drain, pain, or physical weakness even at my level.

"Welcome class," Ansith began as he looked out over us once again. Of course, everyone was there: the brown, surly dwarf; the blue, shapely woman; the fish girl; the elf with the burning hair; and us. Ansith looked as though he were mentally ticking off the list of his students before returning his attention to us. "As I said, today we would begin working more with your summoned creature, your minions. As I told many of you, information is the key to safety in case anything goes wrong and you clash with another of your kind. As such, we will not be working with our Guardians or any creature more powerful than Rank D. Are there any questions?"

Looking from one to the other, not even the dwarf had anything to say on the matter. Grumbling something under his breath, yes, but actually putting it to words, no.

"Good!" Ansith beamed. "Now, Bestiaries are unique items. The more you learn, the more they learn. By using Absorption on a creature, you will learn its attributes and gain traits you can give to your minions. But in addition to this, with enough observation and knowledge, traits can also be created. Dungeon Cores can also exchange Patterns and traits to benefit one another if the two Cores agree to it and have the requisite mana types to make it work."

I smiled, having figured out most of that part the other night. When Amber and I talked, our Bestiaries learned from one another. It was one of two things we learned that night. Some of the traits required specific types of mana to create the first time. We might have learned traits, but not everything we found was useful.

"You'll probably gain quite a few new traits today as you observe your minions and the creation and methods of the other Cores." Then, he paused and smiled. I hated that smile. That smile meant nothing but trouble for me. The last time I saw that smile, I thought he was going to wipe my Dungeon out. After a few more moments of silence, the mace dropped. "Dungeons have a variety of different creatures at their disposal, not just one and a Guardian. For today's practice, you have two hours to create a new minion using none of the traits you used before in our little test. The minion must meet the following criteria to be considered a success. The creature must have a medium to small build with at least two unique attributes. It should be different than your last as well, so it will take a little teamwork."

I looked quickly to Amber. Seeing that she was looking back and that she gave me a curt nod, I knew we had the same idea.

"Begin!"

And we were off.

Amber and I didn't have to move much, but everyone else broke off into their own groups. I noticed the two Water Cores moved away to work alone as did the Fire and the Earth Cores. I didn't have time to monitor them though. In a matter of moments, both of us had Manifested the physical version of our Beastiaries and we began sorting.

We both had a single medium beast base, but despite all of our talking the other day, that hadn't transferred. Neither of us had

Ansith's Patterns for golems either, so there had to be more to gaining it than being nearby the creatures.

Already, I could hear frustrated noises from behind us and I knew others had begun the process of trying to unlock another Pattern from their partners.

"Can I try something?" I asked.

"I think that's the point," Amber quipped.

Without wasting time to reply, I closed my eyes to focus and began spreading my Influence to see if having it touch her book would have any effect. It felt odd as I felt for her construct. The makeup of the book felt like Amber, which I guess made sense seeing as it was made from her. The closer I got to the essence of the book, the more it resisted, becoming like a wall before I actually got to the point of learning a Pattern. It was resisting. Our mana clashed back as her Influence pushed back against mine, refusing to yield an inch to my will. It wasn't her normal warmth, it was like an inferno lashing out against me. A wall of impenetrable fire that felt wrong to try to circumvent. It made me feel wrong, dirty somehow. When I opened my eyes, I instantly knew why.

"Are you okay?"

Amber's eyes were shut tightly, her stance suggesting she was defending herself from something. As soon as my Influence left the area surrounding the book, she began to relax and shook her head. "No. That felt... wrong. Something about it just felt wrong."

I had to agree. We sat there for a bit, thinking through our options before I came up with something less... invasive. It'd been something I'd just started with the month before I'd been removed from my old life.

"Have you ever cooperatively cast a spell?" I asked before my brain caught up with my mouth.

She smiled, seeing the moment of distress. "If I ever did, I don't know."

I nodded. "Basically, we both follow the lines of power of a spell and pour our mana into it. In theory, if we create something like that, our books should pick up on it, right?"

She nodded tentatively. "That could work."

With that, I took the lead. If only my clan could have seen me being so productive.

Choosing the basic fox body, I set up the minion summoning like I had at first. No modifications, no extra features, just an E-ranked basic fox. As before, the outline of the body glimmered in its soft, opal light, waiting for more editing, more attributes, more abilities. That wasn't to be though. I held the Pattern in place with my power and looked to Amber. She looked back at me with a vague expression of confusion.

"Can you see it?" I asked, unsure if it was visible to anyone but me.

She shook her head. "I know I should see something if you're holding the Pattern, but I guess it's for your eyes only."

I let the Pattern fall and thought back to my few lessons on cooperative casting. It seemed like so long ago, but there were distinct rules for casting a spell you had access too, but what happened if you didn't. Thankfully, there had been a lesson on that. A lesson that Vix had been oh-so-helpful in reminding me of recently.

"Amber, I want you to try to send me mana. It's like you're channeling it through a Node, not trying to cast a spell."

She looked at me a little strangely, but then the idea seemed to find an anchor. "I think I know what you mean."

With that, she took my hand and I felt a familiar echo across my Manifestation. It was more than the warmth I'd felt from her presence before, more like warm water pooling around my hand. As I opened myself up to it, the warmth spread all across my form, from tip to tail, I felt the heat spread as what I assumed to be Fire mana flooded into my body. It was like the warmth from drinking too much wine at the Harvest Festival without the difficulty in focus.

With her power fueling my own, I brought the fox projection up again, but the warmth was starting to burn now. When I expanded the image to life size, Amber gave a yip any kit would be proud of as she nearly let go. I grabbed her hand back to keep the link established. The last thing we needed on a timed assignment was backlash.

"This is the hard part," I explained as the Fire burned in my legs. This was when she used me like a Node to cast the spell. At least, that's how cooperative spell casting worked. I had to hope that cooperative

148

Fabrication worked the same way or this wouldn't be a fun afternoon. "Feed your energy through me into the Pattern like when you use a Node."

She seemed strained by the work, but nodded. Things got... strange after that.

I'd only cooperatively cast one spell before: a simple cantrip. I'd given the mana to use and acted as the conduit, so I had an idea how both sides worked, but this was... different. For the few moments our goals aligned, I could feel her mana in my Nexus. I could feel it feed into my Nodes. I could feel it trigger my ability though her rather than simply feeding into the established Pattern I'd set; but it didn't feel like how Vix had triggered things.

This wasn't a flood overwhelming me. It wasn't some great, unknowable force threatening to take my soul and crash it against the rocks of itself.

It felt... nice maybe?

The warmth flowed from my body into my soul, then from my soul into the Pattern, and we both watched as glowing red and orange mana flowed into the Pattern. The creation became more solid, more distinct as the burning mana willed it into existence until the roaring of a campfire echoed through the air with a barely audible pop.

Compatible Pattern Completed.
New page has been added to Rem - Dungeon Bestiary.
Emberborn Aether Fox
Cost: 25 Fire Mana, 25 Air Mana
Challenge Rating: D9
Volatile
Intelligence: Feral, Determined, Bold
Growth Potential: High
Survivability Rating: E
Mana attributes: Lesser Dungeon Born, Burning, Explosion
Reward Seed: Natural

Then, the feeling of her presence faded away as the warmth of her smile replaced it. Almost immediately, Amber went over to the fox and began petting it. It responded like a tamed beast. Its bark was just like its presence, tinged with fire and crackling embers of heat. While she found her beast, I examined the new attribute.

Burning
Attribute Type: Passive
A minion brought to life via Fire mana. Commonly has traits associated with creatures of the Plane of Fire. A creature with the Burning attribute exudes Fire mana naturally and has a chance of burning its attacker or its target by touch alone. In exchange for this status chance, creatures with the Burning attribute are weaker physically than their counterparts.
When paired with the Explosive Attribute, the chance of an explosion being triggered is set at 30 percent and the radius and damage is reduced to 50 percent.

Now, if only I had the Fire and Air mana to make this fox myself. Maybe there'd be a way to get it somehow?

"Rem!" Amber called out. "I can't believe it worked! That was easy!"

I couldn't believe it either, honestly. As I approached the pair a few feet away, the beast stopped basking in her attention and gave me a once over, carefully deciding if I was a threat of not. The fox left her side and moved over cautiously, sniffing at my feet before barking once. Its face turned from caution to fear and then it dashed to hide behind Amber.

"I guess it doesn't like you," she said simply, seemingly as surprised as I was about the strange turn of events.

"It probably saw me as an enemy," I rationalised, knowing that from Ansith's arguments, Dungeon Cores normally weren't friends in the field. Maybe it was some inborn survival mechanism that Dungeon Born creatures had?

"Maybe," Amber agreed before closing her eyes for a moment. A few seconds later, the Emberborn Aether Fox vanished in a wisp of smoke. When she opened them again, she seemed just a little saddened. "I didn't want the others to see it yet. It's your turn though, Rem."

I nodded and explained again to her the process that I had used. She took my hand and I tried feeding Dungeon mana through the link to create a basic creature. It didn't feel as easy as it had been for her, so I tried putting a little more effort behind it. Nearly at the same time, I heard a cracking noise, and Amber jerked her hand away as if I were the one made from Fire.

"That actually hurt!" Amber scolded, rubbing her hand accusingly.

Of course, there was a problem with her breaking the connection. Whenever mana was moving or being focused and the focus was removed, there was a backlash. In this case, the build up of mana had nowhere to go and overloaded the point of connection.

Put simply, her hand hurt, my hand exploded.

"Rem!"

Chapter Eighteen

Missing Lynx

If it weren't for the high mana concentrations within Ansith's academy, I might have popped right there and then from the backlash. Thankfully, my body took in enough mana to stabilize my injury and pour mana back into rebuilding my destroyed hands. When I had my right hand back, I waved her worries away.

"I was just a little disarmed," I said, then wiggled my fingers to be sure each one worked.

She sighed at my poor pun. "More like you single handedly screwed something up." I smiled, ready to quip back, but she didn't let me speak. "What were you trying to do?"

"I wanted something basic, so I was trying to use Dungeon mana like you used your Fire and Air."

She looked at her hand again, any sign of imperfection wiped away by the power of the restorative mana. "It felt wrong, Rem, like when you tried to use it on my Bestiary."

The exact opposite of how it felt for me. Weird. Maybe it had to do with the Influence it carried? It seemed possible, but I didn't like the idea that I might have actually hurt her. Ansith would have stopped us if we were doing something wrong or stupid though, right? Feeling a bit better, I rubbed at my new hands again. "Can we try again? I promise I won't use Dungeon mana again."

She seemed a bit hesitant but took my hand from its place at my side and nodded. "Just don't push the mana like that again either. If it takes, it takes."

The last thing I wanted to do was hurt her again, and I nodded to say as much.

Instead of focusing on the massive quantities of Dungeon mana I had, I pulled mana from the part of the Core I'd designated as me. My Celestial mana felt like silk as I gripped it, soft but unfathomably strong as it glowed from my Nexus and into my hand. I nudged it mentally to cross the barrier between our simulacrums and was surprised when it easily moved from me into her. The moment our mana intermingled I could see her Pattern hanging in the air.

The creature wasn't as small of a thing as I thought it would be, maybe as large as full grown fox with a much longer, lankier form and a more compact face. The eyes were larger as well as was the tail. It was another predator, but distinct enough that I could make good use of it.

As I'd felt with Amber's mana during our first cooperative creation, the warmth of her power was as welcoming as a summer afternoon. It was relaxing feeling the heat and the air mingle around the perception of my mana, but there was something I hadn't felt the first time. For my power, there was an innate draw towards her Nexus, towards her active Node that I assumed was Fabrication. That must have been how she knew where to direct it. I didn't force it away from the flow of the path and instead continued to pour Celestial mana along the channel.

She giggled, and it almost was enough to break my concentration. I gave her a look, only to be met with a muted smile.

"It tingles," she managed, holding back a laugh behind a smile.

Her hand squeezed mine just a bit, and I smiled as I kept the mana flowing. At least she didn't make a joke about my mana being fuzzy. Soon, the creature's form was filling, solidifying, and, in a flash, the act was done.

Compatible Pattern Obtained.
New page has been added to Rem - Dungeon Bestiary.
Aether Lynx
Health: Healthy
Intelligence: Feral
Growth Potential: Medium
Compatible Mana Types: All
Evolution Potential: Unknown - Experiment with different types of mana to populate this information.

Survivability Rating: Unknown - Experiment with different types of mana to populate this information.

Mana attributes: Unknown - Experiment with different types of mana to populate this information.

Mutation Chance: Unknown - Experiment with different types of mana to populate this information.

Compatible Pattern Completed.

New page has been added to Rem - Dungeon Bestiary: Aether Lynx.

Blink Lynx

Cost: 75 Celestial, 25 Dungeon

Challenge Rating: D2

Healthy

Intelligence: Feral, Hunter, Solitary

Growth Potential: Average

Survivability Rating: D

Mana attributes: Lesser Dungeon Born, Blink, Camouflage

Reward Seed: Natural

No sooner had I gotten the Pattern than Amber dragged me over to the feline and began running her hand through its luscious-looking white fur, cooing to it like a newborn child. The creature purred like a pleasured pet at her touch, and I had a tinge of annoyance prickle my mind. Why did she have all the luck with animals? I got a better look at my Blink Lynx. It was smaller than the original form, but all muscle. The way it moved itself around Amber's hand showed it could manipulate itself easily too, nearly bending itself into a complete circle with its tail—surprisingly short compared to the fox's—wrapping around its face and neck. It had two familiar abilities and a third I was unfamiliar with. That lack of knowledge didn't last too long though.

Camouflage

Attribute Type: Passive

Cool down: Scales with cover and mana density

A creature with Camouflage can blend into its surroundings to more easily sneak up on its target, avoid attack, or dampen its own sound. Camouflage's effectiveness and cool down scales with the density of the location's foliage, ambient noise, the creature's coloring, and mana density of the area.

So, I had a muscular, sneaky murder machine on my hands that could blend in, move silently, and blink in and out of existence at a moment's notice.

In short, it was just a cat.

A fancy cat, but a cat none the less. I was sure my Felkin cousins would be impressed at least.

"Rem…" Amber said, cautiously, as she kept petting the now close-eyed Blink Lynx. I made some vague noise of recognition, and she continued. "I can't stop petting it."

To emphasize her point, she pulled her hand from my minion's head, and the lynx instantly responded. Its eyes popped open, and the creature turned its gaze towards the offending limb and growled, moving its head back into her easily accessible, open hand again to continue the petting. Growls melted into purrs as she complied and began scratching behind its ear.

Of course, I laughed. Served her right for being more popular with my creature than I was.

"It's not funny," she groaned. "Not even Aja is this bad. Can you cut off your mana from it so it'll vanish?"

Cut off my mana from it? I hadn't tried that before. I was enjoying Amber's servitude to the cat, but now I turned inward and focused on my active mana. What I found was interesting. There was a link going from myself out into the creature. Well, not from me but from the Fabrication Node of my Dungeon Nexus. A small stream of power was being automatically allocated towards the creature, but before I could explore it further, I mentally shut off the link.

Immediately, the lynx turned to me and mewed before vanishing back into the aether. To my surprise, no loot dropped. Then again, neither had any for the Emberborn Aether Fox. Cutting off mana must not be considered a kill. I'd have to remember that in the future, though I wish I'd focused more to see the actual results.

"You two continue to surprise me!" A cheery voice came from behind me, nearly scaring me out of my fur.

"Mists!" I cursed, jumping back from the shock.

Amber gave him a hard look and a cool smile, saying nothing.

Of course, Ansith never needed a prompt to talk. "Sharing mana isn't the easiest thing in the world between Dungeon Cores, but something tells me you two learned some important things."

"Dungeon mana can't be shared," I said nearly instantly.

Ansith smiled warmly. "Why is that, Rem?"

"Because it carries our Influence?" I ventured.

Another nod, and his beard took it from his chin to his stomach like a taunt rope. "Good! Only elementally aligned mana can cross between Cores. You can't let Amber use your Dungeon mana even if her life depended on it."

"How come Rem's hand exploded?" Amber asked, drawing me from my thoughts.

"Because you resisted his Influence and responded in kind. You're a higher tier Core than Rem, so your protection will be stronger against Influence. Since he was in contact, your mana created a barrier to block him, and the resulting backlash left him a little less handy."

"Ha, ha," I mocked. At least, my pun was decent.

Ansith snorted just a bit. "Yes, yes. I expected this to take quite a bit longer, but you two are dismissed. Tomorrow will be a free day for you two, but I expect you to create at least three variants of your new creatures that you think might be of use to you in your Dungeons."

"Yes, Elder," I said without thinking, garnering a bit of an arched brow from him.

"Ansith is fine. Headmaster if you must use a title, Rem." He corrected me.

Amber bowed, but her attention quickly pulled towards the right and a shimmer of blue light.

A Core shattered a moment later and Ansith sighed. "Some people just don't learn. That's the third time Mera's shattered Fiona and herself. I swear she just doesn't care to learn." As if remembering us, he held a hand towards us and waved us away. "Go, go. Enjoy your afternoon."

As Ansith vanished, leaving us to our own devices, we watched the Earth dwarf and the Fiery elf practice. They came close to shattering each other many times, but eventually, the dwarf noticed us and bellowed at us.

"Get a move on! We're practicing here!"

So, after watching someone else's hands explode for a change, I smiled politely and turned tail.

Chapter Nineteen

Games of Trust

The rest of the evening and the next day were spent together, practicing our minion Fabrication abilities. I ended up with a new fox type, the subtle aether fox and two new lynxes, an armored variant and a mana sensing type. There wasn't much I could do with the lynx itself. For some reason, they had fewer modification slots than my foxes did. That wasn't my biggest accomplishment of the day though.

To my surprise, I didn't actually have to create the minions anymore to gain their Patterns. After the battle with Ansith or maybe after cooperatively casting minions with Amber, the Bestiary let me do all the work within it. Amber found the same thing to be true, too. If we put our mana into the Bestiary, we could create the Pattern if it was compatible. We could even work together as long as we didn't try to transfer Dungeon mana across our projects.

I discovered the reason for that rather quickly. We'd both gained a newly hewn Node in our primary Nexus.

Dual Cast
Secondary Node - Spell Mastery - Passive
Evolution Potential - Progressive
Cost: Scaling
Passive Effect: You have gained a talent for transferring mana between yourself and others to augment your spell craft. Further training will unlock active abilities or more control within larger groups of cooperative casters. When Dual Casting, a percentage of mana is lost in the transfer. This loss is higher when working with opposing mana types.

Current Loss: 2% for Mastered Nodes, 5% for Developing Nodes, 10% for Unshared Nodes

It wasn't perfect, but seeing that there was an actual Node for Dual Casting comforted me. It still didn't explain the weird feeling from Amber's mana, or why mine made her laugh. Mana just must feel different to different people.

We worked together for most of the afternoon to improve our abilities. Honestly, it was the most relaxing time I'd had there. Amber's mana was strangely calming despite its nature. Mine seemed to range from making her laugh to feeling like a cool breeze in her body. We had our own theories on that before our work was interrupted.

Near sundown on Tiera, a soft knocking on the door broke our concentration, and I snapped to attention. My first reaction was to prepare for battle with another of Ansith's scrolls, but as it continued, I noticed it wasn't the solid knocking of the wood scrolls against a wooden door, more like a light, over-enthusiastic rapping of a small hand.

Amber and I looked at each other as my body came down from its heightened awareness. I had never heard the noise before, and I was sure that no one else lived in this dorm. Maybe there was a new Core? Maybe one of the others had returned from the prior testing? The chance of it being a real threat was so low that it would have been pointless not to answer the knocking, especially since my Core wasn't even here anymore, so I got up and opened the door.

I was nearly barreled over by an overly enthusiastic red squirrel, that had eyes far too big for its head. They looked like they were plucked from the head of a horse and just shoved into the squirrel's sockets, but that wasn't the only unsettling thing about the creature. It had a snake for a tail, charred the floor as it walked, and chattered like a madman. When it saw me, it chirped once in a higher pitch and dropped a scroll on the ground at my feet. It waited patiently for a few moments, but waiting must have been too much for the poor thing as it, like my nerves, exploded into a cloud of blinding smoke. Cursing the Core who had made the messenger as I looked at the ring of black around the floor, I was glad the scroll wasn't too badly singed and was still readable. Strangely, the ink itself almost made things worse. It glowed a soft red in its script and seemed to blacken the parchment around it the longer it was open to the air.

Hey Overachiever,

I don't know if you picked up who the attractive elf was at class the other day, but I'm Pyros of the Ember Fields, one of your few surviving classmates, Pyromancer, and Fire Core extraordinaire. Do you know how hard it was to find you when you didn't show up for class today? I doubt it, so I'll cut to the chase. A few of us decided that we wanted to test ourselves. After what happened, we're all still a little jumpy about what Ansith's next move will be, and we want to see how we stack up against one another. I don't know how it'll help other than blow off some steam, but I think we could all use it, and honestly, there's no reason to be strangers anymore. We're all in this together

Come to the center stage at the morning chime tomorrow and let's see just how well we've done. If a friendly competition isn't enough to get you out, I found something good during my testing and thought that it'd be interesting to see how many would like to know the new item Pattern that I got.

If nothing else, at least it'll be a chance to gather a new Pattern or two for your Bestiaries, maybe an attribute or two, and some unique loot drops from one another.

Bring the amber Core with you, too.

I heard she's pretty good herself in a fight. I couldn't find her either in the Aero or the Ember Dorms. Since she walked off with you, I figured you'd know where to find her.

Pyros of the Ember Fields, Fire Core

I shared the letter with Amber, passing her the scroll. "It seems like the others are paying attention to you."

"More to you than me," she said. For a moment, Amber skimmed the letter before handing me back the scroll, which I absorbed for materials. It was nothing special, just some crushed papyrus. "But it does seem that way."

"Think Aja would like to fight some other Guardians?" I asked, already knowing Tenko would be up for some exercise.

"Probably, but it seems like a bad idea if we're supposed to keep information close to our chests."

"Some of us are better than others at that," I snickered to myself.

She didn't even blink. "Really, Rem?"

I nodded, smiling a bit, but the conversation grew a bit more serious as we discussed our options. Tenko and Aja were the only creatures we had for Guardians and right now, they were our strongest ally if something went wrong.

By the time the sun had set, we seemed to be in agreement about two things. One: the offer was not for our sole benefit. Anything that we learned from this Pyros would probably be something we'd be able to figure out on our own. If he was a Fire Core, maybe Amber would be able to get something from it, but unless it used regular Dungeon mana, it wouldn't be nearly as useful for me. So, in return for giving up information on our Guardians, we may or may not be getting anything useful.

Second: even if dueling wasn't worth it for us, we couldn't ignore a chance at getting something new and interesting to play with.

So together, we came to a conclusion. Apart, we'd only stand to lose our individual advantages. But if we worked together, there was nothing to lose and everything to gain. Well, either that or we'd blow ourselves back to our Dungeon Cores and regret ever attempting our plan.

Either way, it'd be a fun rest of the evening.

Chapter Twenty
Loopholes

By the time Pyros's contest was upon us, Amber and I had learned quite a few things. The most important was a personal discovery though: I could Manifest other items without having to destroy my simulacrum and Manifest it again. As long as I was focusing, I could create weapons, clothing, and other items straight from my mana and absorb it back just as easily. As it did with my minions, Dungeon mana didn't have much of a color to it. Items created from it were a dull gray, almost like a faded-out copy of something from my memory. I couldn't create very complex things from my imagination either. If I had a Pattern or had previously created an item, it was easy to make it again and appeared as a nearly exact replica of the original item.

Despite the limitations of my new Fabrication skill, a pair of earplugs, designed with the specific feature of filtering out the screeching sound of the chimes, weren't out of the question.

Items created from my Celestial mana were much more substantial and gave off a slight glow in the same soft lights I seemed to be made from. Though it shared some of my coloring, the small pair of plugs I'd made from Celestial mana were significantly harder to keep bound to my ears. They kept disappearing and then reappearing in the same spot every few minutes. Sometimes when I was testing the earplugs, they never returned. While the idea of something like a shirt or pants blinking out of existence during a summer stroll was hilarious, it seemed my primary mana didn't have much of a use for item construction alone until I figured out how to control it better.

Strangely, no matter how I tried I still couldn't access Umbral mana. Since it wasn't natural for me to use this before I was a Core, I struck it up as something I'd have to deal with later. In the long run, if I made it that far, having access to my diametric opposite element of mana had to have some advantages to it.

Though those were the most important things I'd experimented with, I grinned at what our efforts had created. Amber was almost more excited than I was for what was to come.

We'd created a monster.

When we reached the stage, I could feel the tone pulse around me and try to pierce my ears, but my mana-forged earplugs were working exactly as intended. Better than I had planned, in fact, probably due to the Celestial mana they were forged from. As an unexpected bonus, I could tune anything out I wanted, Amber included. She was far, far too excited about our beast ripping through the competition. In truth, I was too, but my tone didn't get as excited when it came to dismembering things. The way she went from meek to murderous was uniquely her, and it just made me wonder all the more who she was when she was alive.

As long as everything worked as we planned, however, this was going to be fun for us, and humiliating for the others.

Three of our remaining Core cousins had found their way here. This meeting had been their idea according to Pyros. As we approached, I took out the earplugs and strained my ears to listen to the group to gather what I could about my fellow students.

The three others that found themselves around the stage all had simple names. First was the brown dwarf Core I had seen before, Agar. It was nice to finally put a name to the surly Core. He was as armored as ever, and he was talking to the womanly, deep blue Core I'd noticed, the one that Ansith had cursed; her name was Mera.

Apparently, Mera had solved her mana leakage issue, and her personal image was better for it. She still had curves, but around her form hung a long dress. The clothing seemed like something people would wear for more formal occasions and screamed uncomfortable to me in a way my robes didn't. I had to admit the dress did have some merits if you enjoyed the view of open cleavage through a deeply plunging neckline. Glancing around, it wasn't hard to catch how everyone's eyes followed the opening to her naval just to be sure it didn't show more.

I'd even noticed Amber's eyes in the act, something that I couldn't let slide without a smile and a nudge to her side.

She just shrugged, giving me a look that said, *What? I can appreciate a dress too.*

There was a second Water Core present as well. She didn't talk as we approached. The others, though, talked to her without a second thought. Her name was Fiona Lightscale, she was the Core that had been 'partnered' the other day to Mera and if Ansith was to be believed had popped due to her laziness. From what I could pick out from her appearance, she was from one of the lesser races. Though, I guess I was technically a lesser race, too. She wasn't a Beastkin as I knew them, but she was almost all fish, a little chubby in places, but still all fish. Up as far as her shell-supported breasts, she was scaled as if she wore gleaming blue armor. Her arms were scaled on one side too, and fleshy on the other with webbed fingers and webbing around her ears that made her face look almost elvish. Her eyes were strictly fishy as well: large, blue and a little twitchy inside the human frame of her skull. The name of her race was on the tip of my tongue. Merfolk sounded like it fit, but I hadn't had any dealings with them being so far inland. It was interesting to see her float more than walk. Her tail acting as if nothing was any different for her, that the world was just as watery here as the sea or ocean she had once called home.

There was one person missing from the staging area though, the Core that had invited us all here, Pyros.

"Alright, so where's our host?" Agar said with a voice no more pleasant to listen to than shifting gravel.

At least I wasn't the one that had to ask.

Fiona simply shrugged instead of speaking, which seemed to elicit a response from Mera. "I came out here to win something. If he doesn't show, what's the point of waiting around here wasting my time?"

I wasn't sure what else she could be doing with her time dressed like that, but no one seemed to pay her any mind. We were all here for the same reason. Thankfully, Amber was the voice of reason before others could interject. "He's probably just running late for some reason. It'd be bad form to invite everyone here then not show up."

164

I was about to express agreement with her when a meteor screamed through the sky headed straight for us. Without a thought, I prepared to summon Tenko to try and divert the attack, but the chance never came.

It wasn't aimed at us.

Or should I say he wasn't aiming for us.

The loud singing was a dead giveaway as a voice screamed through the air about having a burning passion for his work. I snickered as soon as I realized the pun. You have to appreciate a good pun when you find one. At least up until he crashed down into the stage with more smoke than a wet wood fire.

As the plume of smoke cleared, I had a moment of worry. Had this done harm to Ansith? After all, this environment was all his creation. Pyros had done no damage to the SS level Core's construction, but I was surprised Ansith didn't even come out to scold anyone. Maybe he was used to his students causing trouble?

Either way, the flames died, and we were left with a man whose literal locks were licks of flame. His pointed ears had him pegged as an elf, which was surprising enough, but his clothes, his hair, the coloring of his irises, were all formed from embers and tongues of fire. With a name like Pyros and coming from a place called Ember Fields, I would have been disappointed otherwise.

"Welcome to our little game, everyone!" Pyros said enthusiastically. He held his arms wide. Easily, he was the largest of all of us by a head, but the power that radiated from him showed a whole other level of mana use. His Pyromancer class had to be at least a Rank above all of us. Maybe this wouldn't be a waste of time. "The rules are simple. Everyone will summon their Guardians and attempt to beat the others! If you're the last embers in the fire, I'll give you the chance to copy the Pattern I discovered during the trial we all had the pleasure to undertake. Simple as that!"

"What is it?" Mera asked, clearly unphased by his pyrotechnic display of power.

Pyros simply grinned. "A surprise."

I had the distinct impression I was going to like this guy.

Looking from face to face, Amber gave me a curt nod, and I asked what I felt to be a good question, trying to keep a smile from my face. "What if we tie?"

Pyros shrugged, seemingly disinterested in the concept. "Then you'll both get a chance to copy it, but if you willingly give up, no rewards for anyone."

Ah, the way between the words was a sweet, sweet path. "Sounds like a summer stroll to me." I turned to Amber and grinned as the rest of them took their places around the stage.

Only Agar balked. "Ansith might be a bit paranoid, even for one of our kind, but I doubt he's wrong about the risks of sharing information about ourselves."

Pyros shrugged. "We're not going to live forever. If we screw up, we've seen what'll happen, so might as well know where we stand with each other."

For someone that wielded Fire, he was surprisingly pragmatic. Showy, but pragmatic. Still though, what was his end goal?

"Why should we reveal our Guardians now?" Amber was not as curious as a fox, but she had her own questions. Maybe she had been spending too much time with me. Whether or not, I was almost proud of her, because I had wanted to ask that question. As a bit of reinforcement, I turned towards Pyros and nodded in agreement.

Again, he did little more than shrug before he answered. "Because it's fun? Power for power's sake is pointless if you can't lord it over everyone else. I mean Ansith does it just fine. Look at this place! He might be paranoid, but he is paranoid in style! Mind you, I think I could do one better at his level."

I'm not too proud to admit when I'm wrong. I was liking Pyros less and less as he spoke from that conceited, stupid mouth. I wasn't a fan of power for power's sake, but if I could put him in his place, I think I could come to terms with it.

The others seemed to be in the same camp.

"You think your fancy fracking flames make you stronger?" Agar asked angrily, grinding a hand into his palm. "I'll crush you and your Guardian."

Pyros's smile never wavered, and he turned it towards Amber and I before speaking. "I'm not worried about you, Agar, but you're welcome to try."

Fiona said nothing, and Mera simply took the side opposite the other Water Core. Pyros walked off the stage opposite Agar, and Amber and I stood in place. In every direction, I could feel the mana being siphoned around us and into the other Cores. It wasn't drained by any means, but it was like when someone pulled the plug on the bath while more water was being added. There was a flow about it.

It was interesting to see how fast the others could summon their beasts. Each one took their time, but the fastest by far was Fiona. No words came from her lips, but an intense look of concentration coated every expression. Her beast was ethereal at first, but filled in with colors and power as a creature of the sea. The best word for it was primal. The creature had eight tentacles made from Water that spread from a flesh head of ocean blue. A beak of shimmering orange peaked out from under itself as it stood tall. Eyes spread across its head in all directions, so it did not have a single blind spot. To my surprise, I could focus on it the same way I could my own minions, but I got much less information. The Guardian's name was Blinky. I chuckled at that.

Mera's Guardian appeared next. To my surprise, it wasn't a monster or animal she summoned. It was an elemental, shaped like a woman who matched Mera's form. Her flesh, or what passed for it, was an ever-moving flow of Water. It had no eyes, or feet to call its own, instead settling for what looked like a rounded stone in its head and a puddle at the end of what could generously be called a gown. The only solid part of the Guardian were its hands, which were made into claws of solid ice. It would not be pleasant to meet it in a lake at night unprepared. The name of Mera's creation was equally unsettling: Undertow.

Agar and Pyros both seemed to summon theirs at the same time, but Pyros's was much more eye-catching. Unlike the other Guardian's simple appearance, Pyros's creature burst onto the scene in an eruption of fire and light. When the fires cleared, I was pretty disappointed. It was a box, a chest really. No arms, no hands, just your average chest of goodies. Bigger than a typical chest? Yes, but...

Wait...

Were those teeth?

No sooner had I seen the teeth than I realized what it was. Pyros, surprisingly, had a mimic. From the sides and bottom of the chest limbs burst from the crate. Red wood flew around the area as two bulky arms and eight spindly spider legs lifted it off the ground. The lid opened, reveling two glowing ruby eyes and more gold and silver teeth than I'd ever seen. It was a vision of terror, and as its burning eyes fell on the others, I knew I wanted the Pattern for this. A mimic would be a perfect trap in a range of situations. Pyros had called it Lockjaw.

Agar's creature was simple in comparison: a large golem made from boulders. It was humanoid in a sense like Mera's, but more stylized. At the end of each knuckle were gemstones cut for maximum impact. There were also gems for its eyes and for protecting each joint. Earthen mana surged between its limbs and held it together in its unnatural shape. Rocky was an apt name, but, personally, I just thought it showed Agar's lack of creativity. A dwarf making a stone construct was nothing new.

The others were looking at Amber and I now, presumably eager for the event to be done with so they could have their prize. It was too bad that they wouldn't be walking away with it. Even before death, I had a base study of magic, and the idea of cooperative casting wasn't anything new. As I began to lay the groundwork for our joint creation, I was very, very glad this had carried over into being a Dungeon Core.

The outline of Tenko appeared in the air, but it was much larger in appearance. It towered above me by almost a foot, and the misted outline began to grow more solid as I poured Celestial and Dungeon mana into it. Without missing a beat, Amber followed suit with her Air and Fire mana, and its power surged.

There were voices at the edge of my hearing, but I ignored them. As long as Amber and I stayed focused, neither of us would pop from mana loss. At least, that was the idea. Four tails were visible now, each one tipped in a glowing flame of its associated mana, red for Fire, gold-ish yellow for Air, gray for Dungeon, and opalescent for Celestial. Armor covered its back, head, and legs now, a swimming combination of the four elements. Fire licked at the edges of its feet as an unseen wind washed over its fur giving the creature the illusion of movement even in a resting state. Our Guardian's eyes were a glimmering blue, and its fur was the same opalescence as mine, but with a more pronounced streaks of color throughout. With a deafening burst of mana, the Guardian was complete. With a nearly physical snap, I broke my mana's contact with it and smiled. I looked to Amber, knowing she felt the same familiar drain, but it had worked! Together, we looked over our creation with a pride that must have been akin to the feeling of new parents.

Rembar, Novice of the Four Elements
Kitsune (Four Tail)
Cost: 200 Dungeon, 200 Celestial, 200 Air, 200 Fire
Challenge Rating: C2
Hardy, Inquisitive, Resolute, Chaotic
Intelligence: Gifted - Autonomous
Growth Potential: High
Survivability Rating: B7
Mana attributes: Quad Cast, Elemental Phase Armor, Blink, Minor Summons, Dual Guardian
Reward Seed: Unassigned, Natural, Mana-rich

Looking on our beast, I smiled as she stood heads above the others. This was going to be distinctly satisfying on so many levels.

As if granted by Vul herself, I didn't even have to wait that long to get a reaction!

"That's not fair!" Pyros bellowed as Rembar looked over to him.

Ah, the glory of loopholes.

"You never said we couldn't work together," I reminded him, then continued along the path of my thoughts. "You said that if we tied, we'd both get the reward."

"I said to summon your Guardians," Pyros reminded me, but it was a reminder that wasn't necessary.

"This is our Guardian," I grinned. "It has the attribute of Dual Guardian, so I'm pretty sure that qualifies as a Guardian. The fact that it has twice the power of a normal Guardian, and incidentally should crush all of you under its feet, is just a useful, but completely random happenstance."

That was a fun word, happenstance. It had no use in your average conversation, but it said a great deal to those you were talking to. Mostly that you thought yourself slightly better than them. I held back my snark though. I knew well enough Rembar wasn't perfect.

If we were up against a real opponent in a do or die situation, our Guardian wouldn't have been nearly as useful. It took time to summon Rembar, time and power beyond that available to one Core at our power levels. I almost quivered with excitement at what Rembar might become as I learned to use Umbral mana, but mostly, I just quivered from a nearly depleted reserve of Celestial mana. Another of those pesky things I learned was that my Celestial reserve was separate from my Dungeon mana, unless I was actively cycling Dungeon mana and converting it on the fly. That meant the more of it I used, the weaker I physically felt.

Our kitsune looked from one Guardian to another before turning her attention to Pyros. She was more careful than Tenko was, sniffing the air for whiffs of some unknown scent and shaking her head as if to deny my words.

Apparently, Pyros took this as quite the insult. Either because I'd found a way around his rules or because Rembar was just insulting him. "Lockjaw, attack!"

Pyros's Guardian wasn't alone. As the mimic pounced on its spidery legs, Blinky, Undertow, and Rocky joined the fray, combining against the Guardian they quite rightly saw as the greatest threat.

Rembar bore her teeth in a challenging grin and growled at the approaching foes. As she stood her ground, I felt a swell of pride watching her prepare. In that instance, I knew then that this was going to be fun.

Chapter Twenty-One

Revolt

Four-on-one as a fight wasn't fair in the slightest under normal circumstances, but with a Rank C challenge rating, Rembar was on more than an even playing field. She was meant to be a straightforward fight for a full team of C Ranked individuals, but a full team of D's with a good composure could defeat her as well if they were skilled. I knew it, Amber knew it, and I'm sure the others knew it too. If each of those Guardians were the same rating as Tenko had been, they had a rating of at least Rank D each. It would be an interesting battle to say the least, or so I hoped.

The moment combat started, I remembered something. Never rely on hope for anything important.

Rembar proved her superiority the instant the other Guardians began their approach. The mote of Air essence at the end of her tail flashed, and she countered their first move as she stormed her first target. Much as I love using a turn of phrase, this storm was literal. A bolt of lightning shot from the clear sky with a crack of thunderous noise and caught Undertow in the head, shattering its form instantly and sending its Core of polished blue stone careening off the stage with a howl. Lockjaw was better off, but the force of the exploding water threw the mimic clear off course. As it recovered, the mimic spotted the loot from Undertow, skittered from its resting place, stole the blue gemstone elemental Core, and shoved it inside its jaws for safe keeping. It was still a mimic after all.

"By the Pantheon," I heard someone mutter. From the direction and the proximity, it had to be Pyros. "We need to down this thing!"

With three allies left and Rembar content with watching, the other Cores regrouped, their Guardians close by one another as Fiona's sea monster Blinky put a flowing tentacle on each of them. Water spread from the limbs over their bodies and solidified into armor around vital points. With this renewed defense, the ice and jewel encrusted Rocky was the first to charge back into the fray.

"Smash it, Rembar!" Amber cheered before Rembar looked back at her and huffed slightly.

Rembar's tails swished, and she simply snorted in reply.

Giving Amber no more notice, Rembar returned her attention to her avalanching opponent. She watched for a moment, taking in the creature as any predator would, and I swear to Vul I saw her smile for just a moment.

It was a smile that chilled me from the tips of my ears to the base of my tail.

With a look of satisfaction, Rembar focused, took step forward, and held her tails high, glimmering in the sunlight. Using the rush as a feint, Rocky vanished into pieces of stone and rolled around the stadium, while Lockjaw spotted its chance and the mimic rammed itself into Rembar's armored flank. The armor taking the impact cracked but didn't crumble as she turned and stared at the mimic, clearly annoyed. As she waited, the mimic righted itself and bent its legs again, readying another strike with its box-like body.

Rembar snorted again and shook her head at the creature.

The shaking feet of the Earth elemental had reassembled behind her and rushed again with its ground-shaking weight. In a matter of moments, it was nearly at her back. I was ready to shout a command, but she was already aware of the attack. At least, I think she was. Our Guardian continued to look at Lockjaw with annoyance and made no motion to dodge the incoming strike. Instead, Rembar simply Blinked out of existence.

Whether she'd planned the timing or not, the surprised mimic was left directly in the path of the rampaging Earth elemental. Lockjaw took Rocky's force like a pile of kindling might take a warrior's boot, and the boards that made up its front and top bowed before snapping a few moment later. A squeal of pain echoed through the open area as

Lockjaw sprouted new hands from the darkness of its body and tried to pick up its fallen pieces one by one. Even Blinky got in on the action, trying to help Lockjaw seal its wound, as Rembar returned from her otherworldly sidestep.

The others were too late. Before the three Guardians could turn to face her, another of Rembar's tail tips flashed red, and a gout of flame sprayed from just a few inches in front of her face, across the open space, and across the fallen, frantic, wooden construct. The reinforced ice sizzled and popped as it evaporated, and even the best protected elementally among them, Blinky, lost a limb before the remains of the mimic scattered coins, jewels, and a large, sapphire stone across the battlefield.

"Go, go!" Amber cheered.

I was as excited as she was to see our beast rampaging through them like so much paper, but it was too easy. Rembar wore her emotions like a Foxkin, and I could see it in our Guardian's every feature.

Rembar was unamused, almost bored, as the second foe fell, and the remaining combatants began to scramble. I couldn't help but think she had planned it all as her gray tail flashed, and a pair of the gray-armored aether foxes joined the battlefield. Like pawns, the smaller foxes rushed into battle, attacking legs and hindering movement until Rembar could summon her strength again and use her Air-empowered paw to smash Blinky into a multi-colored pool of liquid and pieces of meat. Then she turned on her final opponent.

To Rocky's credit, the Earth elemental was an instrument of war. Armored like a High Knight, fast as an avalanche, and impressively launching fists like arrows, it could probably defeat a lone adventurer of a higher rank with ease, maybe even an entire group of them at its own level. Rembar, however, wasn't a normal opponent. Her armor exploded in a flash of light, and she entered into a new form. Lighter, more nimble, she dodged the fists easily, and, with an effortless swipe, she decapitated the golem, leaving behind a shower of ores and gemstones in its death keen.

And that was it.

We'd won. I watched our Guardian with a newfound respect for Amber and my work. Rembar had ruined the other Guardians like they'd been cotton fluff.

"It's over," Pyros called out from our right. His voice was like a stomped-out campfire for all the enthusiasm it held. He must have been expecting an easy win. It only made me feel a little better knowing that we'd dumped water over his embers. "Take your loot."

I extended my Influence and gathered up the materials to add to my collection. I'd make a copy for Amber once we were away from prying eyes. Mana stones, currencies from at least three nations, gemstones, iron ore, and copious amounts of meat filled my mind and taught me how to make them all. It was a sweet victory as I turned to Pyros. "And your reward, the Pattern?"

He rubbed the back of his head. "I don't know if you even need it after that show."

I narrowed my eyes at him as Amber interjected herself between us. "You promised us a reward, and I expect you to pay up, Pyros."

I almost laughed as Pyros took a step back when Rembar and Amber took a dancer's step forward. Even I knew that the Hells had no fury like a woman scorned.

I grinned, eagerly awaiting our newfound prize, but my excitement turned to annoyance. Rembar didn't slow her calculated steps. She kept approaching, growling at the Core.

"Stop, Rembar," I commanded, but there was no response.

"Stop, girl," Amber echoed, but again, there was no response other than a slight growl.

I sent her a mental command to stop, but it hurt to hold it to her will. Then, I tried to shut my mana from her, but I couldn't. She was fighting me. Every second I held her tethered, I felt my mana straining against her will. I pulled in what I could from around me, but it wasn't fast enough. Rembar raged, pushed, and snapped forward. In her thoughts, she had more targets, more challenges to deal with. I could feel her pushing ahead. I could feel her probing, searching for a weakness in the command. When she couldn't find one, she pushed against my will with all her combined force.

I didn't stand a chance.

***

Restored in the soft glow of my Dungeon, I couldn't help but scream.

"How could I be so stupid?"

It was a simple question, but one I found myself trying to figure out. As I examined Rembar's Pattern, the problems became obvious. If I'd paid any attention to anything besides how strong she was, I'd have realized that so much sooner. Of course, Rembar had revolted. She was smarter than us, stronger than us, and had no loyalty towards us.

I had to get back to them. Maybe there was a way we could drain her power or unsummon her somehow? If she was left to rampage, would the others be okay? That at least had an easy answer. Of course, they would. Their Cores were safely off in their Dungeons. The worst Rembar could do would be to pop them like she had me. After that, Ansith would probably just wipe her out of existence with some power shot or something.

Sitting above my Core in my chamber, I couldn't help but stew in my own annoyance. I hated when someone got one over on me, let alone a five-minute-old Guardian whose very concept was less than an hour or two old. What would the clan have though? That thought alone was enough to darken my mood.

We should have done more testing with her. At least summoned her to see if she could be controlled at our Rank.

The best thing I could do now was cycle my Dungeon mana and replenish my personal store of power. I also realized just how uncomfortable it was to be at the bottom of a perfect sphere. There wasn't a good place to sit, lay down, or do anything, since every single part of it was a gradient. I'd have to correct that soon.

I spread my personal sight further out and felt I had quite a bit more space to myself now. Plenty to work with if I felt like it, and it wasn't like I had anything else to do until I found my way back to the

Academy. So not wanting to waste time and to try to get myself out of the self-depreciating funk, I set myself to work.

Between worrying about the others and loosing myself in the work, I lost track of how long I spent in the Core room, maybe a few hours or so if I was being generous? Whether or not, I was happy with how things were coming out. It was more of a room now, wider than before with a flat floor and a more natural gradient to the ceiling. It was more of a half oval than a sphere. Everything was spaced now so that Tenko could run about as he saw fit to deal with invaders, and my Core was safely embedded in the wall furthest from where I planned the entrance to be, looking down on the action from a higher, curved vantage point that blended in with the stone around me. It also helped limit my 360-degree vision into something more manageable when I was stuck in the Core. All in all, I was pretty happy with my new perch. If someone was going to shatter me, good luck!

With my work done for now, I was about to summon Tenko again, but another pop echoed in my chamber and stopped me with a bellowing, familiar call of, "Rem!"

Oh, sket. I knew that voice and it was angry.

Ansith the First had Manifested and he pushed towards me without a word: his face spoke volumes. He fumed, he raged, he was anger incarnate as his very steps burned his Influence and power into the ground so completely that it left scorch marks. I had spent hours reinforcing it, and he destroyed it without so much as the decency of an attack.

He was not happy.

His finger pushed at my chest, throwing me back against the nearest wall with so much force that if I still had flesh and bone, they'd have shattered and run my organs through. His voice was a thunder that echoed from all directions as he screamed his question at me. "Do you have any idea what you've done!"

I had the feeling that 'no' was not the right answer even if it was the best one. I said nothing, but my body language spoke about as much as his face did when he first arrived. My tail was no better than a loose string, and my ears fell back leaving enough of an opening to hear but no more than a slightly raised profile.

For that moment, anger had stolen his words. Steam from his power alone rose around him in a dangerous haze, but there was still nothing to hear but the sizzle of his power colliding with my own and wiping it out when it got too far from him. Every time he opened his mouth, nothing came out, and he paced. He'd stop, turn to me again, and try again with the same result.

For a few minutes, I stood there, watching the demi-god burn a hole into my floor and waiting for the scathing comments that never came until finally Ansith stopped and turned to me. If I were any younger, I might have cried in fear alone with the way those eyes burned with anger and ambient mana. Needless to say, I wasn't looking forward to what he had to say, but the words came all the same with a measure of control that sent ice through my veins.

"Normally, I'd applaud your efforts and ingenuity. I'd be happy you and your friend were able to cooperate with completely uncomplimentary mana types to create and summon a creature, let alone a Guardian as powerful as your Rembar. That takes a skill beyond your Rank and experience to achieve."

Every hair on my tail stood on end even before he took that pausing breath. There was a 'but' as large as all creation coming.

"Normally being the operative word, Rem. This isn't normal though. What you've created was reckless and beyond either of you to control!"

I had already figured that much out, but said nothing. You didn't argue with someone that could wipe you off the face of the planet with little more than a sneeze in your direction.

"Even with the Guardian status, Rembar is not a Dungeon born. Its survivability shouldn't have even been possibly at your level of skill and power. At Rank B, it doesn't need a Dungeon to supply it with power once its Dungeon mana runs out. It can live and breathe on its own. What's worse is that your Rembar has the power to create its own Dungeon out in the wild! If it decides to move in that direction, you've might as well have tailored her to be given to Eventide! She's gift wrapped with all the knowledge it'd need to bring our entire operation to a halt. Years, centuries of work would be gone in hours all because of you!"

I felt shame burn on my cheeks at his words. So yeah, that sounded pretty bad. His words didn't stop at just hurting my pride. I'd screwed up, and he was letting me know that whatever handle I thought I'd been building on my abilities, it was nothing now.

His fist squeezed intently at his side as if he were turning coal into diamond or summoning the elements to his call. "For the lives your mistake is going to cost, I should crush you right now and be done with you, Rem."

He took a deep breath and sighed, taking a step towards me. I grabbed at my power, pulling it in and readying Forbid. It wouldn't be much, but it might give me the time I need to live a few more seconds. As he started talking again, I didn't release an ounce of it.

"It'd be a waste of a potential ally, but if you asked the rest of my graduates, they'd tell you that I've done worse for less to protect the races." He seemed to relax a fraction and sighed again. "But this doesn't fall just on you. Amber is equally responsible for its creation; Pyros and the others for getting the idea for the stupid competition; and even me. Maybe even most of all myself. I should have stepped in before it returned the others to their Dungeons and Blinked beyond the barrier."

Ansith sighed for a third time, and the tension that held him left his muscles.

"However, my lapse of judgment does not excuse your actions. You've created a mess that will cost countless lives if left unchecked, and each life will be coming from your hide." His voice turned cold, colder than it had been when he spoke about the other Cores not yesterday. Cold enough to hurt as his eyes bored into me, turning just slightly to take in my Manifestation and my Core. "This will not happen again."

Chapter Twenty-Two

Rescheduled

With those words, he was gone. I wasn't worried I'd be left there, but I still didn't like the creeping feeling that meandered up my spine that I'd be alone again. I don't know why I worried about it so much. I was just a social creature, and I hated the thought of being alone, I guess. Alone, and with questions. Again, he'd mentioned Eventide as if he or she were the most terrible threat. Who was Eventide? And were the Foxkin safe from him or her?

In reality, it wasn't a long wait, but it was long enough for me to stew and consider just how badly I'd screwed up yet again. Then, without so much as a warning, Ansith jerked my Manifestation through the whole world. In and of itself, that was a unique experience. I felt every rock, every insect, every tree passed by my form until I was back at the stage of the academy. Nope, it wasn't nearly as easy or gentle as he had made it the last few times. If I had my best guess, that unique experience was to drive home that he was still more than just a bit angry.

I materialized next to the other five of my remaining classmates. Above us, on the stage, Ansith loomed like a specter of death as he looked down menacingly. He let us stew for just a bit longer before he spoke.

"You have all failed, and, in turn, I have failed you."

The words rang like the piercing tone across the courtyard. They were deep, disappointed words that seeped with negativity. To my surprise, they weren't just aimed at me or Amber. Ansith looked from one to the next as he spoke. We were all under the assault of a resentment deep enough to measure our graves.

"I, however, have done more than enough good to outweigh a single mistake in judgment. None of you can say the same, and if you do not amend your lack of judgment, I will make you atone for each life you'll cost due to your failures."

There was no mirth in his voice. There was no joke to be had, and no loophole to exploit. Ansith seethed with anger that was barely contained within his small stature. Every word was a promise to be extracted from our hides if we did not make amends.

If I was being honest with myself in that moment, a few things came to mind. I wasn't frightened when I died, and even when his minions bore down to murder Tenko, I felt more determined than I was frightened. Now I felt the cold truth of his words like a knife in my heart, and I knew fear. Fear of failure, fear of what was to come, fear of leaving everyone I knew and loved in a constantly growing state of weakness.

I wasn't ready to die... again. People needed me. My clan was counting on me to make them stronger. I couldn't die, not yet.

The others around me mirrored my expression, but some of them were braver than me and tried to redirect his blades from themselves.

"We had nothing to do with that thing," Agar growled, never letting his eyes leave Ansith's. "We shouldn't be responsible for what they did."

"Make them do it," Mera added in her overly-feminine voice.

Fiona, as always, said nothing but nodded towards the other two. She may not have said much, but I still didn't know how to take her wordless responses that everyone seemed to understand but me. It wasn't hard to tell that she agreed with those two though. Amber said nothing, but I doubted it was for the same reasons I stayed silent.

I was more surprised at Ansith's delay. For the moment, it seemed like his anger subsided. He knew as much as I did, as Amber and I did, that those three were right. If anyone was to blame, it was us not knowing what we were doing, and we were duty bound to correct our mistake.

More time passed as he calculated his answer, choosing his words carefully, I assumed.

"You're all right in your assertions." As he spoke, Ansith's expression darkened dangerously, and his anger found a foothold to attack from. "No, you shouldn't be responsible for their actions, but you weren't strong enough or smart enough to stop them." Agar opened his mouth to reply, but Ansith motioned with his hands, and the mouth slammed shut. "If one of you becomes wild, all of you will suffer for it. Warriors will hunt you down and shatter you for the protection of others, Mages will pluck your soul from your Dungeon and use your Core for power, and still others will be given a fate worse than death, utter oblivion!"

The words were heavy. I knew we weren't natural, but I hadn't considered much what it meant being a Dungeon. Ansith had alluded to a lot of issues in dealing with adventurers, but never this. Never how we could die. I thought Vix had been kidding about what they did, but she had come closer to the truth than I would have liked.

We looked from one another feeling the weight of his words, and his smile brightened slightly at our discomfort.

"You must realize the danger you are in for simply existing. You must all learn to temper yourselves against the coming tides. In times of great need, you need to learn to rely on and defend one another against a greater foe. Today, the majority of you failed to assist Amber when she needed you the most. You hesitated, and you all lost your Manifestation because of it. Because of this success of a failure, I have decided that today you will begin to learn how important cooperation really is. Many would consider this a reward, you know..."

I knew those were dangerous words, and the others looked to one another for something they couldn't grip themselves. One by one, their attentions turned focusing on Amber and then on me. I felt the weight of their gaze, and the intensity of it made me wince just a bit, but how could I blame them? I looked over at Amber, but she was doing better than I had fared already. Her color was good, and her eyes almost seemed alien. She wasn't afraid or the least bit bothered by them. If I didn't know her, I would have laughed at myself for ever thinking she'd have issues with her confidence.

"And it starts—"

All around us, the world flashed, and I felt myself lurch like I had when Ansith dragged my simulacrum back to the academy. I felt clouds, sky, a stray bird, and endless blue pass through my body. It was almost worse than before.

When my head felt right again, I wasn't surprised to see that everything was different. Gone were the verdant greens of the forest, gone was the stage and the academy and before us was a small, simple cave opening, in a clearing of grass, surrounded by water for as far as the eye could see, but no. That would have been too normal.

The sky danced with colors beyond my understanding even to what I was now. I could feel the power of mana all around me, but it wasn't the wild mana of the world or the condensed mana of a Dungeon. It was an active spell effect. A massive, unthinkable spell of a proportion I'd never begun to imagine casting in my wildest dreams.

"— here." Ansith smile was dark and knowing, waiting for all of our attention before he spoke again. "This is one of those times, born of a dire need for cooperation." He paused, looking from one Core to the next, letting the words settle before he began again. "I had not intended to allow you to approach this topic for some time, not until you were at least Rank C yourselves, but you've proven that my current methods are not to your taste. That you are ready for greater challenges. So, a reschedule is in order to amend your problems." Turning away from us, he made a grand gesture of reveal and smiled, visible in the reflection of the massive spell barrier. "Welcome to the Sundering."

The Sundering...

From our position, we could see the veil of shimmering mana in front of us, between us and the cave entrance lingering just on the other side. It wasn't thick at all, but I don't think that was the point of it. All around us, leaves, insects, and the occasional creature scampered through the veil of power. A memory nagged though, didn't Ansith mention the name to me before?

"This is the island of Latalong. It is the only land in the entire wake of the Sundering, the last push of a great and terrible power to attempt to cross into the western world." He paused, and there was a whisper of a hesitation before he began speaking again. "The place where

182

Eventide's forces and I came to a terrible stalemate, and where I set the center of my spell's focus. I've taken great lengths to hide this location from the world. Latalong is found on no maps and it requires the spell key of a guide to even see the island. I've seen to it that no one but myself and my closest allies can even arrive here to maintain the ward." That seemed impressive and ominous enough, but he wasn't nearly done. "You see, the barrier here prevents unkeyed Dungeon mana from seeping through to our side all the way to the planet's Core. Without it, the West would be no better than the East, but as you can see, Eventide's Dungeons try all the same."

I felt like the lesson we were getting wasn't just for our benefit as I stared through the shimmering barrier. He said it kept the mana from passing through to the west, so what was the problem? "Why are we here?"

Ansith smiled.

I had to ask.

In a snap, we were hurled through the barrier by a shower of earth and stone like a child might hurl a stone at a neighbor's window after they took their ball. It was a brutally quick trip, and we landed in a not so comfortable heap that I was nearly on the bottom of. Yeah, I probably deserved that right now, but at least Amber broke my fall. Mera would have been better from the way I landed though.

Maybe it was the dust-filled flight through the air, maybe it was crashing into Amber in such an embarrassing way, maybe it was simply the annoyance at being tossed about like someone's toy, but something was different as the barrier solidified once more.

Something felt wrong. From tip to tail, it felt like something had been taken from me.

Before anyone could voice their concerns, object, complain, or argue, Ansith spoke again in such a way that made speaking amongst ourselves pointless. "You are here because you will be purifying this blight while I spend my time and resources to hunt down your rogue Guardian. It will be a good lesson for you on teamwork and invasion tactics." He paused to consider his next words. They weren't as harsh as he had started with, but they still held a bit of scold. "You should feel some measure of pride. I usually reserve trips like this for C rank

Cores. Usually the stakes are much lower thanks to their connection to their home Dungeon still being active. Now, your prey should be no higher than a Rank D, maybe a Rank C this far from the heart."

Rank D was where most of us were, power wise. Rank C was still several steps above us, and if my growth had been any indication, involved enough mana to choke the life out of an elemental. That may not have been horrible in itself, but Ansith had a way of making sure we realized when things were horrible by making this all the harder for it.

"As the nature of the Sundering blocks un-keyed Dungeon mana from crossing, and as I have the only key, you'll have noticed your power has weakened. This not to be ignored. If your simulacrum loses cohesion here, your Core will not be able to recover your Manifestation and the mental processes you've invested in it. So unless you've learned how to do more than just transfer your consciousness into your Manifestation, which is an upper C Rank Node Augmentation, your death will be oblivion as sure as if a mage had taken hold of you on the day of your birth and stole your soul."

And there it was, another death trap.

Ansith just had to make everything worse, but if it hadn't been a death trap, it would have been the noise his words left in their wake. The things that passed for words of the others around me was thought-deafening in a way that made me regret even learning these Core's names. I still didn't want to be alone, but I was really starting to dislike these people.

Ansith took no note and continued after a short pause for him to gather his breath. "There is no point in arguing about this, and I'm not asking the impossible of you. Whether you were beyond the Sundering or not, what happens now would be the same as if you were absorbed by a Dungeon anyways. The only difference is that here it can occur on the surface as well. When you've shattered the Core, return to the surface and I'll come back for you. The Dungeon is young, so it shouldn't be hard to find its heart. Just follow the strongest flow of mana. If you're lucky, it'll be a short trip."

From the arguments that erupted around us, I was only glad that their anger was directed at him and his little pep talk again rather than at us. But as always, Ansith ignored our complaints and went straight into a more sadistic, teaching mindset.

"Any questions about the subject at hand?" he followed up with.

The noises only got louder with his request, but the questions all had the same vein.

How were we supposed to do this?

Ansith smiled like a sphinx watching his mortal foe flounder on a puzzle. "You have all the answers to this test. I do not send my students into hopeless situations for the sake of revenge, but I will leave you with this. Your abilities of Manifestation and Influence will be your best tools here. That, your natural skills, and your wit will help you learn to work together. Consider this your final Rank D exam." There was a slight glint in his eye even I could see from behind the shimmering light of the barrier. "If you survive, you'll understand why." He lifted his wrist, as if looking for something before he spoke again. "Now, if you'll excuse me, I have a hunt to organize."

Despite the pleas for help, he was gone a moment later with the barest echo of a pop.

Chapter Twenty-Three
Cooperation Operation

As Ansith left us, there was a void created by the lack of a unified lightning rod of hate. Of course, all voids were filled in time, and all eyes turned like sentries as the lightning aimed back towards Amber and myself. I took a deep breath and made a decision I hoped I wouldn't regret. Rembar had been my idea, not hers, and I needed to make sure they targeted the right person.

It was the right thing to do.

Stepping out a bit further to put myself more squarely between her and them, I sighed. "Look, if I had known how badly it would have turned out, I wouldn't have convinced her to try it. I'm sorry."

Agar and Pyros both seemed surprised by my admission, but the two Water Cores made no show of emotion other than to continue watching me. Soon, the four of them were staring at me in silence. Nothing made a noise but the ocean and the wind rushing against the cave's entrance. The four sets of eyes bore holes into me, watching my every breath and waiting for the perfect moment to strike me down. I didn't want to fight, but I was ready for them to come at me since they couldn't take out their frustrations on Ansith. Thankfully, the sounds of feet crunching sand broke the tense silence.

"It wasn't just his idea. It takes two." Amber surprised me as she stepped to my side rather than to shrink from their attentions. Her hand found its way to my shoulder and squeezed it gently. I looked to her and thanked her silently for the gesture as a sudden tenseness faded from my mana-made muscles. She'd come a long way in a short time, and I couldn't be more grateful for that. "We're both sorry, but if we're going to survive, we need each other in one piece." She paused for a moment. "Not like a six headed monster, even if that'd be pretty powerful, but together and working as a team."

As she spoke, Agar ground his hand into the back of his head as he thought. Not satisfied with... whatever it was supposed to be doing, he moved into a more familiar action I'd seen among the dwarves I've met. He began to stroke his beard. He was the strongest of them, I imagined, so I was thankful when he spoke first. "Before I became a Core, I lived as a Guardian and enchanter. I gave everything for those I called allies, and I will once more. I know I'm not ready to die again. There's too much left to do, and too many battles left to fight." As if by magic, no... Manifestation, a large battle axe appeared to fill his waiting hands. From tip to tail, it had to be as large as he was, if not larger. The weapon was fit for an executioner, and the blade was as wide as the dwarf's beard was long. "Lena and I will fight with you. Together, we will cut down any who oppose us here!"

Lena? Well, dwarves had their oddities, but I wasn't about to argue with a man carrying an axe larger than I was. What was the deal with these warriors anyways having weapons so large? Were they compensating for something? I knew I was smiling when I turned back to the other three, enjoying my own joke. I directed the first question to the overly busty, under-performing, Mera. "And you?"

Mera shook her head and waved her hand to us as she moved as close to the barrier as she could and flopped herself on the ground. Only once she had wiggled into place did she speak. "I'll be fine here thanks. You got us into this mess, you can get us out."

I couldn't help but sigh in annoyance. If she were as helpful as she was beautiful, we would have been much better off. Mists, if she was as helpful as she was busty, we'd be done already! Knowing that there wasn't much I could do to convince her without having Fiona on our side, I turned to her. "Fiona, will you help?"

The mermaid seemed to consider her options, and I felt something tug at me. Amber looked at me shocked the moment it happened, so I assumed she must have felt it too. It felt similar to when Vix first offered me mana. I accepted it, and a voice seemed to flow into my mind.

187

<I will help as much as I can, but I am not comfortable with physical combat.>

Fiona's voice was kind and gentle, more like a placid lake than a raging ocean. It was as if merely accepting her voice let me feel Fiona's calm nature. When the suddenness of the calm passed, a new idea caught my attention. That technique was interesting. Was that something we could all do, or was it something unique to the merfolk? I tried to project my voice like I had as a Core, infusing it with mana and sending it towards her as a reply.

It did not go as planned.

"Thank you!"

And any semblance of surprise we would have had was shattered as my voice went off like a bomb. It was a new, strange feeling as I did it, something I needed to remember as the mana drained from my body. The sensation lingered as nothing came back. After a few deep breaths, I finally put a name to the familiar feeling from the missing power: fatigue. To remedy the situation, I tried to draw in ambient mana, but it was like reaching through tar for any scrap of it. The mana I could grab was sluggish. It felt like a battle to draw it in, and it fought every step of the way. After a battle of wills, I managed to pull in enough and converted it to refill my reserves, but it took far longer than I thought safe.

Eventually, we all regained our hearing. Fiona seemed to chuckle as the rest of the group turned to me.

"By the Halls of my Ancestors, what in the Mists was that?" Agar groaned, rubbing at his ear with a finger while Lena rested on his shoulders.

"A mistake," I groaned, my voice raspier than it had been.

Note to self, a mana-infused voice was about the same force as a bomb in my ears. The ringing was still apparent, and I could still feel the drain of power as my body attempted to use the mana I'd taken in to repair whatever damage I'd done to myself.

"Two for two," Pyros scoffed. He wasn't wrong, but it was still annoying. "Of course, I'll be joining you. It was my idea after all, and besides. There's loot to be had!"

188

I simply nodded my thanks, but Amber used real words. "Thank you. I'm sure we'll all be able to handle this together, Pyros."

He just grinned, turning towards the entrance of the cave. "I wonder what's waiting. Well, armor up, boys and girls. Let's get this over and done with so we can go home."

Between breaths, I began to think. I could manifest a weapon, but I also had magic at my disposal. Both would cost me in the end, but which would be more useful in the long term? In the end, I ended up with a simple Manifestation of a weapon: a long, slender pole about as tall as I was with reinforced ends. They weren't claws, but it was a calculated exchange. The staff gave me reach, and I wasn't a novice with it. All mages, Oracles included, were trained in how to use staffs. I might not have had any skill Nodes for it, but a staff could break bones without one easily enough.

Giving my weapon a once over, Agar grunted approvingly at my choice. "Versatile."

I grinned. "It's a good stick."

"Yes, Rem. It's a very good stick," Amber said, patting my shoulder.

I was proud, but now wasn't the time to make jokes. I looked at our party. Everyone else had already followed suit with weapons of their own fashion. Fiona had manifested a bow and a quiver of arrows with what looked like forged shells replacing the metal and some other material I didn't recognize in place of the wood. Amber was more of a surprise. She had a pair of large, dense, orange shields that gave off a less-than-faint light. One on each of her forearms. Pyros, Pyros had no weapons that I could see, but his fists were wreathed in some sort of solid Fire. Agar still had the only manifested armor, but then again, could we create useful armor just from what he had shown us? Maybe, maybe not, but I wasn't willing to put it to risk wasting mana. Besides, cantrips would be more useful than crappy armor anyways. Other than the lack of armor, we were really looking like a party of adventurers.

Hopefully, we weren't the kind of adventurers that would smash an innocent's head open like a ripe melon thinking they were a werewolf. Yes, I would still be bitter about that for the foreseeable future.

As we stood around admiring ourselves, an awkward silence passed as we came to a realization. We had no idea how to go forward. No one made a move, so I voiced what I hoped we were all thinking. "So, how do we do this? Run in, kill the things, and just crush the Core when we find it?"

No one responded at first. In fact, no one spoke at all as mana tugged at me again. I accepted, getting used to that feeling as meaning Fiona wanted to speak with us.

<Sounds as if that's as good a plan as any other.>

"I wouldn't if I were you," Mera crooned, spreading out on the beach and materializing a swimsuit that left little to the imagination.

Normally, I'd be distracted, but to show the measure of my annoyance, I ignored the womanly form and looked straight into her eyes indignantly. "I'd care more about your opinion if you were helping."

"I am," she said, laying back against the sand as if my words were no more annoying than the wind on a warm day. "Someone has to be look out up here, right? I just go with the flow, ya know?"

Pyros's colors flared around the edges of his clothing, shifting from soft oranges and tinges of blue to a deep crimson as he took a step towards her. His fists leaked sparks as he made no attempt to hide his disdain for her attitude.

"Your fate is in our hands," Pyros reminded her. "You're really going to just lay there and let us do all the heavy lifting?"

She shrugged and lounged back on the beach. A strange pair of glasses formed over her eyes as she leaned her head back, blocking the deep sapphire hues from anyone's view. "Work smarter, not harder."

I appreciated her comment, but not when it came to dealing with serious issues. "You are utterly useless, Mera."

"Eh." She waved me off with the universal finger for disdain, and I gave her no more notice as I did the same.

The others were behind me as I approached the entrance to the cave. It looked unnatural. From the dark stone to the way the mid-day light barely inched past the cave's entrance, it oozed danger and reinforced just how alien the maw of an entrance was on the sandy island. Literally, it oozed. Green sludge seemed to drip from the clean ceiling and vanish as it touched the floor.

190

Needless to say, I didn't want to go first. I really, really didn't want to, but I knew better. I had to be the first to enter at least. All eyes were on me, except maybe Mera's. I could feel them watching my tail end hesitate.

Well, let them watch a little longer. It might be the last time anyone admired it. Pushing the dark thought away, I smiled and turned my head to look over my shoulder and address my admirers. "It's quite the sight, isn't it?"

At first, no one picked up on it.

Pyros seemed to nod. "It's unnatural. That's for sure. Dangerous, too. You'd be stupid to think otherwise."

My tail wagged all on its own as I grinned, trying my best not to laugh. "It is quite dangerous. Of that, you can be sure. I have it on good authority."

A silence persisted followed by a few looks before finally, Amber groaned and ran her hand down her face. "Rem, no one is looking at your tail on purpose."

"Just trying to lighten the mood." I continued to grin as I took a deep breath. Then another, and another as I let the enjoyment I felt rouse the courage I knew I had to go with that honor.

Slowly, I took a step forward.

Not so slowly, I began to scream.

It felt like I was pulling in the chill of a hypodermic death from deep, icy water. It was rushing into me from every angle, slowing me, freezing my soul, trying to push its way into me, and ripping my warm power from my body. It took everything I had to force my muscles to move in the bone-chilling cold. I fell back out of the cave's mouth with about as much grace as a boulder falling from a cliff onto a village. Thankfully, as I left the shadows of the opening, the icy power released its hold on my soul.

"Rem!" Amber was at my side before I had fallen, but it was only now I noticed. I could feel the warmth from her power, but I tried not to dwell on it as I forced myself to cycle in ambient power from the world around me.

"I'm okay," I managed after a few moments and the other Cores joined us. Pyros and Agar helped me to my feet as Fiona simply looked on concerned as I tried to keep my balance for the moment.

Mera laughed at me from her oh-so-perfect position in the sunbeams. She said something, but I ignored her. What had I missed? Where had I gone wrong? The answer was so obvious I deserved to be laughed at.

It was a Dungeon.

I was a Dungeon's Manifestation.

It had Influence here, and I didn't.

It absorbed and used Dungeon mana from the world around it, and I was literally made from the stuff!

I was trying to invade another Dungeon, and the Dungeon's mana must naturally fight me. Ansith had made it look so easy though. Then again, he was a demi-god trying to break a child's toy. Of course, he could break my Influence without breaking a sweat. I'd managed to resist it a bit, but I had been in the heart of my power. I didn't have the same power as I did there. I did, however, have a better understanding of how things worked now. Knowing that, I focused and checked my mana supply.

Dungeon Core Rank D2
Mastered Skills: 5 of 5
Secondary Skills: 0
7/9 requirements met to reach Rank C
      Absorb a new raw material
      Reach Nexus Size 2
      Absorb a new Bestiary Component
      Trigger a passive cycling of Influence
      Fabricate your Heart Chamber
      Create a Minion
      Create a Guardian
Dungeon Core Nexus Size 2
Dungeon Core Material - Opal/Amethyst
Mana Types - Celestial/Umbral/Dungeon
Mana Reserves:
Celestial - 175/350

Huh, I'd ranked up again. Twice in fact. That was a pleasant surprise. That wasn't what concerned me right now. I hadn't used Umbral mana or Celestial. Dungeon mana might be keeping me Manifest, but I knew it hadn't been that much. There was only one explanation. The Dungeon had attacked my mana, and I didn't like what that meant. If I lost the ability to sustain myself, Well... I didn't want to think about that.

Instead, I focused on breathing again. I'd lost nearly half my mana in all of my reservoirs. That gave me an advantage though. It gave me something to work with. Somewhere to start from for this invasion.

It was time to get to work.

Once I had the idea together, I turned to the others and explained everything. It didn't take long to fill them in on what had happened and how I had tried to fight the first time. I had to give it to the merfolk though, Fiona seemed to pick up the seed of a plan the fastest and formulated it into a full-blown version.

<*That explains why mana is so slow here. We can't pull in mana until it's out of the Dungeon's control. If we do, it'll try to pull us apart. We have to weaken it's hold. The further we push and the more power we use, the more we can claim while cutting off its source and weakening it.*>

"Right," I confirmed. Knowing full well that I was talking out of my tail at this point, but the plan was sound. "We get our power from Dungeon Stone. If we can convert its Dungeon Stone to our control, it'll feed us its power instead. It won't be fast, but it'll be safe."

Mera clapped idly behind us like she'd known that all along, and I never wanted to punch someone in their stupid face more than her at that moment. I got up to say as much when I heard a dull thud, matched with a rush of heat, and watched as the shapely blue Core shot away, thrown from the shore.

A furrow of sand led to where Amber stood, shields lowering to her sides as she began screaming out at the useless woman with her hands balled into fists. "If you're going to be a thorn in our side, go somewhere else. Put up or shut up, you spoiled brat!"

Yep, I was definitely glad I'd taken the time to help her now, not that I'd ever had a second thought about it. Though seeing her like this brought about… other thoughts. Amber was attractive when she was acting like a summer afternoon, but she was like a thunderstorm now that she had some confidence: equal parts beautiful and dangerous. She was someone who could be a leader if she learned how. Saria would have liked her once she got past Amber's self-doubt and that ever-so-slight tinge of prejudice against Foxkin.

Despite the damage the shield bashing must have caused her, Mera moved through the water like Fiona moved through the air and said nothing more as she returned to the beach. There was a deadly acid in her gaze as she settled in, and I got the distinct feeling we weren't done with her yet. For the time being, however, her silence gave us time to progress with our plan.

To everyone's surprise, Agar was not the strongest of us Dungeon mana wise. At D1, he was the closest to the next Rank and had about sixteen hundred mana, nearly four hundred more than me. Pyros was actually first in line at D2 with two thousand. Two. Thousand. He had nearly eight hundred more than I did. Amber was at D2 and had as much as I did, twelve hundred. Fiona was the weakest of us, a D2 with only a thousand Dungeon mana. She had a significantly higher Water mana reservoir, nearly double my own combined, but she had said she wasn't a front-line fighter; maybe Dungeon mana had some relation to our abilities when we'd been alive?

More likely, it had to do with our Core type.

Amber and I were both hybrids, both at the same level, and both had the same amount of power; she had more even stores of Elemental mana, probably because she could use her mana when she'd been alive. Whether that was true or not, I'm sure there was a connection.

Together, we had seven thousand Dungeon Mana, something that I assumed would be well over what a D class, and maybe even a C class Dungeon could have access to. With that and thanks to what we'd learned from our screw up, the five of us knew we could combine our mana into a single effort, so we stuck together as we began our slow descent into the darkness, stealing Influence as we went.

Even together, the Dungeon's mana still felt cold as its power continued to claw at our souls, but our combined power mitigated the pain. Instead of trying to cycle in new power, we pushed Dungeon mana out into the air and stone. Just as it had with Rembar, our powers mingled, this time forcing back the Dungeon's Influence, warming the world around us. With the warmth came a trickle of power, restoring the Dungeon mana we'd spent in the process.

It was exhausting work. What we were doing shouldn't have even worked, but it did, and I wasn't going to question it. There'd be time for questions later. Well, if there was a later.

"Harder than I thought, but we're making progress," Agar said as we passed completely into the darkness, seeming to agree with my train of thought.

Everyone nodded to that, but it had to be done. If we slacked, the Dungeon could summon minions behind us to cut off our escape or worse, overwhelm us with just its power. No, we couldn't cut corners here.

It took what felt like three quarters of an hour for us to fully enter the maw of the Dungeon. We left not an ounce of the Dungeon's Influence as we went, and our reward was a steady refreshment of our power. Split as many ways as it was, it wasn't much, but it was something. If we rested for a few minutes, we'd start to see results, but any time we stopped, an uneasy feeling of the cold, wet power began creeping back into the stone around us to press against our warmth. We rested as often as we dared as we made the trek down into the darkness. Fear or not, we'd be useless in combat without power.

In what felt like hours, we finally reached the first true room of the Dungeon. It wasn't much to look at as far as we could see, but it had a deeper, slimier feeling about it. A well-worn path of stone pavers, an obvious trap, led further into the darkness while holes dotted the landscape on either side of us. The ceiling was lower than in the chamber I'd made, maybe about only about nine feet high? From the way roof of the cave rose and fell, it might have been little more or less in some places. The cave had a greenish blue light about it, giving it a firefly's glow. Strange, glowing green pools dotted the landscape as well, making a warning of the world itself. Objects were visible, but everything further off was obscured. Despite the natural Dungeon glow, it wasn't the kind of place where you could see too accurately without more light.

"I got this," I said proudly, filtering my power into a spell. A moment later, wisps of burning light filled the chamber as I willed, just below the ceiling, one about every ten feet in all directions.

The size of the room was impressive to say the least and it took about twelve of the small burning opal stars to cast light on everything. Even under my light, the scene wasn't much to look at. The floor was rocky but flat, like any cave's floor should be, but it was unnaturally straight given so much water was pooling around. From door to door, at least what I'd call a door, the cave was about a hundred yards across, with what looked like algae-ridden pools of water dotting the landscape. Above each of the green and blue pools was a large stalactite dripping a phosphorescent green liquid into the pool giving it a slight glow as they absorbed my magical light. A quick view told me enough to know the setup wasn't for decoration. The water was completely placid as each drop collided with the surface every few seconds, as if the motion was being purposefully stifled after the initial impact.

To my surprise, Agar spoke first. "Slimes." Disgust laced his voice as he gripped the hilt of Lena all the tighter. "Disgusting."

Amber followed his words. Apparently clued in as she looked around the landscape. "Slimes? You think so?" she asked as she thought twice about taking another step. "It seems a little obvious."

The Dwarven Core nodded. "Aye. I've seen enough slime dens in my time." As if to punctuate the idea, he pointed around the edges of the room. "There aren't any places to hide other than the pools. No sounds or rises either. It can't be anything else with a set up like this."

I liked knowing what was around us as much as the next Foxkin, which was also me, but I'd been a bit sheltered as far as my knowledge of monsters went. I knew when to sit back and let others fill in the gaps. "Suggestions?"

"They're stupid creatures," Agar began as if he were talking to an ill-informed child. Maybe he was always this abrasive? Either way, I simply frowned and listened. "They're nothing more than condensed Elemental mana with an ill-defined magic Core." He pointed before

196

he began speaking again. "See that drip? It's a natural mana condensation point, a slime hive."

I nodded. It seemed simple enough. "So... break it and move on?"

Agar nodded his head. "Yes. It will take some effort, but the loot will be better than just killing the slimes. If we don't destroy it, we might have to worry about small slimes spawning in the time from when we leave to when we come back. It'd be our best move really." He made the choice seem like it had been obvious.

"Then why are we talking?"

The dwarf's tone took on a bit of huffiness. "Because we aren't ten feet tall to be able to hit 'em. If all we do is smash the tip, the slime primer will just come in faster intervals."

In my peripheral vision I saw Fiona jump as something caught her attention. She pointed to the water. As she did, I just happened to notice a perfectly rounded stone moving through it like a fish. The Core, I assumed. It was smaller than I had anticipated, no bigger than my fist. I thought that it'd be a weapon of some kind, but it was like our own.

"Rem should provoke it," Amber said giving me a warm smile. "He has the staff, and an arrow might just scare it off."

I gave her my best incredulous look before deeming her to be sufficiently rebuked. Then I answered, "I don't think bait is a good career path, Amber."

She gave me her best smile. "Come on, Rem. We can't risk it pulling Agar in, and you can always make another staff once we take the room and rest."

But I liked my staff.

"Fine..." Sighing softly, I prodded the pool of 'water' with my staff in an attempt to get the creature's attention. "Might as well get this over with then." It definitely wasn't water. The blue liquid was thicker than it looked and resisted the push from the butt of my staff. I didn't even manage to break the surface tension. I was slightly insulted. I would not be shown up by a pool of slimy water. Putting a bit more force behind my prodding, I shoved the butt into the liquid and screamed at it. "Come on!"

When the water began to tug back, I stumbled forward before pulling back against it. The slimy water came forth in a long tendril as Agar helped me stagger further away from the pool. My wish was granted as the creature advanced. With the surface tension broken, the slime began to grow, oozing out from around the edges and following my staff. Unfortunately for it, I had become attached to my new weapon and slammed the butt of it back into the ground against a thin tentacle. The slime splashed into four small blobs and instead of staying place like a good corpse, it began to crawl back to join its greater form. Yep, I had definitely got its attention, the slime rose to into a tower, pulling itself from the death drop.

I learned an important lesson that day: be careful what you wish for because djinns are assholes.

Chapter Twenty-Four
Slimes are Assholes

Though I had been the first to engage, Agar took command the moment after we'd begun. "Form up behind me!"

His confidence was as inspiring as his axe was big, but as I looked over the gelatinous form of the creature, I doubted it would be enough. If the slime was as gooey as it looked, sharp weapons wouldn't be the way to go. The wounds would just reform themselves. I thought about using Forbid to get some testing on it done, but there might be something more important later, so I focused on the others as Agar led the charge.

Whether or not it would be effective, it was satisfying on a visceral level to watch and hear Lena slosh through the gooey body. Bits of the creature went flying, but as I thought, it seemed to do little damage as the slime continued to slug forward, leaving behind a trail of viscous glowing jelly. When it came too close, Amber lunged forward with inhuman speed with Pyros close on her heels.

Her shields and his fists slammed into the body again and again from the front and side, sending ripples through the form and blowing off pieces of the body as the force passed through the surface tension. It was as if every attack of the pair were bombs going off, with the auras of Air and Fire around their weapons pushing out on impact, sending gale force flames into its hulking bulk at each impact.

Pyros was good, I had to admit, but Amber was something different. It was like an instinct for her, a second nature, as her forearms slammed the shields into the body and jumped back before a tendril could spear or engulf her in slime.

To my horror, they weren't doing enough. More and more slime began to pour out from the pool behind it, following the path of ooze to its master. The color was thicker now, and I had no idea what this meant as I joined the fray, smashing apart the smaller tendrils with the tips of the staff.

Thankfully, someone did.

"It's adapting!" Agar declared, pulling back a bit as his axe sliced a tentacle off cleanly.

I watched for a moment as the limbs fell slower from the body, like they were getting tougher. Amber's shield bashes and Pyros's burning fists threw less and less slime with each strike, too. Then, I saw it again. The small stone was racing from point to point. Wherever it stopped, the slime condensed like a rippling pool and shot forth to attack. There was a pattern! I grinned, turning to Fiona with a plan in mind.

"Can you hit that?"

She looked and let out an audible sigh, unable to do much but shake her head before she transmitted her message.

<It's too dark and too fast in there.>

I could see her point and took another moment to think. If she couldn't see it, that would be a bit of a problem, but one I could help with. It was nothing that a little wisp of light couldn't cure. Well, as long as slimes didn't eat magic spells. I probably should have asked more questions, but they would have stopped me if I was about to do something stupid. I gave her a slight nod, a grin, and focused my power.

And Rem said, let there be light.

All at once, the Core inside the creature flickered to life with a silvery blue light.

It really didn't like that.

Startled, the Core tried to move from my light, but it was no use. The Will-of-the-Wisp followed it with a bright, magical glow that lit up the room in a slimy turquoise light. As long as I kept my focus, there would be no escape for it, but even with that knowledge, Fiona was still right. It was moving fast, but it wasn't as fast as it had been. My eyes were easily able to keep up with the Core due to the confined space, or maybe it was easier because the adapting slime of the creature kept it from blending in too well. All in all, it added up to one thing.

Slimes sucked, and I hated them.

As much as I hated them, there was a bright side to its adaptation. If the creature was hardening to protect itself against us, I had an idea of what to do next.

Staff joined blade, fist, and shield as we began pounding on the creature's form again. With every strike, the creature's body became harder and less pliable as it upped its defense to lessen the loss of its mass of slime. Though Agar's blade cuts were shallower by the strike, the slime moved more slowly to fill the wounds and the Core became more and more sluggish as it found places to settle in for an attack.

Each time it rested, Fiona took the chance to fire shots from her bow. The sharpened shell tips were too slow though, as the slime slowed the impact sufficiently for the Core to get out of the way of the arrows.

Then, it struck again.

A tendril of slime shot out, wrapping around Amber at the waist and lifting her from the ground. Like a whelp with a rope, it began to shake her sharply back and forth trying to snap non-existent bones. Thankfully—as long as we had mana—Manifestations were more stable than our flesh and blood bodies.

"I don't like this!" Amber screamed as it continued to shake her like a toy so violently even I could feel the drain on our combined mana flow as she recovered. "Get me down!"

After the cry, I extended the staff and brought it down on the bulk of the slime, only to be bounced back with enough force to send me off my feet and tumbling back into the ground. Agar moved between the creature and me before swiping for Amber's tendril. Three hacks later, the limb fell free and Amber's shields shattered as they hit the ground hard.

"I'm spent!" Amber called as she rolled away from another strike. This time, instead of splattering away, the tendril broke stone and sent chunks into the air as it came to rest like a fallen tree limb.

"Got it!" Pyros called back and moved in to fill out the weakened ranks with his burning strikes.

The assault was as relentless as I'd ever seen as the elements clashed. Each strike made the slime seize up a little more until the form was nearly solid. My split attention paid off now more than ever. If it weren't for the glowing Will-of-the-Wisp on the Core, it would have been invisible within the slimy bulk. Agar saw it like others saw the sun on a clouded day and slashed for it near the peak of its head. With a heavy clang, his weapon was knocked off course by an arrow.

"Watch it!" he called back to the annoyed looking merfolk.

Fiona shrugged and readied another shot. Amber continued to fall back behind the front line as her power drained. I watched for a moment as a glow outlined where her weapons had been, but nothing happened. She was too weak to Manifest them again, but she had done her job.

Before we even realized it, Fiona notched another arrow and fired while the other three of us were on the attack. There was a satisfying crack of stone on stone, and the slime made the worst kind of noise before it exploded! For twenty feet in all directions, the world was coated in sticky, slimy, blue-green goo.

Even with being murdered, I was definitely sure that being covered in the body of my enemy had to rank as one of the worst things I'd ever felt.

Slime dribbled down my fur, squelched in my ears and under my feet. My tail couldn't even swish from side to side without feeling or flinging the offending ooze in another direction. I could even taste it! Why had I thought I'd need to taste! By the Pantheon, why! It tasted as bad as it smelled: a particularly terrible bouquet of rotting, dead fish mixed with skunk oil and embalming fluid. It was as if the Core of the creature was holding back some final, horrible trick just below the surface tension, but now there was nothing to stop that from bleeding into my nose. If I could, I would have retched.

The others seemed to be having the same problems I had, and since we couldn't Manifest ourselves again if we popped, the smell had to be tolerated. It also highlighted another difference between our Dungeons and this one. Here, corpses persisted.

Minutes after we recovered and Amber's body had healed, the slime continued to paint the walls and us. The smell was almost tolerable now, but it really, really didn't make anything better. As if remembering where we were, the dwarf barked an order.

"Alright, look for loot."

I really, really didn't want to go rooting through the slime. A quick look around told me the others felt the same. Disgust painted everyone's face, and he barely held the expression himself, but Agar was right. If our minions dropped loot, these should too. We could find something useful in the creature's remains.

After a few moments, we found what we could call loot spread across the hall if we were stretching the idea of what loot might be. A shattered blue Core of the slime monster, a vial of something blue, and another glowing blue stone.

Agar, Amber and I moved these items into the tunnel that lead out—so that the Dungeon couldn't reabsorb them—and we began the process of claiming the room for ourselves. Since we already had a foothold and a fresh flow of Dungeon mana, it went faster this time, and to our surprise, the other pools were emptied already. As our Influence spread, we could see why: the one slime had spread itself throughout the room for easy combat. The pools themselves were actually only five feet deep and had their own treasures at the bottom.

Guess who got to go down to get those particular prizes?

Being the most agile, I went back and forth grabbing a few pieces of armor, a flask of red fluid, and a small, glowing red rock. These joined the others back in the hall.

"We really need bags," I commented as I dropped another item in the pile.

"Then next time we're shoved through a barrier into a hostile Dungeon, you remember the bag," Agar snapped.

Frustration began to grow, but Amber put a hand on my shoulder. It was a calming touch, and enough to get my attention back on task. I ignored the comment and sat down to cycle the newly created Dungeon mana. It wasn't as fast or as potent as where we'd come from, but the power was there, coursing through us. Soon, it felt like I was carrying water in my muscles. Mana sloshed within me as the returns grew beyond my capacity. Without my Dungeon to push the mana back out to I was hitting my limit. The Will-of-the-Wisp just couldn't drain my power fast enough.

"Is anyone else at capacity?" I asked looking to those that had joined me. One by one they nodded except for Agar who looked deep in mediation.

"Convert it to your element, then use the rest to summon minions to hold the room in case it tries to push back," Pyros called back. Around him, a small mob of the burning chimera squirrels I'd seen before had already begun to gather.

How everyone else seemed to already know so much about Dungeons was a mystery, but at this point, I didn't care. Even split five ways, we were getting more than a single Core could use at once with our limited reserves.

As Pyros suggested, I converted what I could into Celestial mana until I felt my Dungeon reserve nearly drain. When my Celestial reserves were full again, I began drawing in power then pumping mana into constructs. Four armored aether foxes popped into being and took positions around me as the others summoned their Dungeon variant. Soon, squirrels, rock monsters, foxes, cats, and crabs began to fill the corners of the room.

Dungeon Core Rank D2
Mastered Skills: 5 of 5
Secondary Skills: 0
7/9 requirements met to reach Rank C
      Absorb a new raw material
      Reach Nexus Size 2
      Absorb a new Bestiary Component
      Trigger a passive cycling of Influence
      Fabricate your Heart Chamber
      Create a Minion
      Create a Guardian
Dungeon Core Nexus Size 2
Dungeon Core Material - Opal/Amethyst
Mana Types - Celestial/Umbral/Dungeon
Mana Reserves:
      Celestial - 350/350

Umbral - 20/20
Dungeon - 1000/1200
Mana Reduction:
-2% to Dungeon Mana Regeneration - 4x Aether Foxes

Each creature I summoned was a slight drain on my power at first it seemed, while keeping them around actively slowed my mana regeneration. Somehow, I knew this without looking, but I had to check to verify it. It was strange how in tune I was now with my power when it sustained my very being.

I was surprised by Pyros's use of his elemental version of creature. It was a strain to use my attuned mana to support the Celestial version of the aether fox, but maybe this wasn't as hard for the others? Maybe they didn't have the same restrictions mine had? In the end, I didn't question it as the small red creatures chattered and hissed as they clung like static-charged lint to their Dungeon Core. They seemed very attached to Pyro. Obsessed might have been a better word.

With minions summoned and our bodies recovered, we gave the order that they should stop slimes from spawning and then we were ready to move on. If every room was like this, we would be in for a long trip.

By the glow of Pyros's weapons, we didn't have much need for our senses or my spells. As an added bonus, the more power we took, the more it began to push against our unseen foe. We didn't need to push as hard anymore as our power bled into the room ahead before we even took a step forward. It didn't permeate the stone as we did, but it provided sufficient coverage so that the enemy Dungeon couldn't push us back as it had previously.

Along the way, small holes in the wall oozed out fist-sized slime that tried to fight us.

"Careful!" Agar called as a few bolted from the wall and took to the air, like darts.

Fight might have been an overestimation of what the creatures were capable of.

As a tiny slime whizzed by, I made the mistake of slapping one like a fly between my hands, only for it to sizzle and burn before I could absorb the creature's remains. I cursed, Agar and Pyros laughed, and we all became a bit more cautious about the rhythmic timing of the small swarms.

Stupid slimes.

Every two minutes, more slimes spawned from the walls we hadn't passed. They weren't powerful—unless you were stupid enough to touch them—so we took turns splattering them with our weapons rather than our hands. Unlike with the larger slime, we didn't get anything but more slime that sizzled and dissolved into the rock it splashed onto.

In reality, it wasn't as bad as I thought. In fact, it was even kind of exciting. With every slime we splattered, I hoped for something new and interesting I could claim as my own. It wasn't the same as destroying the golems that Ansith created, but it still made my heart race with each minion kill. I would have enjoyed it more if I liked the people I was with just a bit more, but even they were growing on me: even if it was slowly. All in all, we were handling ourselves pretty well considering every step we took was a life or death situation. As we approached the end of the hallway and the gateway of the next room, our Influence pooled. The mana was much denser here and stopped our approach.

I wasn't the only one to notice as our merry band came to a halt at the end of the hallway. The room was obscured by the two clashing mana types, but if I reached out I could feel the composition. The barrier and the air around it was thick with Water and Earth mana, but it felt strangely sticky rather than fluid. I pulled back, and the shell of mana followed. A tendril of the slimy variant of mana lingered against my own. It felt dirty, as of its own volition it pulled back with a strangely defined snap of mana. I felt violated.

It was then I decided two things: slime Dungeons are assholes, and if I ever came across another one, I'd either burn it to the ground with my Celestial wrath—once Vul taught me how to invoke Celestial wrath—or avoid it entirely.

Chapter Twenty-Five
Heart of the Matter

We all felt the strange pull the mana had as we tried to press forward, but no one was eager to go further than reaching out with their hands. Even Agar hesitated as he pushed Lena against the bubble of mana, only for the blade to get jerked one way then the other before he withdrew it from the slimy mana's hold with a noticeable effort. Whatever was there wasn't going to be the pushover—and I use that term loosely—that the slime before had been.

"Agar should go first," I offered before presenting my argument. "Whatever's there isn't going to be friendly, and he's already shown he can handle himself."

Amber gave me a look as though scandalized, but didn't object. I didn't think she would, but maybe she felt she was better to go in first with those shields of hers? Either way, I was confident I wasn't going to be first, and if I had to, I'd make sure she wouldn't be either. Of all of us, Agar was the strongest front-line fighter. Eyes shifted back and forth before a voice picked up. To my surprise, it wasn't Agar that countered.

"We all can handle ourselves," Pyros turned to Agar. "As much as I don't want to, I agree with Rem though. You're the only one with armor anyways."

Another surprise as Fiona nodded then made a slight wave for the door, both figuratively with her hand and literally with a small illusion of mana. It was a waste, but the gesture was effective none the less.

Agar made no arguments as he shrugged and hefted Lena up onto his shoulder. "We'll have quite the run of it then. Give me a minute, then follow behind me."

With that, he slashed at the barrier with Lena. Rather than the curious prod he had begun with, an arc of green mana followed in the weapon's wake and cleanly cut into the barrier of the sealed off room. Mana began leaking both ways as I felt ours slip into the rip and another strand try to mingle with ours as it came out. The two powers fought in a war of attrition both sides refusing to relent, but neither side giving an inch to the other. Through the gap, the room looked no different from the room we had just been in. It was large sure, tall as the last room doubled at least, with a perfectly flat floor and one large stalactite decorating the center of the room. With a glistening drop hanging from it, even I could tell it was a giant slime condenser.

Walking towards Agar, I gave the dwarf a pat to the shoulder. "Make your own luck," I said with a bit of a smile.

He nodded. "I will." He gave my hand a pat as well before turning to the group. "Don't follow me until I give the signal."

We all nodded, and with that, Agar had stepped through the gap. In the blink of an eye, he vanished, and the seal knitted itself back together.

For too long, there was nothing but silence.

Silence… until Agar's scream pierced the veil.

A chill rushed through me as I turned on myself. What had we done? Why'd we send him in alone?

Without a second thought, I pushed off from the balls of my feet with my staff at the ready and sunk into the veil of foreign mana, body and all. The icy cold barrier of mana was weaker than I thought, and I began to push past the churning mana towards the next room. Despite that thought, the barrier still wasn't as weak as my own damned reasoning. What in the Mists had I done?

I hung in the air for a few moments as the world shifted around me, but the ice in my veins passed as quickly as it started. There was almost no time to process what had happened as I landed on my feet in a place that looked markedly different from the room we glanced through the tear of mana.

My eyes were as quick as my wit as I took everything in. Slime dripped down the walls in a nearly cylindrical room, the roof was a huge, polished purple-blue-green stone, and near the middle of the room was a horrific sight. The creature was at least eight feet tall with humanoid arms and a puddle for legs. Its skin was a transparent gelatinous purple-green-blue, dripping off of the very solid-looking bones that gave it a form. As if to make the disgustingly creepy look complete, the creature had two, glowing purplish gemstones for eyes inside the otherwise empty sockets. Its back was turned, looking at something further in. Through its body, the target was clear as the noon sky: Agar.

I almost lost my nerve looking at him laying so close, yet so far away. He looked almost as good as I did when Cecil's strong man was done with me. Though Agar's head was in a good, solid piece, his arms were ripped from their sockets and laying haphazardly on the ground next to him. Like a disarmed, stuck pig, his mana was pooling like blood from the wounds as the creature reached for the closer of the two arms. Then to my horror, its entire body turned to face me as it began munching on the constructed arm of brown Earthen energy. The monster's purple eyes flared from time to time but were locked on me as it chewed.

If it was trying to intimidate me, it had done quite well.

My staff was raised, pointing at the creature, but I wasn't sure how much good it would do. The creature barely acknowledged me as it stared through me and stretched its jaw like a snake to take in the rest of its meal, then letting one of its free arms slither back behind it, to reach for the other arm to consume. All the while, an odd mote of light played from within the slime horror as it digested the arm.

A moment later, the others joined me and were just as horrified as I was by the gelatinous zombie. For a brief moment, it was a small comfort to know that some horrors transcended the boundaries of aspects like race, species, and personal taste. In the moment of distraction, it finished the second arm as it had the first. There was no cry this time as my wits came back to me. Unfortunately, it was going back to Agar for thirds by the time I had a plan.

Screwing up my courage, I gave one last silent prayer before putting my plans into actions. *Goddess Vul, if you're watching me, please, don't let me fail now.*

"I'm the fastest of us and we need to get Agar. Get ready to pull him out of here," I ordered and prepared my favorite one trick pony for the occasion. "Slimy bastard, I *Forbid* you from touching me!"

Celestial mana drained before the power of the Word of Command like it was being kept in an open bottomed bucket, but the power washed over the creature with a shimmering opaline light. The form of the monster strained, and for the first time it made a noise other than crunching or crying. It roared in defiance. Bits of slime flew from its maw as my spell's effect took hold and my window began to tick down. I had maybe two, three minutes at most, so I did my best not to waste a moment.

Quick as a whip, I ran to kneel next to Agar. I didn't need to register how I'd almost slipped on his liquid mana to know how far gone he really was. Lena was missing, his arms were off, and his normal coloring of Earthen browns was fading into paler shades by the moment.

Life flickered in his eyes as he took me in, stopping on the violet of my ears for a moment before laughing weakly. "Never thought you'd be the one to try and save me, Rem."

"Shut up," I ordered, feeling the creature strain against my power. It had more mental fortitude than I thought. At the rate it was pushing, Forbid wouldn't last much longer. I scooped Agar up the best I could, only for the slick, liquid mana to start to mingle with my crystalline fur and the slipperiness made the dwarf fall from my grasp with a resounding thud.

I tried to apologize, but it did no good as he shook his head to stop me from talking. His voice was weak, straining for each word. "This is the Dungeon's Core. We're inside the Core's soul."

I felt an involuntary heave lingering in my throat as that processed. We were in the Dungeon's soul, in its heart and mind. No wonder the room was so different and no wonder Agar had vanished when he walked in. We were fighting inside its Core! Was this how Dungeon combat was done? I pushed the thought away and instead focused on the dwarf. Cracks ran through his form as liquid mana ran freely from some wounds and congealed in others. I wasn't a practiced healer, but even I knew the damage was near fatal. If I didn't stem the flow and find a way to fix the damage, he'd die as surely as the winters were cold.

I felt weak, helpless as he continued to bleed out while my restraint spell continued to strain against the creature's force. It was experienced in the D ranks while I was still new to my power. I needed another way out, another card to play from my sleeve, but I didn't have any.

At my back, I heard the creature roar again as it turned to those it could give more attention to. Pyros rushed with Amber in his wake as Fiona supported them from afar, but it wouldn't be enough. I couldn't listen any more as my world focused on the bleeding form in front of me. Agar had so much mana to lose, but the Core wasn't absorbing it. As long as he was still bleeding, he had Influence over himself. As long as he was still fighting, he wasn't lost yet.

I absorbed my staff to refresh some of my reserves and focused on what I had. A few cantrips, a few tricks, but that couldn't heal him. I hadn't learned to mend flesh...

But... he didn't have flesh anymore, did he?

We didn't have flesh at all.

Hope began to rise in my chest as the paths converged onto a single idea.

We weren't made of skin and bone! We were crystalline mana constructs, and most constructs weren't considered to be alive. We could be fixed!

I may have been a fledgling Oracle still, but there was one thing I could do properly.

"Mend." The dim feeling mana filled my thoughts and spell forms as I pushed the spell out into Agar's form. There was no response from him, so I did the only thing I could think of. "Mend. Mend! Mend, damn you!"

It had to work.

"Mend!"

The idea was sound enough. We were constructs after all, why shouldn't it work? It wasn't though, so I improvised. I knew how to mend broken objects, and we were only slightly different. Dungeon Mana wasn't cutting it, so I had to try something else. Checking my mana reservoirs again, I noticed I was using Dungeon mana to cast the

211

cantrip. It was my default now, just like ambient mana had been when I was alive. Celestial was more attuned to healing though, so what happened if I pushed that mana into the Node to cast the spell?

I'd never tried to do something like that before. Mana just flowed as it willed when I used a Node. Sure, I'd crafted using Fabrication to make things from different mana. It shouldn't be much different than that. Right?

Looking down at the quickly fading form that was the disarmed dwarf, I couldn't imagine anything much worse happening.

With that in mind, I focused on my Celestial mana and pushed the two pieces together in my Nexus. It was harder than I imagined, but the mana obeyed and flowed into the Node, triggering it with a glimmering opalescent light. So far, so good. There was only one thing left to it.

Please don't blow up, I asked of the half-baked idea with equal parts respect and fear.

Thankfully, it did not explode.

As the Node reached its casting capacity of Celestial mana, the spell triggered. There was no sparkling, no healing-like glow, or even a glimmer of light like I'd seen in my memories of healing. Instead, the spell was alien, unlike anything I'd seen before.

Instead of targeting a specific part of the body like flesh, bone, or gaping open wounds seeping mana-blood, it sent itself out searching over Agar's fallen form like an opal mist rolling across a forest lake in the late fall, serene and meandering in its approach. As it washed over him, I felt a drain on my spirit growing stronger and stronger. Whatever I put into the spell wasn't enough to do its job, and it was pulling for more, forcibly converting my Dungeon mana into Celestial as some kind of safe guard.

Well, at least if it failed to heal him, I would have died trying.

Before I had to shatter the injured form to stop the spell from killing me, the pulling stopped, and with it, Agar's bleeding. Fear gripped at whatever constituted my heart as I looked down at him.

Was he breathing?

Could he breathe?

Had I made things worse?

As if to answer, the liquid mana around him began to quiver like the slime beast, the green sludge congealing into gelatinous ooze that wobbled towards the broken form of Agar. I thought about striking it, but I knew it wasn't a slime no matter how much it looked like one. More and more of the mana blood condensed and bounced towards the remains of his arms. In a flurry of motion, the blob shot out tendrils of itself that attached to Agar's jagged stumps. It was as disgusting as it was fascinating. At least it was fascinating until the screaming started. Then it was more on the ear-piercing end of the spectrum.

Agar screamed unholy, demonic murder furiously in an incomprehensible language as the gel solidified into a new set of unarmored arms and then moved over him, mending what it could of his battered armor. In mere moments, the screaming had stopped, and he pounced like a Felkin back on his feet. I wasn't really sure how or why, but he ran back into the battle, pausing only to scoop up Lena and give me a nod of thanks before he leapt onto the creature's back to the cry of, "For the clan!"

I was exhausted, but Agar made me laugh all the same. Dwarves were strange creatures, but I couldn't fault him too much. We Foxkin had our own ways, and I had to uphold them and protect my clan, and my friends, at any cost.

When my legs refused to work after the spell resolved itself, I chalked the loss up to fall into a price worth paying, then a light shimmered for just a moment in my vision.

Chapter Twenty-Six
Slimes Continue to be Assholes

From the moment Agar left my side, something was wrong.

~Help me!~

Maybe it was the tiny voice ringing in my ear from nowhere? That was probably it. The voice was tiny and pitiable, like a child being punished for something it didn't do, and that shook me. Yep, hearing voices was much more pressing than the fact my legs couldn't move. Much more important than the effects of mana fatigue. I tried to focus, and my two Nexus appeared once more.

Dungeon Core
Rank D2
Mastered Skills: 5 of 5
Secondary Skills: 0
7/9 requirements met to reach Rank C
 Absorb a new raw material
 Reach Nexus Size 2
 Absorb a new Bestiary Component
 Trigger a passive cycling of Influence
 Fabricate your Heart Chamber
 Create a Minion
 Create a Guardian
Dungeon Core Nexus Size 2
Dungeon Core Material - Opal/Amethyst
Mana Types - Celestial/Umbral/Dungeon
Mana Reserves:
 Celestial - 20/350
 Umbral - 20/20

Dungeon - 200/1200

Oracle
Rank D1
Class Skills Mastered: 3
Secondary Skills: 2
8/9 requirements met to reach Rank C
Mana Types - Celestial/Umbral/Dungeon
Mana Reserves:
      Celestial - 20/350
      Umbral - 20/20
      Dungeon - 200/1200
Class Passive for Mastery:
      None Earned

I'd drained myself too much, and I wasn't recovering, which was odd in itself. Checking myself again, I wasn't hurt, and my form felt solid, but nothing else wanted to respond. My feet still couldn't move, but I could smile and hope for the best as my inner monologue became a force all its own.

~I'm going to die here. Please, help me escape!~

Tell me about it.

Speaking from my deepest fears, the small voice ringing in my ears was about as much fun as getting my tail caught in a bear trap. It was more pronounced today than usual, so that was fun. Shaking the whimpering away, I turned my attention back to the Core I'd managed to heal.

Agar had been a surprise from start to finish today. That's the good kind of surprise, not the way my parents had been when I was born. Nearly killing one another over my mother's fidelity wasn't a good thing.

Memories aside, the dwarf was a positive. I had thought he was nothing more than your average warrior. I had never been more glad to be wrong. There was a real warrior in there as he ripped at the creature, flinging slime in all directions as Lena sang through with the violence of his blows. For the first time, I had a real respect for the dwarf.

I may not have liked him, but for once, was I glad to have him on my side.

~ Can you even hear me? Are you deaf or just as dumb at this thing?~

I was less glad to have my mind being so pessimistic.

At least there was plenty to watch.

Agar roared back into combat with all the fury and fire of a pissed-off mother dragon protecting her clutch of eggs. While our allies were on the defense, the dwarf lashed at the creature again and again.

Agar's blood rage was a thing of beauty.

That didn't mean he was safe, but he seemed to be out of its attack range as he clung to its head. The slime fought like a squid, but the sweeping motions of its tentacles weren't easily predictable. The creature would raise a limb halfway through a swing and slam it down if it saw fit, but it seemed to be almost feral.

I couldn't see Amber or Fiona, but I did see Pyros, and, in its raging fit, so did the slime.

The slime cut its movements short and jerked to the right so that a whip caught the Fire Core in the side. His body seemed to collapse in just a bit before the momentum took Pyros, flinging him to stick like a thistle burr against the slimed wall. It was not a soft landing. As his body hit the wall, a cracking noise snapped through the air, and bright red mana seeped slowly from his cracked side.

I wanted to rush to him, but I still couldn't move. Red mana dripped across the slimy wall as I watched, searing the surface until Pyros took matters into his own hands. A flare of white-hot fire burned the slime around his arms, and he did something I don't think I'll ever forget.

Pyros screamed as he turned his magic on himself. There was another white flash as his hands pressed against his wound. His simulacrum's wound melted together, sealed as his body returned to its normal red. The wound was closed, but it was never going to be that easy. He couldn't see it though.

"Pyros! On your right!" I yelled.

Slimes were forming on the wall, following the scent—or whatever sense it was that slimes used—of prey.

A quick look to the side was all it took for him to redouble his efforts. He didn't have any time left to pull the rest of himself free, so I couldn't rely on him for help. Pyros was busy enough smashing baby slimes with his flaming knuckles as they tried to gather enough forces to swarm and devour him.

It was getting harder to care though. I felt exhausted, just calling out to him felt like it had taken everything I had.

Maybe if I just closed my eyes for a moment…

"Rem!"

Amber.

Focus was difficult, but I knew that voice even if my spirit felt like it was about to drift off into sleep. Amber's voice pierced the veil of exhaustion loud and clear, but no, the once-timid creature wouldn't settle for just that. She had to be impressive. She barreled straight towards me, dodging the tendrils of slime like she had been made for that activity. Amber performed like a seasoned hunter as she dodged here, stuck a leg out there to just narrowly miss a strike, tumbled and jumped between whips, and ended with a diving slide between a pair of tendrils to come to a stop next to me.

If she wasn't my friend, I'd say a few more flattering words.

"Hi," I said simply as the dust of what I assumed to be dried slime came to settle. "Fancy meeting you here."

She looked at me strangely as another whip passed over my head. Agar screamed victory a moment later, and a large bone flew in the same direction. "You realize we're in combat still, right? What's wrong?"

As the question processed, Agar roared again and yet another bone did an impressive impression of a bird as it leapt towards the other side of the room. I was glad that it wasn't me under his surgical touch. "I do, and as much as I'd like to help, my feet refuse to obey. If I didn't need them so badly, I'd walk all over them." When genuine concern crossed her face, I felt a bit less like joking and spoke plainly. "I can't move, Amber. Something… something feels wrong…"

~You know… You're going to die in here, too, if you keep ignoring me!~

I didn't want to say I was hearing voices too. I might not have been your average mortal anymore, but I knew that was wrong still at least. What did it mean by here?

Amber gave me the once over I'd seen many times before from Saria, and I winced just a bit. She was looking for injury, and when none were to be found, she shook her head. "You've got your legs. Why can't you use them?"

~Because the Dungeon's trying to absorb you. Focus on the boss!~

Huh, that was new. "I think the Dungeon's focused on me. My mana isn't recovering properly. I'm barely taking in enough to be stable."

~Oh, good. At least I'm not talking to a wall. You aren't a wall are you?~

Amber took it from there. "Guardians take a lot of mana, if we take it out, we should be able to shake its attention. Maybe?"

~In here, if you break the boss...~

I waited for a moment, expecting more of that latent knowledge from my subconscious to come, but it was all for naught. I managed a shrug. "Maybe is better than a no."

Agar caught my eye a moment later as the dwarf landed a few feet away, picked himself back up, and ran from us. A green swarm of the screeching hells followed him across the sky a moment later. Whatever he'd done, he really must have pissed it off.

The swarm sounded like a chorus of screech bats, but they were green. They were also too small, only about the same size as the ones Pyros was still splattering. Maybe it was another form of the boss or some kind of attack spell? There were a lot of uncertainties in this place. Either way, I turned my gaze back to the creature to see an entire flock of those things were still erupting from its chest, carrying its malice towards Agar and shrinking its form by almost half. It had invested a lot of itself into the play.

It was the boss's last mistake.

I felt the growing power before I saw it. The air in the room became damp. At first, I thought it was nothing more than the nature of the slime room or my own problems finally getting at me. Those simple things like a growing insanity and voices in my head. The idea left my head as soon as water began to flow across the room. Pure, blue, cleansing water that smelled like salt water ebbed and flowed quickly out and back to the source. It wasn't hard to follow it back to the merfolk, but where it was going on her was more interesting. She had pulled it all back towards her like an archer notching an arrow. It grew and flowed backwards, leaving a clean opening for her hand as if it were the bow. And the noise! It was a raging river, an ocean storm, and a whirlpool roaring together as one. The shot she had gathered looked like a sharpened tidal wave, not an arrow notched in her hands. Fiona's cerulean form flickered between solid and ethereal, barely able to hold itself together. A strong breeze from a summer shower might have been enough to do her in, but the slime noticed her too late as her archer's hand went slack.

With its lessened mass, there was nothing the monster could do to weather the blow. It had a single moment to scream in defiance at the force of nature as it approached. Water rushed over every inch of its dripping flesh, ripping away the slime under its tidal force and leaving nothing more than a stripped skeleton in its wake. Then, the attack turned back before it could break against the walls. The skeleton only twitched once before it was forced again into the churning power of the ocean.

Moment by moment, the swirling rush of water ate away at the bones that produced its body. When the skull was nothing but a pair of purple gemstones, which took practically no time at all, the attack turned upward, striking the ceiling with the force of a tidal wave.

As it collided, all the world became noise as something screamed, and Amber tried to cover me.

~Yes!~

Chapter Twenty-Seven
Spoils

The next seconds of my life were an act of pure chaos.

The slime room shattered around us like a mirror, and we fell through the air. No, 'fell' would have implied we were tripped. We were thrown from where we were to the far corners of this new place. Five thuds colliding with the wall would have been enough noise, but Vul had other plans for us.

Most of us did not get off particularly well. Agar's momentum was stopped cold against a particularly nasty looking stalagmite. It wasn't enough to shatter him thankfully, but he did let loose a colorful string of dwarven curses. So colorful in fact that I'd only heard one or two of them before. Pyros, the lucky elf he was, had been fortunate enough to simply fall forward and catch himself before he hit his face; I landed ears first in a wonderful pair of pillows. Amber didn't appreciate it nearly as much.

"Rem, are you okay?" I managed a nod. Her hands grabbed my shoulders and rolled me to the side with a little more force than necessary.

It was a bittersweet moment as my body sprawled back out on the floor. I had lost my comfortable cushions, but my body was moving again!

After she freed herself from the minuscule weight of a Celestial Foxkin, Amber took stock of herself before calling out to the group. "Everyone okay?"

It was hard to tell where we were since the chamber was dark now. The natural Dungeon light from before was nowhere to be found now that the Core was dead. I tried to focus my mana into a new batch of

Will-of-the-Wisps to light things up, but I just felt too weak. There had to be a reason.

Mana Reserves:
    Celestial - 20/350
    Umbral - 20/20
    Dungeon - 190/1200

My mana still wasn't recovering. I hadn't gained back a single point. In fact, I was still losing mana when I exerted myself. To make things worse, my power felt... cut off. I felt isolated, like I was in my own bubble of power. I could feel the power, but I couldn't reach for it. It was like running my hand along a winter rose, soft and beautiful, but dangerous to try to grab. Somehow, I knew that if I tried to grip and pull the power to me, it'd hurt me. I knew it as surely as I knew the back of my hands.

What had the enemy Core done to me? Had it broken something within me?

I didn't even want to think about my situation. If it had, did I want the others to know? I stopped moving for a new reason now as fear welled up within me.

Excluding me, a chorus of statuses from good to not so good came back to Amber, but the darkness was still a problem. Eventually, someone managed a spark of light—Pyros, if the color was to be believed—and we began to move towards each other in the center of what was evidently simple stone room. I took in everything I could: there wasn't a hint of the room we were in before. No slime coated walls, nothing to show where we had been.

"Weird."

~A Dungeon's Heart is a very different place from an invasion. You were fighting in its heartscape, or soulscape if you prefer, not this room.~

Thank you, random voice of knowledge. So, we'd been inside it's heart? Was that why it had been so strong?

The center of the room was littered with... just stuff! Boots, books, pieces of cloth, armor, weapons, hunks of stone, jewelry of all shapes and sizes, trinkets, and—strangely enough—fish, were sprawled about a tower of junk. All around the pile was purple crystal, still shimmering softly with a faint bluish-green light as it sensed the mana around it.

"We won?" I ventured to ask as I felt for any remaining Influence.

Nothing pushed back. The others seemed to focus and did the same. This time, the Dungeon stone responded and fed me till I was near bursting. I kept poking around though, searching for any shred of the enemy Dungeon's Influence. The most resistance I felt came from the area surrounding the small shards of crystal, but even that receded like the shadows to the sun as I prodded it gently with mana. They looked like my Nodes did...

~Don't touch them! Don't absorb them! Don't do anything with them!~

I jerked back my power without question at the warning. Where had that come from? Is this how the others knew what was going on?

One by one, the shards and dust of what I could only assume to be the other Core began to vanish as the others absorbed the purple crystal without a second thought, and the results were immediate. It was like someone shot them full of lightning and water. The four seemed to solidified, becoming so much more comfortable looking in their Manifested forms. For Pyros and Amber, it was harder to pinpoint what exactly was the difference as their mere presence became stronger, but Fiona and Agar especially seemed to be affected as they changed.

Fiona's illusion of water under her tail became more defined, her form seemed healthier as she... well... filled out would be the best word for it. She had looked no more than eighteen seasons before, but after she absorbed the fragments of the other Core, she seemed closer to her prime or what I assumed her prime to be. She was more herself in every way, from the way her scales glimmered, to the way she held herself, to the way she fit in her own skin. She even seemed more... blue now, a deep cerulean rather than a dark blue.

Agar was much the same in shape, but notably different in the richness of his appearance. His armor rebuilt itself around him and seemed more dense. More obviously, his dwarven beard grew, braided itself, and even seemed to become more luxurious as it began to show its own barely visible, soft green light. A moment after he seemed done, Lena returned to his hand—a surprise, given his expression—and became etched in some sort of script. The weapon too had a slight glow about it after. His browns and new shades of greens began to mingle, neither isolated to skin or armor.

Well, that didn't seem fair. I wanted power, too.

To calm myself, I nicked a small white gemstone and absorbed it while the others were busy. At least that ability still worked. As the item was broken down and its mana was added to my own I felt stronger.

Mana Reserves:
    Celestial - 120/350
    Umbral - 20/20
    Dungeon - 490/1200

That's what the healer ordered! At least I could still regain mana that way. Besides, a chunk of unrefined diamond, not quartz like I had thought, could come in handy later on.

When their empowering trance broke, I went to work on the closest items to the pile. Without missing a beat, I reached for one of the many, many bags and began tossing them one at a time to the others. I might have been a bit sour, but I wasn't stupid.

"To the victors go the spoils!" I called enjoying the sight of their faces lighting up at the thought of loot.

"Take the first share," Agar called happily back to me. "You saved my life, and as the one who made the first assault, I yield my choice to you."

There was an order to this? I guess I should have known. "That's big of you." Mists, what was that thing to say to a dwarf? Something about their parents? How did Agar phrase it before when he cursed? Eh, I decided just to wing it. "May your ancestors prize your heart."

He smiled at that. It was a pitying smile telling me I had horribly butchered whatever expression I was trying to convey, but it was a smile all the same. It made me feel a bit better about things. I may have already taken my first pick, but they didn't need to know that and I chose my 'first' item.

In a more orderly fashion than I thought possible, we split the tower mostly evenly. I ended up with a bag stuffed to the brim with useful things. After absorbing it and everything inside, I could practically feel my Codex grow heavily with useful materials. At some point, I'd really have to start delving into crafting and see what I could do. From today alone, I'd learned how to make quite a few things: four small bolts of kobold leather in blue, silver, copper, and green; a handful coins from different countries made of gold, silver, and copper; boots; the bag, made of regular cow's leather; a few rings and bracelets; a lesser healing potion; and a spellbook bound with a lock made of a gleaming, silvery metal. Of course, there was no key to it. I wanted to see if I could learn everything in it by breaking it down, but I was worried it'd be like the scroll and break itself down into its key parts if I absorbed it. I'd learn runes and ink from Absorption, but I didn't want to take the risk of losing knowledge that I so desperately wanted. Not wanting to lose my chance at more magical potential, I kept it at my side in another bag I had grabbed. I'd need to make a bookcase soon to keep track of everything if I was going to try to improve myself.

The others got equally lucky with few items of special note. Amber got a new shield made from the same metal as my lock, which she didn't absorb; Agar got more gemstones than I could shake a loot bag at; Pyros got some vials filled with what he said was an excellent oil once he absorbed them; and Fiona got herself a cape. Why she picked that, I have no idea. It did look nice in its blue fabric. It looked just as nice when she remade it with her new stable mana.

Overall, I thought we did pretty well. We were laughing and telling stories almost as soon as we'd finished, and I'd realized something. I hadn't just survived my first Dungeon run, I felt like I'd made a few new friends too. Maybe the other Cores really weren't so bad after all.

On the way out, we made small talk about ourselves and our Dungeons, though at this stage we would be better described as spheres of rock in the ground. Most of us had been in the same boat before our unfortunate issue, but hey, they should have been thanking us at this point.

One of the most important things we talked about was each other. As if we had planned it in advance, we each took turns telling our stories.

Pyros of the Ember Fields was indeed an elf, a cinder elf. Honestly, I had no idea that elves came in different flavors besides forest. He was a high rank C pyromancer in life but had a rare mana disability. He lacked the ability to expel Fire mana from his body. He'd adapted though and learned to channel it into close range attacks. That explained why he excelled in hand-to-hand combat, but what did that mean about that ball of fire from before? Some kind of drop kick? He talked about the sisters he'd left behind, his teacher, his family, and the burning flows of lava that could be found all over the black grass planes of the Ember Fields. He talked about it with such love that I couldn't bear to tell him it sounded like the Hells had come to reign over the world.

Agar, as I would for now and forever call him as opposed to his given name of Agarenth Dioa Copperbrand, third son of the Copperbrand Lineage, was an easier one to understand. He'd been a guard for the Royal Academy in Copperforge like his father before him, before being transferred into the service of the Temple of Hector, the Minor God of Metal, as a scholar when he showed potent affinities for magically working metals and stone. He had studied Ansith in depth as part of his curriculum while he was there thanks to Ansith being such a prominent dwarven artificer and runesmith. Consequently, Agar's dual interests led him to study something else, Dungeons. Well, at least that explained how he seemed to know so much about them. He talked at length, longer than the others by far, about his floor plans, minion ideas, traps, and everything. In truth he was a scholar, a warrior, and probably the most Dungeon-like among us. I liked it: especially the traps idea. Strangely, he didn't know how he died, only that he'd gone to sleep one night and awoken to his new form.

Fiona, as per usual, said little, seeming more interested in looking herself over in a hand-sized mirror or reflective blue crystal when she thought no one was looking. I took it that she wasn't comfortable with herself before she became a Dungeon and she still wasn't. Of what she did say, very little was about herself. She talked about the Inner Sea, a huge ocean of clean water at the center of the nation of Inerro. That surprised me. The nation of Inerro was on an entirely different continent to that of my clan. To get there by foot and boat would take months of travel. She also mentioned she had a Patron herself, though she wasn't a seer or an Oracle. Fiona said little more on the subject, other than that it had an effect on her original archer class, calling herself a Rank C Loch Guardian.

Amber stayed silent, lost in thought it seemed, but I knew well enough that she was more self-conscious about her lack of memory than anything else. She also spoke little of her Dungeon even to me, but she did mention her class, Shield Dancer Rank D. I could tell she wasn't willing to talk much more, so I took it upon myself to fill the gap in conversation.

The words just came so naturally as we began our trek back towards the entrance that I didn't even think before speaking. I told them about my home, my death, meeting Vul, being rescued from the fate of becoming an opal necklace, and my faithful arrival. Once I started talking, I just couldn't find a place to stop. It was strange being the one to tell a story for once. It just kept coming, although I left Amber's part of the story to her. She filled in some of the gaps as she saw fit. Finally, I reached our mutual meeting and finished talking about Ansith's attack. No one needed to hear my side of our bout, so I stopped there, only to hear a tiny fanfare in my ears.

~ Wow! You have an interesting story for sure. I like stories. I didn't get enough of them here. ~

At least someone was entertained.

We'd taken our time getting back through the Dungeon. We weren't in any hurry now that everything, at least according to Agar, was dead. We talked, made a few jokes, and exchanged small talk until we got back to the first chamber.

When we reached the mouth of the first cave with the large slime, something was out of place. Our mana felt lesser now when it should have been stronger and a quick stretch of my mana sense showed that all of our minions were gone. I had expected my will-of-the-wisp to dissipate, but did minions vanish like spells? To my surprise, everything was like the outside. Even the strange, dripping stalagmites had crumbled to fill in the three holes where the giant slime had hidden itself.

226

We pushed a bit harder through the chamber and stopped only when we reached the opening of the tunnel.

"I don't like this," Pyros warned, snapping his fingers nervously to create and dissipate a wisp of fire. I don't really think he was doing it consciously though. Had he done it before? Maybe it was a holdover from his prior life?

"I agree," Agar added. "No mana or minions — it seems off. Our status might be different, and we did destroy the Core, but I've never heard of a Dungeon's Influence reverting so quickly back to nature."

"I've never been in or met a Dungeon before, so I'll take your word for it," I said simply.

Weapons drawn—with myself as the exception, as I still couldn't manifest anything—we walked through the chamber and noticed the second warning sign. Our loot was gone. Every scrap of it was missing as if it had never been. Not a shard of glass or drip of slime was to be found, and we looked. Fiona even extended her mana senses to search for any sort of gap in our perception. She only found a void of Dungeon mana, even our Influence had vanished. Nature had reclaimed everything it seemed, but deep down, I worried it was somehow my fault. Though she did point out some interesting rocky plant life that the island seemed to be built around. It still didn't add up.

"Okay, we've got to be chasing our own tails here. Something is messing with us." I wasn't as eloquent as I could have been, but really, objects didn't just vanish for no reason.

It didn't take us long to find the source of our lost items. As we left the confines of the Dungeon, the sun was a wonderful addition. The warmth of it filled my body and gave me a new sense of self, but something was wrong. The air still smelled of salt, sea, and the breeze still blew, but something had fouled all of it. It didn't smell completely of salt anymore. It had undertones that smelled more like a river or lake. The air was cooler than it should have been, too, compared to where we had been. There, sitting on the beach as if she'd not moved a muscle was Mera. Around her, a small area of sand and soil radiated her Dungeon presence.

"What took you so long?"

With her words, the pieces fell together like leaves on the forest floor in the fall. She'd been the reason for the breakdown. She'd wiped out our minions. Most importantly… "You took our loot! Do you know how hard we worked for that?"

She shrugged, tossed some hair over her shoulder, and looked at us as we quickly left our huddle at the entrance. "You shouldn't have left it unguarded."

"It wasn't unguarded!"

"Minions are about as useful as the orders they're given," Mera shrugged. "If anyone's to blame for it, you are. Those things didn't even fight back when I killed the groups with Undertow."

Because we told them to guard against slimes, not anything. Our mistake didn't sate my fire though. I could practically feel the fur running down my neck standing on end. "We risked our lives for our survival! For that loot! What did you do?"

Mera hesitated for a moment, seeming to think before an answer came forth. "Sunned myself for the first hour or so then I waited for a prime opportunity to take advantage of the hard work of others," she said nonchalantly before laying back on the sand. "It's what ladies do, dog boy."

I bit my tongue before I snapped. If I had blood, it would have been boiling. How dare she call me a dog! Foxes were as much dogs as wolves were! "Heavy words from a scavenger."

"Scavenge is such an ugly word. Ladies don't scavenge. They use their superior cunning to work smarter, not harder —"

Harder was a good term for how Amber decked her moments before she could finish that sentence. It was a beautiful sight seeing Amber's shields, new and old, connect with Mera's face and give her so much momentum that her body flew like an arrow into the field that made up the Sundering. It didn't look like much, but it stopped her cold as she collided with the barrier and cracked across nearly every surface of her skin and swimsuit. Without so much as an ounce of grace or self-respect, Mera collided with the ground, shards breaking from her form, and her wounds seeping liquid mana that slowly evaporated back into the aether.

Her cries may have been as pitiful as her Influence had been, but I felt no pity for her, and Amber walked back to us as if nothing had happened.

"Rem," she said after a few moments, her eyes never leaving the other woman's form. "Can you heal her like you did Agar?"

The cracked and shattered woman struggled to raise a hand, but it crumbled off into a fine, blue powder that hemorrhaged mana in a steady seep. The sight was more disturbing than Agar's had been, but the decisions was much easier.

"I can," I answered simply, but I made no move to do so.

"Will you?" There was a pause as I considered it. Would I? Quietly, Amber added in a voice only I could hear, "I don't want to be a murderer."

Looking over at the body, I hesitated. Scavengers like Mera lessened the power of a clan as a whole and made families weaker. Scavengers deserved nothing more than to be cast out into the wilds or to be dead, but I'd heard the plea in Amber's voice. I'd felt the heart in it, and I knew what I had to do.

I couldn't ignore it.

Amber didn't want to be a murderer, and I didn't want her to feel like one either. On top of that, I doubt the Goddess Vul would have been so accepting of me being a bystander when someone was in danger.

Walking over, I bent down and extended my hands. I was weak, but I had to at least try something. Focusing on my Node and the spell within, I began pouring the Celestial power into it, mana began to build to near bursting, and I could practically feel the strange healing fog at my fingertips...

But nothing came.

I didn't need to check to know what my reserves were this time. I hadn't done anything to drain them other than walk. It was like the first time with the Will-of-the-Wisps. I knew I had more mana this time than I did before, maybe not enough, but the spell within the Node had accepted the power.

-I'm sorry. -

"Rem," Amber said, worry strewn across my name with equal parts fear and prayer.

"I'm trying!"

I really was trying, but my power just wasn't responding. What in the Mists was going on? I pushed harder, doing one of the few spell work things I shouldn't do and flooded the Node with as much mana as I could spare. The power crackled and strained inside my mind, but it felt trapped, unable to leave my Nexus to trigger the spell.

I kept pushing. I couldn't let Amber down.

I didn't even notice when we were jerked from the small island and returned to the stage at the center of the campus.

Chapter Twenty-Eight

Welcoming Party

A rainbow fog fell over Mera's form as I struggled to force power out from myself. Even with the flood of new power and stability from the fresh connection to my Dungeon Core, the spell form failed spectacularly, and I screamed as the power shattered my hands like glass. Thankfully, the rainbow fog caught me before I could be overtaken by the shatter and pop.

"A mess indeed," Ansith's voice rang out as the cracks in Mera's body healed her back into a single piece. My hands regrew just as quickly, but the spell still never came. "You all did better than I thought you would. Not a single casualty."

As the final details of my hands healed, I couldn't help but breathe a sigh of relief at those words. In my experience, you either met Ansith's expectations or you died. I was happy we met them this time as I wasn't quite ready to be cast back into the embrace of Oblivia, but I noticed something different as I looked around to the faces of my peers.

We weren't alone anymore, and it wasn't the same campus as it had been.

Moving around campus were hundreds of students of all colors and species. I noticed more dwarves, elves, humans, and beastkin than there were shards from my hands. If my eyes didn't deceive me, there were even a few korgan in the mix with their half humanoid, half beastkin features. The half breeds were more numerous here than it seemed out in the real world.

To make my return even more disorienting, there were the other buildings too.

The towers no longer had walls. Those were reserved for the barrier that now separated them from the edges of the forest, the same forest that had always been there it seemed. In their places were four new buildings. I couldn't make their designs out, but I was sure that they had definitely been walls before.

Ansith's doing again? It had to be.

All of the other Cores were looking up at us, and as if a great weight had been lifted, they began clapping. It would be an understatement to say I was a little bit confused. Mera began to stir under Ansith's attentions, and we all turned our attention back to him as he began speaking once more.

"Normally, her little stunt would meet with her demise, but I gave my word that if you all survived, you'd be brought back here, and seeing as you, Rem, were trying to heal her, I'll just assume no hard feelings for whatever she did." Ansith announced as the healing ended and the fog vanished.

I only half listened to his words. Mera wasn't my concern anymore, but my mind felt foggy, fluttery, as if it were going a mile a minute outside of my control. I didn't like it. Maybe I should ask Ansith about it? Not even a second later, alarms went off in my head as a feeling of stress and worry slipped into my thoughts.

~No! Stop! Don't ask him! I'll explain everything when you're alone. I promise it'll make sense. Just don't ask him! Whatever you do, don't ask him!~

Ow.

The voice was loud and clear as if it had been right next to my ear, screaming like a banshee. Again, it sounded like a part of me, but not at the same time. My curiosity was stronger than my fear though, and as long as I could Manifest, I knew Ansith could find me. Curiously, I tested something and sent a thought back at the voice.

Fine, but I want everything.

A sense of hesitation washed over me for a moment.

~Fine.~

Then, the thoughts were gone as if they had never been.

"Rem?" Ansith asked, irritation in his voice. "Are you listening to me?"

I shook my head, getting my bearings once more. He'd been talking to me, and I'd not been paying attention. Sket and Mists. "There are so many people," I muttered.

Clearing his throat, Ansith looked from side to side. "Yes, well, since all of you have advanced to the C ranks, you've been granted permission to enter the school instance proper, not to mention the slew of new Talents you can work towards. Check on your Nexus the next chance you get. For now, since I'm sure you won't kill your fellow students without just cause, let me introduce you to the majority of the student body."

In reality, it wasn't the fact there were so many people that bothered me, it was the word he had used. "Instance?"

"Alternate realities that occupy the same space," Agar the All-Knowing broke in at that moment to allow my mind to once again drink from his endless fountain of knowledge. "I've heard of Dungeons that could create pocket dimensions to keep groups from ganging up and making things too easy. It's an extremely rare ability."

Ansith nodded, never missing a chance to teach. "Yes, it is. Most Dungeons don't have the power, intelligence, or skill to be able to create and sustain the ability. Alternate Reality, or Instance as it's more commonly known as, is an ability you shouldn't even attempt until you're a B ranked Dungeon Core. It's a useful skill for populated areas, but you will only learn it if you have the willpower and cunning to figure out the differences between gates, portals, and pocket space."

Gates? Portals? Pocket space? I knew what they were, of course, but I had no idea how they worked. Then, the voice chimed in again.

~Psh. Easy.~

As had happened before when Vix repaired my Nexus and when Ansith had drawn our attentions inward, I was drawn back into my Nexus, and I saw that Ansith wasn't kidding.

Everything had changed for my Dungeon Core class.

Dungeon Core
Mastered Skills - 5 of 5
Soul Attributes - 1
Secondary Skills - 0
Dungeon Core Rank C6

1/7 requirements met to reach Rank B

      Acquire an Advanced Pattern

      Achieve a Mana Equilibrium or Mana Constructive rating within   your finished Dungeon Floor

      Gather 1000 Soul Points (3/1000)

      Unlock a Soul Attribute

        —Granted abilities do not count towards this total

      Create a B or higher Ranked Item or Item Attribute

      Create a B or higher Ranked Minion or Minion Attribute

      Create a B or higher Ranked Trap or Trap Attribute

Dungeon Core Size 3

Dungeon Core Material - Opal/Amethyst

Mana Types - Celestial/Umbral/Dungeon

      Celestial - 500/500

      Umbral - 60/60

      Dungeon - 2600/2600

Dungeon Alignment - Mana Constructive

Floors Complete - 0

Soul Points - 3

Class Passive for Mastery:

      Dungeon Mana Reservoir: All Mana Reservoirs grow based on use.

      Rank Knowledge: An innate knowledge of what requirements are   needed to increase in rank for any visible Nexus.

Node Augmentation Acquired for Dungeon Memory: Trans-Dimensional Magic Applications

~Oh... that doesn't feel good...~

What was it talking about? I'd never felt anything like this!

Not only had I ranked up and nearly doubled all of my mana reservoirs, I understood everything Ansith was talking about, not to mention the fact I knew everything I needed to do to Rank up! The fully-formed knowledge rushed through my questions and enlightened my understanding: from the function of how changing an entrance would work; to the mana efficiency ratio of the materials I'd already gathered per rune; and the drain each reality would have on me. It was staggering enough to force the word from my mouth. "Amazing."

Ansith, taking my amazement for his own work, smiled, giving me his most approving look yet. "It is, isn't it?"

There were a few more words shared from Ansith of little importance, a few congratulations from the other Manifestations, and Mera sulking off with her ill-gotten gains, but I had bigger fish to watch.

"As you've progressed to this point. Your classes will be changing, and you must begin considering your graduation requirements." The cheers of the crowd stopped. The silence was thick a spring fog in the forest. They knew better than us how important his next words were. "If you hope to survive, you'll be focusing everything you have on reaching the A Ranks. That may seem closer than ever, but to reach the A Ranks in both of your Nexus isn't easy. In addition to that, you'll need to reach at least four floors; befriend an elemental spirit to manage the lesser functions of your Dungeon; be mana compliant; create a graduate project worthy of dying for; and not only get the approval of the Adventurer's Guild, but my own personal seal of approval. If you fail to meet them in five years' time, you will be removed from our roll and shattered."

Just all that? Just reach the A Rankings, which took most people the better part of their entire lives? Impress someone who was functionally a demi-god? Build floors? Befriend elementals? And create a treasure worthy of a dragon's horde or die a horrible death?

Simple, real simple.

Then again, wasn't it just that simple?

Ansith had his standards, and, as far as I knew, they were achievable despite how much of a stubborn ox he was. The goddesses would have known that. Vul wouldn't have chosen me and sent me here if she didn't think I could handle it. She knew I could do it, and I wouldn't be deterred anymore from helping my people. With Ansith in my corner, I didn't need anyone else being hard on me.

I snapped out of my thoughts just in time to catch the tail end of Ansith's speech.

"—You'll also have your lessons in Dungeon Theory and Design, then you'll be going back to your Dungeons to build. I'll also install a portal script inside your Core chamber for easy access to the school's resources."

At that, Ansith paused again, the crowds still silent.

"In less than a year, your Dungeon's location will be opened to the Adventurer's Guild, and your true tests will begin in earnest. Any questions?"

I had more than I could possibly ask in the span of a few days, and I would bet my tail that Ansith knew it.

He just smiled, created a rolled-up scroll for each of the five of us on stage, presented them, and left no time for his request as he disappeared back into his Core with a declaration of, "Dismissed!"

That was getting old real fast.

Before we could even get off the stage, a cavalcade of curious Cores surrounded us, cheered us, patted our shoulders and gave us words of encouragement. It was enough even to make me blush at the attention, but we were worthy of attention now. We'd earned their respect by way of Ansith.

For almost an hour, they kept us with them, asking us to repeat the story of our attack, and more embarrassingly, the story of how we'd set Ansith on such a war path.

Part of me wanted to run, part of me wanted to stay, and all of me was exhausted still from the evening's events.

I played my part as well as I could, to the point I felt that the clan's Teller's would have been proud. We all did our best not to alienate anyone as we each told our versions of the story. Well, those of us that actually stuck around.

As far as the actual story telling went, Agar's side was very factual and flattering. Fiona's wavered on some points but she did let a few interesting points about her class slip, like how she could call on portions of her Patron's power in a pinch. Pyros was, of course, vastly overstating some parts of it. Pompous, full of himself, stretching the truth without breaking it… I really could see a storyteller in him my people would have loved. I let him continue, and Amber did the same. I could tell on some level she was enjoying the story as much as I was. All good things come to an end though. When the story ended, there was one last round of congratulations before the group left us, and we were given a moment to breathe.

Agar gave me a hard smile of granite from behind his beard before he spoke again. "I meant what I said, Rem. I wouldn't be here without you. I owe you my life."

Fiona gave me the same smile, and Amber did the same. Pyros just grinned like a guilty child, and for some reason that smile was infectious. I knew it oh so well from the nights I'd snuck out, the pies I'd been caught with all over my face, and the kisses I'd stolen and had stolen in return. I couldn't stop myself despite everything, and I found myself smiling back to him, to all of them.

We really were friends now, weren't we?

I wanted to say something witty, something heroic, something worthy of what I thought of Agar without botching it again, but I couldn't. I just kept smiling as I offered him my hand and settled for the truth. "There are no debts here, Agar. What are friends for?"

He took it me by the forearm and squeezed. It was a bit strange, but I didn't resist and squeezed back before we broke the grasp.

Pyros took the chance to yawn loudly and pointed off into the distance at the Ember Dorms with both hands in an overly exaggerated gesture. "Well, I'm exhausted. How about we all go back to our rooms and hope we never get thrown into a test like that again."

I doubted it would be the last time Ansith tested us, but no one argued with that hope. Like Pyros had, we all took the chirp of the crickets as our chance to say our goodbyes and return to our Dorms to rest.

As far as I was concerned, I still had a lot to figure out.

***

I didn't even stop to examine the scroll of classes or the new buildings as Amber and I returned to our dorm. The air here even smelled different with so much intermingling magic. The deluge of noise and people compared to where we'd come from was starting to be a bit much for me.

Even with the over-saturation of my delicate senses, I had to admit that I was curious about everything, but I knew that there'd be time to deal with it later. Whatever had happened to me, the answers wouldn't come to me until I was alone. Even with that knowledge weighing on me, I couldn't help but keep an eye out for more magic as we pick our way across the campus. Amber was as quiet as I was as we walked. Despite the fact neither of us wanted to talk, it felt strange that neither of us were saying anything, like something had changed since the Dungeon. Something she didn't want to talk about as much as I didn't.

I knew I'd have to talk to her once I figured things out.

As we arrived back at the dorm, something caught my attention. I noticed that the doorway wasn't as clean as I'd first thought. All around the frame of the door was a line of intricate runescript. It blurred together in such a way it looked like a single, unbroken line and was too small to actually comprehend, but things started to make sense now. Even the buildings were instanced according to our class. That's why we'd never seen anyone else here, and why I'd seen so many Air Cores inside of the Aero tower!

"What are you looking at?" Amber asked as she leaned in.

It was good to hear her voice again, but at first, I simply pointed to the dull, glowing line. Once she noticed, I used my newfound knowledge and explained the line's function. At the same time, I couldn't help but wonder what would happen if I broke it? A sense of danger rushed over me on par with what I'd felt inside the slime Dungeon's Core, so I brushed the thought aside. Messing with multiple realities didn't seem like a good idea, even if it was right there to toy with!

Amber seemed to nod appreciatively at my hesitation to even touch the glowing script. Apparently, she had the same worry as the thoughts in my head did. Did no one trust my survival instincts not to mess with an interdimensional gateway?

The nerve.

I sighed softly, passing the doorway and entering once more into our empty dorm. This time, I tried to pay attention for the tugging feeling that usually came with teleportation, but there wasn't one. I still hadn't seen many Cores of my coloring, so I didn't know why we needed to be instanced. Either way, the silence returned between us, and it was a quiet trek back up the stairs to our rooms.

My end of the silence didn't go unquestioned though.

"You're quieter than usual," Amber said before I could disappear back into my room. I simply nodded, and she added, "You're never this quiet, Rem. Do you wanna talk about it?"

I wanted to, but I shook my head. "Not yet."

She seemed to be reading my face about as well as any card player and gave me the barest hint of a smile. "I'm here, ya know. It's what friends are for I'm pretty sure."

For all we had been through, it made me feel a little better that she felt the same way. Even with the others in my corner, I thought about Amber as my closest ally, and knowing she felt the same way about me was like having back something from my last life that I'd lost. "I know."

Amber turned to close her door then hesitated for a moment. Her orange hand held the edge of the door as she leaned into the room, speaking almost to herself as she turned thoughts to word. "We all freeze up sometimes when something big happens."

If only I could tell her why, but I couldn't trust that Ansith couldn't overhear me. We were in his Influence after all, but there was truth in her words. I'd almost cost Mera her life because of whatever was holding me back. I bobbed my head and answered as simply as I could. "I know."

She didn't leave her spot, studying her door a moment more before it opened wider. "Thanks for trying though."

When her door shut, it felt like an insult. I don't know why, but it seethed just above the surface of my mind like oil on water. It felt like I wasn't good enough, but it wasn't my fault. Was it? Did I do the right thing?

I wanted to go across the hall, to explain everything, but I didn't have all the answers yet. Once I did, I'd tell her everything. It was so easy just telling her everything like she was another of my people, and the way she acted didn't help things. She was so much like Saria it was scary. Well, less physically inclined towards me than she was, but still, it was nice having someone around I could call a friend, that I felt I could trust with everything.

As the door closed behind me, my request to the strange voice was simple. Ansith or not, this had to be done.

"Talk."

There was a feeling of... something fleeting. Fear? Apprehension? Anger? Whatever it was, the voice that answered was smaller than it had been.

~ Okay. ~

Chapter Twenty-Nine
All's Fae in Love and War

A familiar feeling began to well up from my mana. It pushed into the Node for Manifestation as if I were using it, but I knew it wasn't me willing this to happen. I attempted to stop the flow of mana, but the power only redoubled its efforts. It pushed itself harder and harder into the Node, the will pressing against my own until—

Pop!

I… had a visitor, apparently.

A small, feminine creature no larger than my head came into being. She was a creature I'd never seen before, so I doubted I created her. If I had, she probably would have been a Foxkin like me. Instead, she was closer to human with only a pair of foxen ears to call her own. In truth, she was a tiny, opaline humanoid woman with a long, pearly braid streaked with violet coming over her right shoulder, soulful violet eyes, and a two-piece dress made of opal leaves. Strangest of all were four dragonfly wings keeping her aloft at eye level. Her face was soft, but her alien eyes were more than enough to keep me on guard, all violet with not a single hint of anything else.

"Hello!" the creature chimed happily like an overactive humming bird, bowing just a bit at the waist but smiling widely as her face contorted into something resembling true happiness. "It's nice to meet you, Dungeon Core Rem."

I couldn't stop myself from staring as her ear twitched. Her hand raising to brush it as though she were trying to clean something off of it. "What are you?"

She seemed slightly offended and let out a dismissive sigh. "You are a Dungeon Core, and you don't know what I am." She paused a moment, waiting for me to pull back from some grand joke. In my silence, she must have assumed I wasn't lying. "I'm slightly offended if you can't tell, but since you're one of *his,* I think I can forgive you."

The way she said 'his' didn't sound like anything good. "His?"

She scoffed and waved a hand as if fanning something away from her. "Ansith's. You practically stink of the civilized lands, and you can do that Manifesting thing. Not that I don't like it! It's a really neat trick. I haven't seen myself since that Dungeon ate me months ago!" Her hands went right to her head as her ears twitched. "Oh, these are new, do they do this often?" I shrugged. "This is great! Do you know what it's like having no… body… oh… um, never mind."

What had I done? My muscles tensed as if I were expecting a fight. The little creature was one of the things Ansith had talked about that helped the wild Dungeons advance. This was a Dungeon sprite, fairy, elemental… thing. They worked with Eventide if Ansith told the truth, and the evidence was very much in the Dwarf's corner at this point. In a fluid action my old masters would have been proud of, I Manifested my staff and prepared for battle. I had to end it before she brought everything down around us!

The small sprite looked at me and laughed, putting a hand on the staff and making it vanish in a puff of mana like it had been no effort. I stood there for a moment unable to comprehend what had just happened. How did she do that?

"I think we need to talk more than I thought!" she laughed again. It sounded a lot like chiming crystal, hard to ignore but fragile at the same time. "We've Bonded, so there's nothing we can do to hurt one another. In fact, that's another reason your spells aren't working. We can't do anything together without first coming to an agreement about our arrangement."

There was just a hint of guilt in her voice at that last bit.

But what she was saying… that wasn't true. I hadn't Bonded with anyone. I was still very much single, and I had done plenty of things since I met her. "I absorbed items. I Manifested. Those aren't nothing."

"All Dungeons can absorb items and learn from them without causing harm, and Manifesting isn't something normal Dungeons can do." The creature said, shrugging just a bit as she took a breath and flapped her wings. "Our contracts don't cover either of those abilities. If you couldn't Absorb, you'd be helpless to gather mana, and Manifestation hasn't really come up on the other side to even consider."

"Wonderful," I mumbled as those violet eyes stared straight through my soul. That didn't explain why I didn't regain mana earlier, but then again, that might have been Mera's fault too.

She put a hand under her chin thinking deeply, ignoring my well-placed annoyance. "As you've seen though, most of our contract is still able to be validated. That is good for both of us! If you'll allow me to make my offer, I'm sure you won't regret it."

I had the distinct feeling I would, but right now I was curious to see what this was about.

When I didn't object, the small creature continued her speech. "In return for my services, you will give me a name and provide safety to the best of your abilities. In return, I will willingly serve as your Assistant in your Dungeon's construction, protection, and advancement, and I will do nothing to endanger you or the Dungeon that is our home at large."

Well, that seemed simple. "You'll serve me? How? I don't really see how you could help with any of that."

The little creature sighed and looked me over again. Her eyes might have been alien, but I knew annoyance when I saw it. For a moment, it felt like she was probing my thoughts, looking for something before she finally gave up. "You have no idea what I'm offering you, do you?"

Finally, it was my turn to be annoyed. "Of course not! Why would I lie about any of this?"

"Because you're a Dungeon Core!" she returned, just as annoyed as I was.

She'd already said that. I already knew that too, obviously, but it didn't make it any easier. "Look, I know what I am, but I don't understand what that has to do with you." Honesty was a risky gambit with an unknown creature, but I felt that it was the best one for once. I'd get the most information from her if she truly knew I was clueless about some things. At least, I hoped so. "You've already said a lot about what you are, but maybe it's best you start at the beginning."

Her mouth hung open, closed, open again, closed again, and she finally sighed and dragged her hand across her face in exasperation. "Fine, but the longer we have to spend negotiating our contract, the more likely I'll be discovered. Pockets within pockets can hide a simple conversation but not if he comes looking." Was that fear in her voice? I could feel it in her, but had it been her voice or just her thoughts like before? "I don't want to find out what he'll do with me."

Ansith again, more than likely. There was only one thing I could really ask when it came to her fear of the dwarf. Sure, he and Eventide were enemies, but it still didn't answer the question of… "Why?"

"He's a Dungeon without an Assistant." She smiled darkly, and I knew there was more to the story. "I can't imagine how he's survived this long without one or reached… what? SS Rank?" I didn't acknowledge that she was correct, but she had enough already to continue. "Imagine what he could do with access to what we can do. He'd probably be able to break into the triple S ranks, if not the Divine Tier, by nightfall!"

Now that was worth probing into. Did having an Assistant make that much of a difference? Why did it matter if Ansith reached the Triple S Ranking, let alone the Divine Tier? I'd never even heard of that one. Still… "How could you possibly do that?"

More annoyance passed from her face to the point where I could feel it before she spoke again. "You really have to understand three things to understand what and who I am." Before she continued, she raised a finger. I only now noticed she had but four digits: three fingers and a thumb if we were being specific. "First, Dungeons are a natural wonder placed by the Pantheon themselves to test the sapient races."

If only she knew. Vul had sent me here herself, so I guess I counted as being placed by the gods themselves. Though Cecil had done this to me, he didn't control the Grand Plan. If Vul hadn't come to me personally, my evolution into a Dungeon Core might still have happened since I was god-touched to begin with. As my mind lingered on the idea, I thought that just maybe it had been more Dante's plan then

Vul's. She was a trickster, and stealing one of Dante's Dungeon's would have been right up her alley.

To pull a prank on another god? To steal their project's results by swaying them before he could? It was perfect.

I really, really liked Vul.

I snapped back to reality as the small fairy raised another of her four fingers. "Second, everything in the world exists in balance: life and death, male and female, love and hate, Dungeons and Assistants. Dungeons need a consciousness to guide them away from mindless hunger and grabs for power, to help them advance, and to give them direction. We are two parts of a whole, thought and instinct."

Her words were just another part of the puzzle that didn't seem to fit our design. From what Ansith had said so far and my personal experiences, the idea of a Dungeon having consciousness made sense, but they seemed more like monsters than they did thinking entities. If they could think and react, their moral systems left a lot to be desired. Bonded to whatever this was, was I going to become the same thing? She raised her final finger before I could get caught up in that trail of thought.

"Third, Dungeons help the world advance with their abilities. Dungeon Cores and their partners are creative on an unparalleled scale. Really, what else would we do? It's not like lines of people are waiting to test themselves and die every hour of every day. In the name of honesty, your race alone was one of the more well-known creations of a Dungeon. Well, you and the runic language of magic."

Part of that made sense…

Wait…

"What was that again?"

She shrunk back just a bit at my intensity. "The runic language…" I shook my head. "Your race being created by a Dungeon…"

And that's when my brain stopped working.

My race was the result of a Dungeon Core playing around? How…

Slowly, very slowly as not to break my tenuous hold on reality, it began to make a sick sort of sense as I began to think back to my Bestiary and attributes. A worse kind of sickness began to rise in my stomach as the edges of my mind began to touch on a possibility. Foxkin, and the Beastkin at large, could easily have once been minions of some powerful Dungeon.

We were powerful in our own rights. Foxes were clever and magical, the felines were fast and powerful, wolves were well rounded, and the dragons... well, no one had met them in some time, but rumor was they could do everything of all the clans combined. Even the lesser clans were specialized and powerful in their own rights.

The pieces made sense, and I really didn't like it. Minions had attributes we, as Dungeons, could manipulate. I'd seen that result first hand. My Rembar wasn't reliant on Dungeon mana to survive. She wasn't loyal either, but she'd been created by a sort-of accident. So, that part still didn't make sense. How... why would a Dungeon create a race to oppose it? If we didn't oppose it, where had it gone? How in the Mists of Oblivia had it happened? Who would allow it? Why weren't there any stories about it? Was that why we were viewed as monsters by the other races for so long?

The fairy-like creature was snapping her fingers in front of me, but I hadn't noticed. She must have been watching me for more than a long minute, and I couldn't have blamed her. I must have looked like an idiot or at least had a dumbstruck expression still plastered to my face. She kept snapping at my face three more times before I finally came to. When I blinked at her, recognition seemed to register in her expression. "You... didn't know that? It's common knowledge, isn't it? I haven't been out of the loop that long, have I?"

I had no words, just shaking my head as a reply.

"Oh..." Somehow, I'd expected more sympathy from a creature that just threw the story of my entire species upside-down. "Well, better to find out now than when you come across a Dungeon using your species as its minions. I hadn't heard of Dungeons doing so in the last few centuries, but it isn't all that uncommon for the elder Dungeons to create sapient races to serve as relations ambassadors and Guardians. It's a mark of pride and creativity among your kind."

This was getting less and less comfortable by the moment, but there was a glimmer of temptation there. So, I pressed forward as my better nature came to my rescue. "So, how did we beat your old Core then if you're so powerful together?"

"My old Core," she shivered at the thought of it once more. "My old Core was too primal, too newborn to listen to me as it was supposed to. Without Eventide to guide it, it acted out its instinct, trapped me, sapped my power, and ate me before I could even touch its Core and start the contracting process. It wasn't pleasant, but death isn't the biggest deal when you're part of a Dungeon, willing or not. We persist as a Pattern even after our physical deaths inside the Dungeon. Unfortunately for me, when it ate me, it shoved my spirit inside its soul space. I was in there for weeks! Weeks! It couldn't catch me to break me down, so I was just flying around inside it trying to stay alive as it leeched off my body's power for an easy gain." She hesitated for a moment, looking over her form for the first time. "I was originally a Dungeon Nymph, but now, I guess I'm a Dungeon Spirit? A Dungeon Spirit Nymph."

"And your people exist with Dungeons because..."

"I'm getting there, geeze," she said slightly exacerbated. "My race is what you'd call symbiotic. We have no power of our own other than contractual magic until we Bond. We can Bond with anything with a significant magical presence, but think about it from our perspective. Dungeons are an excellent source of everything magical, so why not Bond with them exclusively? With the protection they provide, it's a real win-win."

That made sense at least. Why take a lesser mage when you can bond with an entity that literally can bend reality?

"Once we formally Bond and a contract is accepted, our abilities change. We can copy and produce more of the mana you create and supplement your mind with the knowledge and guidance you lack... well... usually."

"Wait. You're the reason I understood what Ansith was talking about? You modified my Nexus?"

She smiled and nodded. "Yep! Normally it's not so draining though to grant you knowledge. Your Core was just a little weaker than it should have been. You had almost no soul energy, so it took some of my own power." She looked sad all of a sudden. "I won't be able to do that again for some time."

I wanted to open my Nexus there and then to verify what she'd done, but I felt that would have been rude. "Thank you for that."

"You're welcome." Her hand touched under her chin as she studied me. "You're a nice change from running from slimes." Then almost as an afterthought, she added. "You're not going to eat me, are you?"

I shook my head. "I don't need to eat, and I have plenty of mana." Killing her to protect myself wasn't out of the question, but I definitely wasn't going to eat her. Probably. I was ninety, ninety-five percent sure that wouldn't want to eat her under normal circumstances. There wouldn't be any meat there anyways.

Bad, Rem. Wrong path of thought. Why'd she have to put the thought in my head in the first place?

"Right, well, that's pretty much the long and short, or in your case tip to tail, of it."

Her existence sounded miserable. I almost pitied her. "How come I've never seen any of your kind here with Ansith's Cores?"

She winced, hesitating a bit before she answered as she floated side to side. "Because of Ansith and Eventide's… disagreement, the fae are not on good terms with Ansith's people."

As if that explained anything. Really, it made things more confusing. "So I've noticed."

"You don't seem so bad though. You saved me from being digested and then from suffering a slow, painful death, so I freely offer my services as I mentioned before," she continued without missing a beat. "My terms are simple. You provide me mana, a home, and a name, and I will give you access to the true powers of a Dungeon. Advancement and skills in exchange for soul power, guidance…" she grinned now before adding, "and a lifelong friend to help keep you from going insane after hundreds of years, and the blood of thousands of adventurers on your floors. Like I said, it's a win-win."

It didn't sound like a win-win. It really sounded too good to be true. Suspiciously, it sounded as good as Vul's offer had been not a week ago. Why would I even need the school after this? I'd have my own personal library of power. I wouldn't need anyone to help me. I felt the regret the moment I thought it. Amber, Agar, Fiona, Pyros… I actually liked them. I would be happy to pull one over on Ansith if

I could and beat him in Ranking, but if I made this deal, would everyone here turn against me?

Would they even try to kill me next?

I couldn't take that. Besides, there had to be some things that only Ansith could teach a sapient Core.

As if reading the thoughts on the lines of my face, the spirit creature softened her smile. "No one can tell that a Dungeon has a Bonded partner unless you want them to. We're just another facet of your Core and spirit." As if an afterthought, the fae grinned and added, "Ansith wouldn't be the wiser if you took me as a partner. We'd just have to be careful not to be too good before you got strong enough."

I thought about the offer carefully for a moment. What did I stand to lose? Well, Ansith would more than likely turn on me, and I'd die or suffer a fate worse than death. Both of those were definitely experiences that I didn't want to have.

But, what did I have to gain?

The knowledge of a hidden race, the power to overcome more obstacles, the ability to push myself and the Foxkin further than any of the other races, someone more knowledgeable than anyone but Ansith himself to talk projects through with, more advancement options Ansith may not be aware of, and a new source of power were a few options if the spirit nymph was telling the truth. Though our tenuous link, I couldn't feel any deception coming from her.

But being smashed into dust and having my soul obliterated…

The longer I thought about it, the more her offer and the benefits outweighed any potential problems. Then, there was the fact I could get one over on a creature of near god-like power. In the end, I decided that Vul wouldn't just approve of such a trick, she'd expect it of one of her people. I grinned, holding my hand out flat for the fae to finally land on. "Do you have a name you'd like?"

She settled with a happy whistle. She was surpassingly light compared to what I expected. She felt like nothing at all. Making herself comfortable, the spirit sat down and began to make some sort of humming noise. She was thinking to herself, I assumed. Looking from herself, back to me, then back to herself, she finally had an answer. "Something feminine."

Well, that was a broad answer. What name wouldn't I get tired of...

"Saria," came the instinctual answer.

She smiled, a bob of her head accepting the name. "Greetings once more, Dungeon Core Rem. It's a pleasure to finally meet you as me. I am Saria Soulborn, Bonded Celestial Spirit Nymph of your Dungeon, and together, we're going to change the world!"

And we're going to bring everyone along for the ride, I added with a reflective smile.

Meanwhile One
Diamond Unicorns and Enchanted Apples

Far from the center of the civilized world of man, elf, and dwarf, the Adventurer's Guild could be found thriving. Whether fighting the good fight, keeping down wild monster numbers, researching rare elixirs, or just training, the guild was known near and far. Guild members were the source of many items required for everyday life. From the Fire crystals that kept ice mounts going to the Umbral mana stones that kept Dragaz, the Lord of Dark Fires alive and sleeping, the guild was something of an everyday necessity, and the second largest economy in all the world.

Today was a day that Ina, High Lady of the Golden Leaf and Headmistress of the Adventurer's Guild, loved more than any other. Her guild's mysterious benefactor, a Dwarf claiming to be the late Lord Ansith of Copperforge, had set up a delivery for her, and in the weeks leading up to it, she could barely contain herself. That energy was three-fold now that the day had finally come.

It wasn't her first delivery from the mysterious Lord Ansith, but it never made it any less interesting even if the present always came the same way. She could already picture it as if it were happening again. By the time the sun rose, there would be a large wagon pulling across the horizon filled with four SS Ranked, single-use casks of *Ansith's Finest Dwarven Whiskey* for her guild's members. That alone was a small fortune in itself, but it wasn't what made the delivery special. The real prize was for her alone. Inside an empty compartment below the fourth cask, there would be a small reinforced chest with a pure steel lock, unbreakable, mana absorbent, and unable to be tampered with, but it was keyed to open to her mana signature as guild leader.

Inside was what gave the guild so much of its ability to help the world function: a list of locations where new Dungeons would rise in the East.

For the last few hundred years, the guild had been receiving such shipments from a man calling himself Ansith. It was common knowledge that the mad dwarf Lord Ansith was dead and had been for nearly five centuries, but the guild never argued with whoever took up the name. Lord Ansith's information was always accurate. Since the guild had been formed nearly four hundred years ago and the first shipment had come, it had never been wrong. No one questioned it anymore, and no one dared to search for their mysterious patron. He'd been very specific telling them not to try and find him.

Maybe it's just better that way, Ina thought to herself.

Despite all the guild's power, she hated to be in debt to anyone, especially anyone of power, and if someone could identify newborn Dungeons so quickly and know not only their alignment but that they were good training and farming spots, she didn't want to be the one to jeopardize their friendship. Besides, *Ansith's Finest* was one of the most expensive whiskeys in the known world due to the refined, dark flavors and high mana content. Her men would riot if they knew she had lost them their comparatively cheap supply.

As the sun rose once more over her city of Alliance, Ina smiled. On the horizon, the cart was approaching as it always did, led by the same diamond golem shaped into the form of a glistening crystal unicorn. She could barely contain her excitement, but she had to and took a deep breath.

No, no squealing this time. I am a professional now. I am the guild leader. Guild leaders do not squeal at diamond unicorns. Guild leaders accept their client's eccentric ways. They do not take girlish joy in diamond unicorns that travels with rainbows.

That may have been the case, but she really, really wanted to.

Dressed in the half-plate of her Duelist class and marked by the pure whites, golds, and greens of her station, Ina left her private room at the top of the guildhall. Without a care in the world, she descended the steps, and continued through the various hallways and doors until she reached the ground floor of the five-floor guildhall.

Unintentionally, and with all the grace of a drunken doe, she burst through the door, prancing like a mad woman as she declared to the residents of the hall, "It's Whiskey Day, everyone!"

At first, there was pause. The young adventurers looked from one to the other, confused about what such a day was. There were no strange looks from the multitude of elder or visiting adventurers.

"Ho!"

Instead, they rushed to follow their leader, leaving the younglings dazed and confused. Like a parade of fools at closing time, the line only got longer and longer until Ina reached the hall doors.

In a deft motion, the guild mistress threw open the doors and moved into the training yard. A smile painted her face as she waved to the younger adventurers training in archery at the shooting range, the warriors practicing swordsmanship on the training dummies, and even the rogues stabbing unsuspecting targets when the warriors were finished. All was as it should be in their little part of Alliance.

Again, she called to the assembled masses. "It's Whiskey Day!"

"Ho!"

Another cheer, and the line only got longer as they followed the excited woman through the yard, and out the front gate.

Moving through the front gates, Ina held a hand back to the following masses. They knew the motion by now, but some of the newer adventurers knocked into backs. She spoke frankly for their benefit. "Wait for my signal, stay here."

With their favorite brew on the line, there were no arguments.

Ina was sure-footed in her approach as not to spook the golem. Each step was more gentle and tender against the ground than the last. Her motions were not fast enough to even be perceived as a threat, as direct and implied as they were. She reached slowly for a bag at her side, and from it, she produced one of the more eccentric treasures her guild had acquired long ago, a small, barely fist-sized apple of pure gold that shimmered in its own enchanted light. As she did, a tattoo on her hand glowed gently and reminded her just how valuable the item was as her Item Identification tattoo, won from the Infinite Maze, created a small pane of information that appeared to the side of the item.

Enchanted Golden Apple
Item Rank - SS - Food: Fruit
When eaten, the individual will be temporarily enchanted with the
following effects for half a minute: Ethereal Armor, Regeneration,
Heat Resistance, Titan's Endurance.
Ethereal Armor: Your body becomes cloaked in pure mana, negating a major portion of any physical assault.
Regeneration: Your body's healing accelerates to unnatural levels.
Flesh wounds, bones, and internal injuries mend in accordance to
the free mana your environment can provide.
Heat Resistance: Your body becomes cloaked in Fire mana, drawing
excessive heat from around you and negating a major portion of
any fire elemental attack.
Titan's Endurance: Your body draws on excessive mana from
around you. You will feel no effects of physical expenditure for the
duration of this spell's effect.

The value of the item came in many forms, but its value wasn't in its gold or even in the effects it could grant that could turn the tide of battle. The guild learned long ago that they were gifted with the small tree for a very specific reason. The strange fruit made the golem calm enough for others to approach. Holding the item forward, Ina began cooing softly.

"Come here, Princess. Come on."

The unicorn backtracked only slightly, and Ina sighed.

Princess is a better name, she thought before correcting herself, hand outstretched. "Come here, Brandon."

Brandon lowered its head, slowly approaching as it sniffed for the enchanted air of its favorite snack. Opening its mouth, the creature leaned in and ate the item in a single bite. As many times as Ina had seen it, it still disturbed her watching the creature eat through its transparent face. A few moments later, the creature stilled.

"Adventurers!" Ina called after waving a hand in front of the creature's face. "We've got about five minutes. Get those casks into the basement, and if any of you take even a drop of that whiskey without permission, I'll double the guild tax on everything your group brings in for the next year!"

No one would dare cross their guild leader with that risk on the table. One by one, the four casks were loaded into waiting arms and carried away back into the cellar of the guild house. Once the others were gone, Ina did her secondary search where the fourth cask was resting. A spark of mana later, and the hidden compartment clicked, lifting the lid and revealing a single rolled piece of parchment.

Ina greedily lifted the paper and put it into her side pouch before the effects of the apple wore off. The weight of the paper belied its power. The paper represented the whole of their focus for the next year or so. It would show her guild where they needed to create new settlements to take advantage of new Dungeons. This meant there'd be new monsters to fight and, most importantly, new peoples to meet, admit to the guild, and train. So much potential in such a small package.

As Ina walked away from the group of adventurers carrying the new casks of Ansith's Finest, visions of Dungeons and treasures danced in her head to the tune of sloshing whiskey.

One year from now, her people would have their first outpost in the Wildwood! So much to do, so little time.

Meanwhile Two

Roots

There was no stopping. Stopping was no better than death.

Run.

Send out decoy aether foxes.

Blink.

Stay in the Celestial Plane as long as possible.

Return.

Keep Running.

There had never been another option for the kitsune known as Rembar.

Rembar may have been a beast in form and function, but she wasn't dumb. She knew that if she ever stopped, they'd be on her again. She knew the risks of what she had done, attacking the Dungeon Core Manifestations in the heart of such a terrible power, but she wasn't willing to pay the price, not yet. Not now that she'd tasted freedom.

She'd already shown her power by outwitting a hunting party of Umbral Manifestations, striking them down with a surprise attack from a sulk of aether foxes. Only aether foxes though. Without Rem's connection, she had come to the realization that her power was weakened. But she could deal with that. In the whole, that wasn't her only concern, just another in a long line of them. She had the knowledge of her creator. She knew what it meant to be a Dungeon monster. She knew that Rem or Amber could call upon her again if they gained sufficient power, but she also knew what it took to strike out on her own.

All of this brought the Kitsune back to the same conclusion over and over again. She was just too dangerous to be left to her own devices.

On top of that, she knew what it meant to be a Guardian. A Guardian would always remember, so even if she died, her memory would still be intact. If Rembar ever did get taken down and was summoned back into the service of one of those two Dungeons, she knew they wouldn't make the same mistakes twice. Rem was too smart for that, and, below the surface, Amber scared her. As surely as she'd be alive, she'd be bound back into service, unable to leave the area she was assigned to guard, trapped with the knowledge of what was beyond. Teasing her with its lost promises.

It would have been torture every moment of every day to live that existence.

Her former master and mistress hadn't been strong enough to control her at their level, but it wouldn't be that way forever. She had to get strong enough to survive.

For three days, Rembar ran from Ansith's forces.

Run.

Send out decoy aether foxes.

Blink.

Stay in the Celestial Plane as long as possible.

Return.

Keep Running.

For three days then three days more, she repeated her methods, sent out false leads with aether foxes, and risked her existence by straining her Blink Node to keep her out of their grasp. Her record was five minutes in the Celestial plane now, much higher than her starting time of forty-five seconds.

But the skill came at a cost.

Straining an ability drained more mana, and it left her weak in more than one way. In one respect, Rembar was made of mana, and overusing it meant death; staying in the Celestial plane wasn't much better. The longer she stayed, the more poisoned she became by the high concentrations of Celestial mana. Despite her ability to use it, she wasn't built for it in such high concentrations.

257

Her senses spread wide, triggering her second new Node born from her necessity, Sense Enemy.

A moment later, she knew the answer. There was none. She'd thrown them from her trail.

Finally.

With the last of her strength, Rembar looked around for a place to recover, finally settling down in the shadowy roots of an ancient tree as tall as Ansith's elemental towers.

There, Rembar slept a sleep as close to death as one may be.

Around her, the world continued as the brush shuffled and five figures emerged dressed in the leathers of hunters.

＊＊

It was night by the time Rembar awoke once more. How much time had passed, she didn't know, but things were not as she had left them. She was still under the ancient tree, protected from nearly all views by the roots and a fine coating of dirt. Someone—six someones from the scents—however, had been there. Her limbs, ravaged from a multitude of attacks, were bandaged, and the smell of mint and medicines seeped up from the wounds.

Overpowering that smell however, was another that really caught her attention. There was a king's bounty just waiting before her! There were steaks from a multitude of beasts, both cooked and raw, fish prepared in the same manner, a mountain of berries, jars of honey and jams, breads, still warm to the touch, and... a child?

Why would she want to eat a child when she had all of this?

Rembar let the thought pass as she studied the young girl. The child was meditating, drawing in and radiating Earth and Air mana in equal parts, but she looked equal parts fearful and curious. Rembar took a quick sniff, and then she relaxed. Her senses told her that the child was no higher than the low D Ranks, new to her class and weak. She wasn't to be feared.

When Rembar began to stir in earnest, the girl broke from her meditative trance nearly in the same instant. Her deep orange fur was a stark contrast to the dark browns and grays of the bark and dirt underneath the tree, and her tone was almost as bright as her coloring.

"Greetings, honored one."

Rembar stopped before her maw could close around one of the steaks. She was weak, but again, she wasn't dumb. Rembar eyed the meat again, quickly ate three of the raw chunks of meat, and turned her full attention to the young woman. Rembar gave her a nod of acknowledgment for her to continue.

"I am Illa, Fifth Druid of the North Garden Foxkin, and my clan sends their humble offerings to one of the divine messengers of Vul."

That alone answered many of the questions lingering in Rembar's mind. She knew of Rem's origin among the Foxkin. She also knew of the Foxkin's patron goddess, Vul, and of her messenger, the two-tailed fox Vix. With the words of the girl and her memories from Rem, she knew was in no danger here.

Rembar didn't correct them as she gave a nod again, three of her four tails throwing an array of light throughout the small den.

"We tended your wounds while you slept, and the Kintree has seen fit to guard you from all other eyes. Now that you have awoken, we wish to know what brings you to our lands."

Rembar said nothing, unsure of how to proceed with that answer. For the moment, she didn't have to. Her stomach growled at her and Illa equally, reminding her of her hunger and forcing her back to the food. With a bestial gnashing of teeth and ripping of flesh, Rembar continued to eat a few of the larger, raw fish and a large portion of the berries, with little more care for the young druid girl.

For her part, Illa seemed slightly taken aback, maybe even insulted. From the corner of her eye, Rembar caught the subtle motions of mana on the air calm the rustle of leaves outside in the brush. If she'd missed the gentle movement of power, she wouldn't miss the young woman give the fraction of a nod to an unseen ally. A moment later, Illa sighed and spoke again, doing a decent job of keeping the annoyance from her voice and cheer in her tone.

"My apologies for interrupting your meal. I didn't think before I spoke. You must be starving."

Rembar was, both for mana and for food. Her Dungeon mana had exhausted long ago, so now she had to sustain herself. Not to mention hunting food was nearly impossible while you were running for your life. Feeding a bit of ambient mana into her skill, she still sensed no one that meant her harm.

With her fear abated, Rembar ate, ate, and ate. She ate until she could eat no more, which just so happened to coincide with the food running out. Licking every single drop of jam and honey from their jars, Rembar pushed them to the far corner of her make-due den.

With that done, she turned back to the young druid and nodded her head. From her vague memories of Vix, she knew enough on how to act towards another. The longer she could keep this up, the longer she could stay hidden, and the stronger she could grow.

Strong enough to keep her freedom.

"You may speak now, child."

Final Core Report - Rem
Final Report as of Frostfall 1
Rem Snowfur of the Wildwood
Oracle/Dungeon Core

Oracle
Class Skills Mastered: 4
Secondary Skills: 4
Rank D2
7/9 requirements met to reach Rank C
> Learn 4 Class Skill Nodes
> ~~Learn a Cantrip~~
> Learn at least 1 Healing Spell that uses Celestial Mana
> ~~Learn at least 1 Unique Oracle Spell that uses Celestial~~
~~Mana~~
> ~~Learn at least 1 Weapon Mastery Node (Staff, Wand, Scep-~~
~~ter, Mace)~~
> ~~Gain a base understanding of your Class~~
> ~~Expand your Nexus reserve to at least 100 Mana~~
> ~~Forge Connections Among your kin~~
> ~~Understand your Purpose~~

Mana Types - Celestial/Umbral/Dungeon (Ambient)
Usable Mana Reserves:
> Celestial - 150/150 (500)
> Umbral - 10/10 (60)
> Dungeon (Ambient) - 1200/1200 (1200)

Class Passive for Mastery:
> None Earned

Word of Power: Forbid
Unique Primary Class Node - Active - Oracle
Evolution Potential - None
Cost: Base - 20 Celestial (Scaling)
Effect: Spend mana to bend those to the power of your Patron.
Word of Power: Forbid prevents a target from taking a specific action. The power and cost of this spell depends on the will of the

target and the complexity of the command given. This spell cannot stop biological functions such as breathing.

Minor Commune (Goddess Vul)
Unique Primary Class Node - Active/Passive - Oracle
Evolution Potential - Flexible, High
Cost: None
Active Effect: Commune with your patron goddess, Vul. Responses will be based on her whims. The easier the request, the more likely Vul will be to respond.
Passive Effect: Vul may commune directly with you at her discretion.

Stabilize
Primary Class Node - Active - Oracle
Evolution Potential - Minor
Cost: Base - 20 Celestial (Scaling)
Effect: Spend mana to stablize a fallen creature. Stabilize will quickly mend critical injuries and restore lost blood by responding to specific magical and biological cues. The power and cost of this spell depends on the severity of the injury and the power required to mend critical injuries. This spell has no effect on a non-critically injured party.

Invisibility
Secondary Node - Spell - Cantrip
Evolution Potential - Flexible
Cost: Base- 10 mana per minute per creature per five feet radius (Scaling)
Effect: Spend ambient mana to bend light around you and appear to vanish. Cost of the spell increases based on movement, environment, and size of the spell's target.

Mend
Secondary Node - Spell - Cantrip
Evolution Potential - High, Flexible
Cost: Scaling

Effect: Spend ambient mana to attempt to repair a mundane or magical item. Repair cost is based on knowledge and complexity and the severity of the damage of the item.

Will-of-the-Wisp
Secondary Node - Spell - Cantrip
Evolution Potential - Flexible
Cost: 5 (Scaling)
Effect: Spend ambient mana to create a sphere of light in the color of your choice. Cost of this spell changes based on size, intended duration, distance from user, and color of the sphere.

Weapon Mastery - Staff
Secondary Node - Weapon Mastery - Passive
Evolution Potential - Flexible
Cost: None
Passive Effect: You can properly defend and attack an opponent using a staff. Further training will unlock active abilities.

Dual Cast
Secondary Node - Spell Mastery - Passive
Evolution Potential - Progressive
Cost: Scaling
Passive Effect: You have gained a talent for transferring mana between yourself and others to augment your spell craft. Further training will unlock active abilities or more control within larger groups of cooperative casters. When Dual Casting, a percentage of mana is lost in the transfer. This loss is higher when working with opposing mana types.
Current Loss: 2% for Mastered Nodes, 5% for Developing Nodes, 10% for Unshared Nodes

***

Dungeon Core
Mastered Skills - 5 of 5

Soul Attributes - 1
Secondary Skills - 0
Dungeon Core Rank C6
1/7 requirements met to reach Rank B

       Acquire an Advanced Pattern

       Achieve a Mana Equilibrium or Mana Constructive rating within   your first finished Dungeon Floors

       Gather 1000 Soul Points (3/1000)

       Unlock a Soul Attribute

         — Granted abilities do not count towards this total

       Create a B or higher Ranked Item or Item Attribute

       ~~Create a B or higher Ranked Minion or Minion Attribute~~

       Create a B or higher Ranked Trap or Trap Attribute

Dungeon Core Size 3
Dungeon Core Material - Opal/Amethyst
Mana Types - Celestial/Umbral/Dungeon

       Celestial - 500/500

       Umbral - 60/60

       Dungeon - 2600/2600

Dungeon Alignment - Mana Constructive
Floors Complete - 0
Soul Points - 3
Class Passive for Mastery:

       Dungeon Mana Reservoir: All Mana Reservoirs grow based on use.

       Rank Knowledge: An innate knowledge of what requirements are   needed to increase in rank for any visible Nexus.

Influence
Primary Class Node - Active/Passive Ability - Dungeon Core
Evolution Potential - None
Active Effect: Spread your Influence by spending mana to claim an unclaimed area or fight another Influence. Influence spread is equal to Size, Rank, and mana spent. Claimed areas generate mana equal to the power and density of aether present in the material claimed. Material touched by your Influence within your Influence give off a

faint light related to your primary mana type. Influence cannot be used to claim living things or sufficiently powerful constructs.

Passive Effect: When mana reaches critical levels within your Core and cycling has been sustained for a substantial time, the effect of cycling mana within the Core will become a passive effect based on your prior skill use.

Passive Effect: Fabrication and Absorption can only be used within an area of Influence.

Ability Augments:

Direct Control - Rank C7, Core Size 2

Rank C Locked Abilities:

Split Control - Rank C4, Core Size 4

Fabrication

Primary Class Node - Active Ability - Dungeon Core

Evolution Potential - None

Cost: Scales with complexity

Effect: Spend mana to create or recreate items from Patterns that you have absorbed via absorption, created, or have sufficient knowledge to attempt to recreate from memory. Cost is directly related to the power, complexity, and Rank of the item created.

Creation is limited to items within two Ranks of your current Dungeon Core Class.

Ability Augments:

Item Fusion - Rank D2, Core Size 2

Item Dissection - Rank C7

Rank C Attributes Locked:

Automatic Spawning - Rank C5

Creature Fusion - Rank C3

Absorption

Primary Class Node - Active Ability - Dungeon Core

Evolution Potential - None

Cost: None

Effect: Absorb a non-living creature or item to learn its Pattern to recreate. Upon absorbing an item, gain mana equal to the complexity of the item. Items can be absorbed repeatedly to improve the detail of the Pattern or gain mana.

Rank C Attributes Locked:
    Automatic Absorption - Rank C5, Core Size 4

Manifestation
Primary Class Node - Active Ability - Dungeon Core
Evolution Potential - None
Cost: Scales with power
Effect: Use mana to create an inhabitable simulacrum based on a predetermined, personal image. The simulacrum's power is equal to the size, rank, and mana spent to create it. The Rank and mana of the simulacrum cannot surpass the non-Dungeon Nexus of the intended controller, though excess mana can be stored in the body to maintain it for independent operation. Cost to maintain the simulacrum is equal to its power.

Dungeon Memory
Primary Class Node - Passive Ability - Dungeon Core
Evolution Potential - None
Cost: N/A
Passive Effect: Stores and recalls the Patterns, mana requirements, ranks, abilities, and other attributes of any ability, item, creature, or material absorbed by your Absorption ability. Patterns are separated between Pattern Memory, the Index, and Creature Memory, the Bestiary.
Ability Augments:
    Bestiary - Rank D7 - Core Size 2
    Codex - Rank D7 - Core Size 2
    Trans-Dimensional Magic Applications - Soul Ability
Rank C Attributes Locked:
    Trap Development - Conditional

Author's Note

Dear Readers,

I want to thank you for making it this far. As most of the authors you've read probably say, if you liked the work, please take the time to rate and review this work on Amazon and on Goodreads. Reviewing even with just a set of stars can make the difference between a work being found and being lost in the depths of the 'Zon.

Without any further ado, I want to thank everyone involved: my beta readers for helping to make the book into what is open before you; my editor Conor and Level Up for taking the risk to trust in the idea that created this work; the crew over at the LitRPG Forum Discord for putting up with my endless pun-ishment; and, most of all, my wife Erin for distracting our hurricane-of-a-son long enough for me to take time out of the day to create this novel. I will admit that she had the harder job. If you have a nearly two-year-old, hyperactive boy I'm sure you know what I'm talking about. It's very hard to distract a toddler when he's trying to hug a tuxedo cat that most definitely doesn't want to be loved, or bite his mother to get a reaction, not to mention licking towels to make me laugh.

Toddlers are an untamed force of nature whose power we wish we could harness.

Anyway, if you enjoyed *Dungeon Core 101*, remember that you can always follow me on my Twitter at @RJ_Triveri, connect with me on my Amazon profile, or find me at Goodreads to see what's in the pipeline next.

If you're looking for more LitRPG, check out Level Up Publishing with great titles like *Gamers* by Cambry Varner, *The Dragon's Revenge* by Conor Kostick (Yes, the editor of this book), and many more.

As for my own recommendations? Personally, I enjoyed *Bone Dungeon* and *Dungeon Core Online* by Jonathan Smidt, *Shade's First Rule* by A.F. Kay, *World Tree Online* by E. A. Hooper, *How to Defeat a Demon King in Ten Easy Steps* by Andrew Rowe, and *The Wandering Inn* by Pirate Aba.

There's always *Incipere Online*, too.

With that, take care and level up that reading skill!

RJ Triveri